MARGERY
HARLEQUIN

CW00758521

MARGERY Sharp was born Clara Margery Melita Sharp in 1905 in Wiltshire. She spent some of her childhood in Malta, and on the family's return to England became a pupil at Streatham Hill High School.

She later studied at Bedford College, London, where she claimed her time was devoted 'almost entirely to journalism and campus activities.'

Still living in London, she began her writing career at the age of twenty-one, becoming a contributor of fiction and non-fiction to many of the most notable periodicals of the time in both Britain and America.

In 1938 she married Major Geoffrey Castle, an aeronautical engineer. On the outbreak of World War II, she served as a busy Army Education Lecturer, but continued her own writing both during and long after the conflict. Many of her stories for adults became the basis for Hollywood movie screenplays, in addition to the 'Miss Bianca' children's series, animated by Disney as *The Rescuers* in 1977.

Margery Sharp ultimately wrote 22 novels for adults (not 26, as is sometimes reported), as well as numerous stories and novellas (many of them published only in periodicals) and various works for children. She died in Suffolk in 1991, one year after her husband.

FICTION BY MARGERY SHARP

Novels

Rhododendron Pie (1930)*
Fanfare for Tin Trumpets (1932)*
The Flowering Thorn (1933)
Four Gardens (1935)*
The Nutmeg Tree (1937)
Harlequin House (1939)*
The Stone of Chastity (1940)*
Cluny Brown (1944)
Britannia Mews (1946)
The Foolish Gentlewoman (1948)*
Lise Lillywhite (1951)
The Gipsy in the Parlour (1954)
The Eye of Love (1957)
Something Light (1960)
Martha in Paris (1962)
Martha, Eric and George (1964)
The Sun in Scorpio (1965)
In Pious Memory (1967)
Rosa (1970)
The Innocents (1972)
The Faithful Servants (1975)
Summer Visits (1977)

* published by Furrowed Middlebrow and Dean Street Press

Selected Stories & Novellas

The Nymph and the Nobleman (1932)†
Sophy Cassmajor (1934)†
The Tigress on the Hearth (1955)†
The Lost Chapel Picnic and Other Stories (1973)

† these three shorter works were compiled in the 1941 anthology Three Companion Pieces

Children's Fiction

The Rescuers (1959)
Melisande (1960)
Miss Bianca (1962)
The Turret (1963)
Lost at the Fair (1965)
Miss Bianca in the Salt Mines (1966)
Miss Bianca in the Orient (1970)
Miss Bianca in the Antarctic (1971)
Miss Bianca and the Bridesmaid (1972)
The Children Next Door (1974)
The Magical Cockatoo (1974)
Bernard the Brave (1977)
Bernard Into Battle (1978)

MARGERY SHARP

HARLEQUIN HOUSE

With an introduction by
Elizabeth Crawford

DEAN STREET PRESS

A Furrowed Middlebrow Book
FM56

Published by Dean Street Press 2021

First published in 1939 by Collins

Cover by DSP

Shows detail from an illustration by Eric Ravilious

ISBN 978 1 913527 67 9

www.deanstreetpress.co.uk

Introduction

Reviewing Margery Sharp's novel, *Harlequin House* (1939), the *Manchester Guardian* intimated that she was second only to P.G. Wodehouse as a comic novelist, welcome praise for a writer, still young, who had determined from an early age to become a self-supporting author and who, over a period of about fifty years, published twenty-two novels for adults, thirteen stories for children, four plays, two mysteries, and numerous short stories.

Born with, as one interviewer testified, 'wit and a profound common sense', Clara Margery Melita Sharp (1905-1991) was the youngest of the three daughters of John Henry Sharp (1865-1953) and his wife, Clara Ellen (1866-1946). Both parents came from families of Sheffield artisans and romance had flourished, although it was only in 1890 that they married, after John Sharp had moved to London and passed the Civil Service entrance examination as a 2nd division clerk. The education he had received at Sheffield's Brunswick Wesleyan School had enabled him to prevail against the competition, which, for such a desirable position, was fierce. Margery's mother was by the age of 15 already working as a book-keeper, probably in her father's silversmithing workshop. By 1901 John Sharp was clerking in the War Office, perhaps in a department dealing with Britain's garrison in Malta, as this might explain why Margery was given the rather exotic third name of 'Melita' (the personification of Malta).

Malta became a reality for the Sharps when from 1912 to 1913 John was seconded to the island. His family accompanied him and while there Margery attended Sliema's Chiswick House High School, a recently founded 'establishment for Protestant young ladies'. Over 50 years later she set part of her novel Sun in Scorpio (1965) in Malta, rejoicing in the

Mediterranean sunlight which made everything sparkle, contrasting it with the dull suburb to which her characters returned., where 'everything dripped'. In due course the Sharps, too, arrived back in suburban London, to the Streatham house in which Margery's parents were to live for the rest of their lives.

From 1914 to 1923 Margery received a good academic education at Streatham Hill High School (now Streatham and Clapham High School) although family financial difficulties meant she was unable to proceed to university and instead worked for a year as a shorthand-typist in the City of London 'with a firm that dealt with asphalt'. In a later interview (*Daily Independent*, 16 Sept 1937) she is quoted as saying, 'I never regretted that year in business as it gave me a contact with the world of affairs'. However, Margery had not given up hope of university and with an improvement in the Sharps' financial position her former headmistress wrote to the principal of Bedford College, a woman-only college of the University of London, to promote her case, noting 'She has very marked literary ability and when she left school two years ago I was most anxious she should get the benefit of university training'. Margery eventually graduated in 1928 with an Honours degree in French, the subject chosen 'just because she liked going to France'. Indeed, no reader of Margery Sharp can fail to notice her Francophile tendency.

During her time at university Margery began publishing verses and short stories and after graduation was selected to join two other young women on a debating tour of American universities. As a reporter commented, 'Miss Sharp is apparently going to provide the light relief in the debates', quoting her as saying, 'I would rather tell a funny story than talk about statistics'. Articles she wrote from the US for the

Evening Standard doubtless helped defray the expenses of the coming year, her first as a full-time author.

For on her return, living in an elegant flat at 25 Craven Road, Paddington, she began earning her living, writing numerous short stories for magazines, publishing a first novel in 1930, and soon becoming a favourite on both sides of the Atlantic. Her life took a somewhat novelettish turn in April 1938 when she was cited as the co-respondent in the divorce of Geoffrey Lloyd Castle, an aeronautical engineer. and, later, author of two works of science fiction. At that time publicity such as this could have been harmful, and she was out of the country when the news broke. Later in the year she spent some months in New York where she and Geoffrey were married, with the actor Robert Morley and Blanche Gregory, Margery's US literary agent and lifelong friend, as witnesses.

During this hectic year, Margery maintained her output of short stories, as well as writing *Harlequin House*. The novel's star is 'lawless' Mr Alfred Arthur Partridge, one-time manager of Peters Library, a lending library in the seaside town of Dortmouth. The library's name and, indeed, that of a butler ('Peters') on duty in a London house, may constitute a nod to A.D. Peters, the author's new British literary agent. 'Harlequin House' is the soubriquet for the top-floor flat in Paddington taken by Mr Partridge and the two young people, irresistible Lisbeth, who 'took up a great deal of the Life Force's attention', and Ronny, her ne'er-do-well brother, with whom his life becomes entangled. Perhaps Margery's lengthy US sojourn, during which time she may have been working on the novel, encouraged her to allow Lester Hamilton, an American 'engaged in the film industry', to take Lisbeth to the altar, rather than the 'admirable' army captain to whom she was engaged. In his summary of the year's fiction the *Manchester Guardian* reviewer reprised his praise, 'Words are felicitous, distortion is discreet, life is comically but temperately out of focus, and the plot, always under control, twists and somersaults exhilaratingly' (1 December 1939).

During the Second World War, while Geoffrey was on active service, Margery worked in army education, while continuing to publish novels. The couple took a set (B6) in the Albany on Piccadilly, where they were tended by a live-in housekeeper, and from the early 1950s also had a Suffolk home, Observatory Cottage, on Crag Path, Aldeburgh. The writer Ronald Blythe later reminisced, 'I would glance up at its little balcony late of an evening, and there she would be, elegant with her husband Major Castle and a glass of wine beside her, playing chess to the roar of the North Sea, framed in lamplight, secure in her publishers.'

Late in life Margery Sharp, while still producing adult novels, achieved success as a children's author, in 1977 receiving the accolade of the Disney treatment when several stories in her 'Miss Bianca' series became the basis of the film *The Rescuers*. She ended her days in Aldeburgh, dying on 14 March 1991, just a year after Geoffrey.

Elizabeth Crawford

CHAPTER 1

1

THE refining influence of natural beauty, particularly upon members of the Anglo-Saxon race, is a fact universally admitted, particularly by Anglo-Saxons. It provides their moral justification for taking the week-end off. Every Friday afternoon all over the globe iron-browed proconsuls, bleak-eyed captains of industry, write a last memorandum—"Martial Law," or "Call in strikebreakers"—and rise wearily from their desks. On Monday they return, changed men, and tear the memos up. Or such is the theory. If true, it accounts for much. But it does not account for Mr. Arthur Alfred Partridge.

Mr. Partridge inhabited—not at week-ends only, but all the year round—Dormouth Bay; and he could have chosen no spot on earth more morally beneficial. The magnificence of the Alps, the sublimity of the Himalayas, could not hold a candle (from the moral viewpoint) to the conscientiousness of Dormouth Front. Within its boundaries the white cliffs of Albion lived up to their name. The walk along their top was bounded on one side by a row of equally white palings, on the other by a stretch of perfectly-kept lawn adorned with moon- or star-shaped flower-beds. The beds made patterns on the lawn, the flowers made patterns in the beds, geometry and horticulture clasped hands. Upon all these things the sun, as Mr. Partridge sallied forth on the second afternoon in July, shone brightly down. (It had to: Dormouth Bay boasted a higher average of sunshine than any other town on the south coast.) The sea lapped gently in a neat blue crescent. A passing schoolchild stopped to pick up a paper bag and deposit it in a box marked LITTER. Every object in sight conformed unhesitatingly to either natural or municipal orders. Only Mr. Partridge was lawless.

His very presence on those lawns, at that hour, was a scandal. Already three infuriated subscribers had clamoured in vain at the door of his twopenny Library in Cliff Street; already two widows and a maid were facing the prospect of a lonely evening unsolaced by literature. One of them, who had just discovered the works of Miss E.M. Dell, and who had hastened back for more, rattled the knob with such violence that the BACK SHORTLY notice fell to the ground. This would have annoyed Mr. Partridge had he known, for he considered the phrase "Back shortly" to be the commercial equivalent of the social "Not at home"—something to be accepted without question, and with a good grace. In this, as in so much else, he was of course wrong. It was part of his lawlessness.

He did not look lawless. In height he was five foot four, in shape oval. His attire was inconspicuous—pepper-and-salt trousers, black alpaca jacket, panama hat—except about the feet. Mr. Partridge wore brown-and-white shoes, the white brilliantly pure, the brown chocolate-dark, and scarlet socks; and these added a peculiar touch of frivolity to his whole appearance. They were the single outward sign that the scenery of Dormouth Bay had for once fallen down on its job.

Mr. Partridge strolled across the grass and approached one of the star-shaped parterres. From its margin sprouted three notice boards. Two were municipal, bearing the injunctions *"Please do not pick," "Please keep off the beds"*; on the third, donated by the Dormouth Bay Rose-Growers Association, it said, *"A rose by any other name would smell as sweet. Shakespeare, Romeo and Juliet, Act II, Scene II, l. 43. D.B.R.-G.A."* Mr. Partridge read all three, took out his penknife, and stepped between the bushes to cut a buttonhole. In the centre of the bed he paused indeed, but it was memory, not conscience, that suspended his hand upon a

Scarlet Glory. He had just remembered that it was the tenth anniversary of his wife's death. Regretfully but firmly Mr. Partridge spared the bud and selected a white Frau Karl Druschki instead. He then took a look round, noted that there would be some fine Daily Mails open by next morning, and stepped back onto the grass.

Since he was standing at the extreme eastern end of the lawns their full extent stretched away on the right. On the left the ground rose sharply to Dormouth Head, a small promontory almost entirely monopolized by the Dormouth Towers Hotel. Its two square miles of pleasure grounds were screened from the public gaze by walls and shrubberies; behind which (or so the rumour went) many a celebrity exclusively sported. Mr. Partridge, who had a very lively imagination, often wondered what they were up to. He pictured a good deal of popping in and out of beds, varied by the austerer delights of orchestral concerts and brilliant conversation. There was of course no real reason why he should not have actually entered the place to see for himself; he was not, like the average citizen of Dormouth Bay, overawed by either its splendour or its prestige. He was not overawed by anything. But a deep, sane instinct warned him that the pleasures of the imagination are rarely equalled by the reality. Mr. Partridge therefore contented himself with gazing from without, and there was indeed plenty to gaze on, for the building had originally been constructed, in 1860, to the orders of a railroad millionaire with a taste for foreign travel but a weak stomach. He had crossed the Channel twice, the first time because he did not know what it would be like, the second because there was at that time no other means of returning to his native shore: but the lure of the Continent persisted, and to assuage it he incorporated in his new home all the features which had most impressed him abroad. From where he stood Mr.

Partridge could distinguish the Bridge of Sighs, a minaret, and a portion of the Alhambra. The dome of the minaret was of coloured glass, inset with medallion portraits of the Victorian novelists. These Mr. Partridge of course could not see, which was a pity, for he would have appreciated them; and he would also have appreciated, as a student of human nature, the scene on which they looked down.

Under the eyes of Mr. Dickens, Mr. Scott, Mr. Thackeray and Mr. Trollope, Lisbeth Campion was engaged, as usual, in resisting advances.

2

She was resisting them without harshness. That was the trouble. The earnest young man at her side meant so little to her that she could not even remember his name; she knew only that for the past two days, ever since he arrived, he had been following at her heel with a gun-dog's perseverance and a gun-dog's good manners; and indeed his whole personality was so amiably canine that Lisbeth could not help feeling it was not his fault: someone had trained him to do it. (In a sense she was right, the trainer being simply the Life Force, or—more classically—Venus Urania, or—more familiarly—Mother Nature, Lisbeth took up a great deal of the Life Force's attention.)

"It was wonderful of you," said the young man, "to think of coming up here."

"I didn't mean you to come too," said Lisbeth, with truth; for she had climbed up into the minaret specially to be alone, to try to evolve, by persistent solitary thought, some way of escape from an unbearable situation. . . .

"Of course you didn't. That's what's so adorable about you. You're just like a child—"

Lisbeth backed away. Unfortunately she backed into a shaft of sunlight. The young man drew a quivering breath.

"Don't move," he said huskily. "You look wonderful. You look like an angel. Lisbeth—you don't quite hate me, do you?"

Lisbeth sighed.

"Of course not, darling."

"Say that again! Darling!"

"Darling," repeated Lisbeth politely.

"Do you call anyone else that?"

"Dozens." She thought a moment, and corrected herself. "Hundreds."

"Don't try," said the young man, "to hurt me."

Lisbeth looked at him hopelessly. Try to hurt him—when she was doing her very best to spare his totally unnecessary feelings! When all the time she longed to be alone, because there was no one she could tell . . . For a moment she considered the impassioned young man beside her, mentally testing, as it were, the strength of his clamorous devotion; and unconsciously shook her head. The devotion was all right, but he lacked understanding. He would never be able to comprehend that someone might be a millstone round one's neck, and yet so dear—such a fool—so impossible—such a darling—

Tears filled her eyes. They were very beautiful eyes, grey under dark lashes.

"Dearest," cried the young man ecstatically, "are you crying for me?"

Lisbeth swallowed hard. For once in her life she wanted to wound, to prick with sharp words the swelling bubble of his male complacency; and it was characteristic that her own nervous system prevented her. Sobs choked her throat, she had to bite on her lips to keep them from trembling; she knew that if she opened her mouth it would be to weep aloud. And the young man, all ignorant of his escape, was enchanted. He had not believed himself capable of arousing in her such emotion—as indeed he was not. In another moment his protectiveness would have been let loose and Lisbeth would have found herself, as so often before, being embraced under a misapprehension. But the catastrophe was this time averted. A footstep sounded at the head of the winding stair.

The pointed doorway was just over six feet high: Charles Lambert had to stoop to enter. It was impossible to tell, from his dark ugly face, whether he were thirty or thirty-five or forty years old; and it was also impossible to tell whether he had heard the young man's last enquiry or was observant of Miss Campion's tears.

"Tennis, Lisbeth?" he asked quietly. "There's a court free now, but they're all booked again at four."

Lisbeth nodded, and pointed one toe to display for his inspection the white rubber-soled shoe and short white sock. It was a charming gesture. It indicated that of course she intended to play tennis with Mr. Lambert, that she had attired herself with that object and had been only killing time till he came. None of these implications was deliberate: they were simply byproducts, so to speak, of her need to avoid speech. Another by-product was the sudden crimsoning of the young man's face.

"If you'll tell me where your racket is," said Mr. Lambert pleasantly, "I'll fetch it and meet you on the court."

Immediately the young man was beside him in the doorway.

"I'll get Miss Campion's racket," he announced. "It's in my press."

He shouldered by, clumsy as a schoolboy. Mr. Lambert, on the contrary, was not clumsy at all. He followed, and left Lisbeth alone.

3

The four wise old heads—of Mr. Dickens and Mr. Scott, Mr. Thackeray and Mr. Trollope—gazed benignly down on her. Lisbeth knew nothing about them, but even in stained glass their features were impressive. They looked experienced, and understanding. But they weren't any use. They were all dead.

Round the wall there ran a narrow seat: Lisbeth climbed upon it and pressed her face against the glass of the dome. There at the rim panels of colour alternated with panels of plain, through which she could see out. The view before her included the length of the cliff walk and a distant glimpse of Dormouth Bay.

"Sister Anne, Sister Anne, do you see anyone coming?"

"Fool!" Lisbeth rebuked herself. For you didn't watch from a tower nowadays, you waited by the telephone, or haunted the letter-box. But for a moment longer instinct held her where she was: women—from Bluebeard's sister-in-law to Duchess Sarah—had watched longer from towers than they had waited by telephones. . . .

"Sister Anne, Sister Anne . . ."

But Lisbeth saw no one at all save a small oval figure distantly silhouetted at the end of the promenade.

4

Mr. Partridge turned and strolled on. His objective was a defective slot-machine at the end of the pier, from which, by a certain manipulation of the handle, he had for some days been extracting two packets of cigarettes for the price of one. The sun continued to shine down on him just as though he had been going to put sixpence in the Lifeboat box. A pair of seagulls swooped in from the bay, performed a few masterly evolutions, and swooped off again—no doubt to give the same show a little farther on. Dormouth Bay was renowned for its amusements. The band on the lawns started at three o'clock, and Mr. Partridge knew of two seats from either of which, according to the wind, one could enjoy the program without paying to enter the enclosure. He was approaching the first of these now, and the overture to "William Tell" was distinctly audible. Mr. Partridge hesitated: he had plenty of cigarettes to go on with, and though the bench was already occupied by a lady, her presence was an additional attraction. Mr. Partridge was in the mood for converse.

He turned aside. The lady was elderly, of pleasant, though strait, demeanour. She wore a grey coat and skirt, black shoes and stockings, and a black straw hat embroidered with white raffia flowers. "All her own work," thought Mr. Partridge, looking at this last; and was not surprised, on sitting down, to find the bench strewn with more raffia and the material for a sewing-bag.

But the lady was not working. She appeared to be lost in thought, and as this was no good to Mr. Partridge, who wanted conversation, he unobtrusively knocked a hank of raffia to the ground, and with more ostentation picked it up.

"Oh, *thank* you," said the lady, in exactly the voice he had expected. (It was gentle, and refined, and a little worn. It was the voice of a whole generation. On most occasions it would be hesitant, and self-distrustful: but if a firing-squad were ever to lead its owner out and ask: "Will you, Milly Pickering, deny your allegiance to the dear King and the Church of England?"—then the voice of Miss Pickering would be bold enough as she answered: "No, I won't!")

"Fine day," observed Mr. Partridge.

"Delightful," agreed Miss Pickering, with a touch of reserve. She was always cautious about talking to strangers; but the old man beside her, sitting with his hands folded in his lap and his feet tucked under the seat, looked most harmless. And he was wearing one of the finest roses she had ever seen.

"What a beautiful bloom!" said Miss Pickering. "Did you grow it yourself?"

"No," said Mr. Partridge, with a chuckle. "I have 'em grown for me."

Miss Pickering felt herself slightly, disconcerted—not by the statement, for many of the most unlikely people employed gardeners—but by the sound which accompanied it. Mr. Partridge's chuckle came from very deep down, from the broadest part of his oval; and it somehow implied a vast acquaintance with all the aspects of life least familiar to herself. To hear it was like getting a glimpse through a public-house door . . .

"Frau Karl Druschki," added Mr. Partridge, cocking his head and snuffing at the petals. "Good old-fashioned sort. Plenty of body to 'em. So had *she*, poor soul."

"So had who?"

"The late Mrs. Partridge. I'm a widower. I've been a widower ten years to the dot."

Miss Pickering looked sympathetic. She had a natural feeling for anniversaries, particularly of deaths; moreover, the introduction of a funereal note somehow put the whole conversation on a more respectable plane.

"It must have been a great blow," she suggested.

"Like concussion," agreed Mr. Partridge enthusiastically. "For days and days I couldn't believe it was true."

He sat up; a change came over his appearance; he had extended his feet. The brown-and-white leather twinkled in the sun, the scarlet of his socks irresistibly drew the eye. Before she could stop herself, Miss Pickering had asked a personal question.

"Do you always wear red socks?" asked Miss Pickering impulsively.

"Always," replied Mr. Partridge. "I find them warming to the blood. You ought to try a pair yourself." He looked at the lady's lean black-clad ankles consideringly; and Miss Pickering, who had not felt a male glance on her shins since 1908, flushed.

"That would *hardly* be possible," she said, concealing her embarrassment under a kind smile.

"Not when you're out and about," conceded Mr. Partridge. "But why not wear 'em at night? As bed-socks?"

He spoke so earnestly, so reasonably, that for a moment Miss Pickering could not decide whether it was she or her companion who was mad. To sit there on a public bench discussing night-wear with a male stranger! "I ought to get up at once!" she thought; and was on the point of doing so when Mr. Partridge, as though sensing her discomfort, suddenly embarked on a new topic.

"If there's one thing I'm partial to," stated Mr. Partridge, "it's Human Nature."

"He *is* mad," thought Miss Pickering, tense. "He's mad, and I mustn't annoy him." For Mr. Partridge's eye, as it rested on the now thickening stream of promenaders, was not only appreciative, it was proprietary. He had the air of a benevolent judge. He was looking at those passers-by as though—"As though he'd *created* them!" thought Miss Pickering; and the shock of her own blasphemy rooted her to the seat.

"What I like about 'em particularly," continued Mr. Partridge, "is that you never can tell. You can live with 'em, and study 'em, until you think you know all: but you never do. You can live with a man from boyhood up and then just by chance—by chance, mark you—find out that he once pushed his wife over a cliff and passed it off as a fainting-fit."

For one moment an awful, a breath-taking suspicion blanched Miss Pickering's cheek. She did not voice it—

they were very near the cliff's edge at that instant—but Mr. Partridge read her thought.

"Nay, that wasn't me!" he reassured her. "That was a friend of mine in the stationery trade. I'm just giving him as an example. Take another. Take yourself, for instance—" he fixed her with a bright, inquisitive eye—"you *look* all right, most respectable, a perfect lady; but for all I know you may be a Queen of the Dope Gangs. There's no telling."

"But indeed there is!" cried Miss Pickering vigorously. Rather to his surprise, she seemed to be answering a direct charge. "People know all about me, I have all sorts of friends and connections—many of them in the Church! For several years I was Lady Warden of an Anglican Settlement in Rotherhithe!"

"There couldn't be a better disguise," pointed out Mr. Partridge. "And think of the opportunities. Near the docks— plenty of seamen about—a First Mate drops in for religious consolation, and leaves a packet of dope under the spittoon. Easy."

"There were no spittoons!" protested Miss Pickering.

"Under the clock, then. Or inside your umbrella. I could think of a dozen places."

Miss Pickering began rather nervously to gather up her work. She did not really believe Mr. Partridge to be insane, she did not seriously suspect him of crime, but she had an obscure feeling that he was not quite safe.

"Don't mistake me," said Mr. Partridge hastily, "I've never peddled snow in my life. I wouldn't think of it. At least—I might *think* of it—work out the ways and means, you know—but that's only natural."

"It isn't natural at all," retorted Miss Pickering, with innocence. "It's wrong. As we think, so we become. I hope you keep your criminal tendencies in check." Mr. Partridge considered.

"I do and I don't," he said candidly. His thoughts ranged from his rose to his cigarettes, from his cigarettes to a trick he knew with electric fires. "It's like this: there's times when civilization—all over machines and by-laws—annoys me. I like to diddle it. And in my quiet way, I do."

But Miss Pickering had not been listening. That is the only explanation. So scandalous a declaration, had she heard it, would surely have expedited her departure. Mr. Partridge's self-communings had given her time to slip back into her own thoughts, and out of her own thoughts she now impulsively, yet hesitantly, spoke.

"About people," began Miss Pickering, "and—and what you were saying just now."

Mr. Partridge nodded.

"Gospel truth, every word of it."

"That makes it worse," said Miss Pickering unhappily. "You see, there's a person staying at the Towers who looks as though he might be *anything*; and now you've made me think perhaps he *is*."

Mr. Partridge disentangled this sentence with a brightening eye.

"What does he give himself out to be?"

"Nothing at all. And that's what's so odd, because we've really got to know him quite well, and yet he never *seems* reticent at the time. And of course he's very much attracted by Lisbeth—so many people are—and the child naturally likes attention. In fact, I do feel it such a pity that her fiancé has to be abroad . . ."

"Ah," said Mr. Partridge, shaking his head. "Long engagements, they're trying to all parties."

"Oh, but this won't be *long*," explained Miss Pickering. "Only another six months. And he's such an excellent young man—in the Army, with everything one could wish for—that he's the one thing that's consoled us. In fact—"

She broke off, conscious that her tongue was outrunning her discretion. A faint colour stained her cheeks. Mr. Partridge tactfully changed the subject. The question with which he did so, however, was prompted by genuine curiosity.

"What's it like up there?" he asked. "Up at the Towers?"

"Oh, quite delightful!" said Miss Pickering, responding gratefully to the social note. "Positively luxurious! In fact, *so* luxurious that I quite enjoy getting out for an hour while my niece plays tennis. And the expense!—but of course my niece couldn't possibly have come alone, and to the Maules expense is nothing. I *shrink*, I regret to say, from going abroad. . . ."

She broke off again. The eager interest of her companion had led her further than she meant to go. She once more collected her belongings, and this time succeeded in putting herself in motion. Mr. Partridge rose politely, and politely raised his hat. He did not sit down again, but strolled on till he came to a vacant deck-chair by the side of which lay a discarded but still valid ticket. Mr. Partridge picked it up and established himself upon the superior comfort of canvas. But it was only his body that sat there: his mind had already checked in at the Dormouth Towers hotel.

"Lisbeth," said Mr. Partridge aloud. "Pretty sort of name. Soft."

The passers-by were no longer interesting to him. They were dull.

"A quid a day," thought Mr. Partridge. "More, very like. Can't afford it."

He looked towards the sands. The beach under Dormouth Head was the private property of the Hotel—all except the strip between high- and low-water mark. When the tide was out the British nation, if it so pleased, could stroll unimpeded (save of course by natural obstacles) all round its island home; and from this right of way below the Hotel one could look up and obtain a distant view of a long terrace where the guests took tea. But Mr. Partridge rarely did so: sand, particularly if moist, being notoriously bad for the shoes.

Mr. Partridge stretched out his feet and considered them thoughtfully. They were still immaculate—the white unflecked, the chocolate undimmed. They were beautiful, but that was not all. They were inspiring.

"Even with shrimps," thought Mr. Partridge, "it can't cost a quid for tea . . ."

CHAPTER 2

1

UNDER a lemon-and-white sunshade, in a long lemon-and-white striped chair, Lisbeth Campion lay flat on her back eating cucumber sandwiches. The nonchalance of her pose was highly disturbing, though in different ways, to both her companions, who were the young man (his constantly-forgotten name happened to be Gerald) and Miss Pickering. "Those *shorts*," thought Miss Pickering. They were really quite modest, closely pleated like a fustanella, but they were—well, short. Lisbeth's brown and slender legs were almost fully revealed. So were her equally brown and slender arms. But her neck—"Quite perverse!" reflected her aunt—was closely muffled by a green silk handkerchief, twisted twice round and thrust down the opening of her white silk shirt.

"More tea, dear?" asked Miss Pickering. One had to sit up to drink.

Lisbeth shook her head. Her mouth was full of sandwich; with one slim brown hand she reached out and pawed vaguely in the direction of the plate. The young man hastened to supply her. Lisbeth took two sandwiches at once and held them over her open mouth, retaining the bread-and-butter and allowing the cucumber to drop out. She was behaving like a spoilt, badly-brought-up child.

Miss Pickering glanced round. At the next table sat two very nice people indeed—a Royal Academician and wife; the man's eyes were fixed, in frowning concentration, on Lisbeth's legs. "What *does* he think?" wondered Miss Pickering unhappily. She would have been surprised to know: he was seeing those brown curves, against the white canvas, as the line of a dun moor against snowy hills; whereas for twenty years his moors (which hung in every provincial gallery) had been heather-covered under cloudy skies. Lisbeth's legs had launched him on his second period. . . .

"Damn," said the young man suddenly.

Miss Pickering looked round and saw Charles Lambert. He was wearing tennis-shoes, which was no doubt why she had not heard him approach. The vacant chairs were of elaborate wickerwork; he managed to drop into one, and stretch out his long legs, and settle his wide shoulders, without waking a single creak.

"I believe there's going to be a thunder-storm," observed Miss Pickering; and instantly wondered why she had made such a foolish remark. The air was fresh, and pleasantly animated by a light breeze. Fortunately, no one seemed to have heard. The two men were looking at Lisbeth, and Lisbeth was looking at the sky.

It was thus Mr. Partridge found them; and since he had no false bashfulness he at once approached Miss Pickering with a friendly smile.

"We meet again," said Mr. Partridge.

The lady glanced hastily round. Lisbeth, her eyes suddenly innocent and her mouth curved, looked like an angel who has seen a joke. The young man frankly stared. But it was the expression of Charles Lambert—cool, enquiring, tinged with mockery—that spurred Miss Pickering to social action. She was a lady to her bones: the thorough conviction that Mr. Partridge was an inferior made her all the more determined that he should not be mocked.

"Won't you join us?" said Miss Pickering.

Mr. Partridge at once did so.

2

There were no shrimps, but he made a very good tea nevertheless. He consumed several sandwiches, and two cakes, and a good deal of bread-and-butter; and after the first embarrassment Miss Pickering quite warmed towards him. For he chatted very pleasantly and entertainingly, on just the sort of topics she liked: local history, current fiction (about which he naturally knew a great deal) and the activities of the Royal Family. He seemed to have lost all his queerness; he brought to the party a note of homely cheer which had previously been lacking. Lisbeth sat up, tucked her legs under her, and listened with just the right friendliness; the young man Gerald, reflecting her mood, forgot to sulk. Even Mr. Lambert asked a question or two about the life of Dormouth Bay. He had rather the air, however, of investigating the customs of a savage tribe, or the economy of an ant-hill. Mr. Partridge set out to dazzle him.

"The next thing we're to have," stated Mr. Partridge impressively, "is a Paddling Pool; and if that's not luxury, I don't know what is. There's miles and miles of beach, all good firm sand—"

"But surely," put in Miss Pickering, "for children, a pool is so much safer?"

"If it's all that safe," countered Mr. Partridge, "why are they advertising for an attendant? To stop the youngsters drowning themselves!"

Lisbeth dropped back on one elbow.

"But could you?" she asked idly. "I mean, could you drown yourself in just about a foot of water?"

"Easy," said Mr. Partridge. "A friend of mine—though he wasn't exactly a friend, he was the gas-inspector—*he* drowned himself in about three inches. In the bath. You'd have thought he'd use gas, and do the Company a bit of good; if he'd asked me—"

But Lisbeth's attention was as hard to fix as a child's. She was now staring, fascinated, at Mr. Partridge's feet.

"What lovely socks!" she exclaimed. "Do you always wear red?"

"Always," affirmed Mr. Partridge. "They're warming to the blood. But as I was saying, if you must do yourself in—"

"Aren't they hard to get?" persisted Lisbeth. Mr. Partridge did not like being interrupted, but her intent and serious look made it impossible to take offence.

"Not to me," he explained complacently. "I bought up two gross off a bankrupt the year of Cameronian's Derby. If any lady or gentleman here would like to try a pair, I'd be very pleased to fix them up."

His glance, travelling benevolently round the group, lingered on Miss Pickering, who blushed.

"Nearly three hundred pairs!" she exclaimed hastily. "Where ever do you put them?"

"Under the mattress. Keeps 'em aired. I had quite a job at first, climbing into bed; but they're going down nicely."

Mr. Partridge stretched out his feet, so that everyone could have a good look at them, and lay back in his chair. He faced the hotel; the portion most fully in view resembled an out-size Swiss chalet, with balconies of fretted wood running beneath each row of windows. You could pop in and out there all right. . . .

"Got any actresses here?" asked Mr. Partridge.

"Oh, yes!" replied Miss Pickering eagerly; and she mentioned a very famous name indeed. Its bearer, besides being a great comedienne, was also an exemplary wife and mother; but Mr. Partridge, who did not know this, at once placed her in imagination on one of the balconies, dressed her in a negligée trimmed with ermine, flung her headlong into the arms of a lover, and lit the whole with a full moon. . . .

The young man Gerald grinned.

"She came the same day as Lambert," he said, "and there was only one garage left, so Lambert had to tool out again and park his 'bus in the town. Fame has its privileges."

"So," pointed out Charles Lambert smoothly, "has age."

Lisbeth suddenly yawned. It was not a pretty little *moue*, it was a frank schoolgirl gape that took her and everyone else by surprise.

"My dear!" rebuked Miss Pickering. But she looked worried. She turned to Mr. Partridge. "The air here *is* bracing, isn't it? And yet Lisbeth goes to bed early every night, and—"

"And I'm bone-lazy," finished her niece. "I'm a loafer."

She yawned again, this time deliberately. "Doublebluff," thought Mr. Partridge. "Pretending you're pretending . . ." Miss Campion aroused in him an extreme interest; she aroused the extreme interest of every man she met, but Mr. Partridge, though suspecting this, naturally drew a distinction between himself and the rest of mankind. It was not Lisbeth's slim brown-and-golden exterior that interested him, but what was going on inside. There was doubtless a lot going on inside Mr. Lambert too, and inside Miss Pickering, and inside the young man; but as a case history, so to speak, Mr. Partridge felt he would prefer to study Lisbeth. He wondered about her fiancé, and why she didn't wear an engagement ring: Miss Pickering could have told him that, for it was she who had insisted that Lisbeth's square and flawless emerald should be given into the custody of the manager. A safe was the only place for it, with the child bathing two and three times a day; but already its absence had led to complications. With a certain simplicity, Miss Pickering felt that if only Lisbeth had been wearing her engagement ring, the young man Gerald wouldn't have (so to speak) *begun*. . . . She was glad that Mr. Lambert had seen it the first night.

The talk dropped. Lisbeth was frankly withdrawing into sleep: caricaturing (with one eye on her aunt) the limpness of extreme fatigue. No one spoke for fear of disturbing her. Miss Pickering disapproved, Mr. Lambert looked bored, the young man was restive; but no one spoke. Mr. Partridge felt he was wasting time.

"I believe," he said, "I'll take a stroll round. See you all later, p'raps."

He rose, bowed, and took himself off. First of all he sought out and paid his waiter. The bill came to three shillings, or twice what it would have been at the Pier Café: but then it covered more than tea. In Mr. Partridge's estimation its payment gave him full (though temporary) rights in the entire hotel.

3

Upstairs and downstairs, through the Alhambra, across the Bridge of Sighs, Mr. Partridge wandered. He climbed into the minaret, and admired the stained glass, and nodded with respect to Mr. Dickens and Mr. Scott and Mr. Thackeray and Mr. Trollope. He was probably the only visitor for a generation who was familiar with their works; when he found, under the circular seat, a small handkerchief stained with pink, he at once recollected that both Becky Sharp and Mr. Thackeray knew of a rouge that didn't come off. Mr. Partridge considered the handkerchief thoughtfully;

it was a proof that even people who could afford to stay at the Towers could also have something to cry about; and he descended the winding stair in a very moralizing mood.

The corridor from which the minaret sprouted was strictly Gothic, even to the lift-doors: Mr. Partridge would have pressed the button to see whether the lift itself were Gothic also, but that a notice (in Gothic lettering) proclaimed it to be out of order; so probably it was. At the passage-end a staircase copied from Versailles descended to the main building; as he went down it he had the pleasure and honour of passing the great actress coming up. Unfortunately he did not recognize her. He hardly saw her, for on the flight below followed Lisbeth Campion.

She followed very slowly, pulling herself by the banister—until she saw Mr. Partridge; and then, with a brilliant, friendly smile, she gathered herself together and finished the flight two steps at a time. As she ran down the corridor, she whistled.

4

It was nearly seven o'clock when Mr. Partridge left the hotel, and he went straight to the Three Doves publichouse, and had some drinks, and dined off a cold sausage or two, and spent the rest of the evening playing darts. The complete change of surroundings was highly agreeable to him: he had admired the hotel almost to the limit of admiration, but there was still a lot he liked about the pub. Its decorations (consisting chiefly of advertising matter) might be simple, but they went straight to the convivial point: women and wine (as sang Mr. Gay) should life employ. The actual employments of the company were very different: they drove trams, or painted houses, or engaged in the smaller branches of commerce; but it did not matter. In spirit, and pro tem, they were one with the Georgian rakes. Even the classic phrase of their dismissal addressed them as gentlemen.

Mr. Partridge walked home with a buoyant step. He did not feel tired, but rather stimulated. He wanted more things to happen. Dormouth Bay, however, felt otherwise; it had gone firmly and smugly to bed. Mr. Partridge slackened his pace; if there were a foot-pad behind him he was willing to give that foot-pad a chance. But of course there was no foot-pad. There wasn't even a body on his door-step.

He let himself in and switched on the light. Beneath its untempered glare every detail of the shop was startlingly distinct: he could have counted, from the threshold, every single one of the three thousand odd books whose rental, at twopence a week, furnished in a sense his livelihood. Mr. Partridge did not own the Library, he was employed by its proprietors (who ran a chain of about fifty more such establishments) at a modest salary, with use of premises. The premises consisted of a small kitchen behind the shop, and a bedroom above, and as a rule Mr. Partridge was quite content with them. But to-night he felt strange stirrings. The whole place, so small and bright and familiar, might almost have been called cosy: Mr. Partridge considered these adjectives in turn, and indignantly repudiated them. He did not want to be cosy. The place was too small, too familiar. He yearned not for brightness, but for the dark immensities of the unillumined night.

Without even crossing the threshold he automatically replaced the BACK SHORTLY card, switched off the light, stepped out again, and shut and locked the door. There wasn't much dark immensity about the street outside, for night, at Dormouth Bay, was as bright as science and the rates could make it. Night, at Dormouth Bay, was regarded with suspicion: the moon afforded no useful statistics, did no useful work, but rather loitered with intent. Mr. Partridge looked up at her and raised his hat.

He strolled on towards the front. A cat slipped into the lamp-light, paused long enough to show that it wore a neat collar, and hurried on. It wasn't going on the tiles, it was going home. It was a Dormouth Bay cat.

About fifty yards farther on the row of shops was split by a narrow lane: a mouth of blackness, romantically obscure by comparison with the street. But it was also the mouth of a garage, and as Mr. Partridge came up even that pocket of dark was riddled by light—by headlights, in fact, of the most powerful kind. Mr. Partridge drew back and waited for the car to come out.

It was a two-seater coupé, but so wantonly long in the bonnet that the negotiation of the exit took some time: the monster crept forward, paused, retreated, crept forward again. Mr. Partridge could see its two occupants quite clearly. The driver was the long dark fellow called Lambert, and beside him, looking smaller than usual, sat Lisbeth Campion.

Mr. Partridge's first thought was purely instinctive. Because he acted on it, it was to have far-reaching effects, it was to turn the course of several lives; but it was based neither on reason nor even on common sense.

"Can't have that," thought Mr. Partridge.

For all he knew Miss Campion and Mr. Lambert were simply going for a run along the cliff. If he had stopped to consider, some such innocent explanation would at once have presented itself. But he did not stop. The car had almost drawn clear. Its rumble, open to accommodate an up-ended suitcase, was already all of it that Mr. Partridge could see. He had no time to consider, he had time only to jump forward and grip and scramble over the smooth side. He had certainly no time to settle himself. The car, leaping from first to second gear, did all the settling for him.

It wasn't going along the cliff. It was going to London. It wasn't a Dormouth Bay car.

CHAPTER 3

1

"THIS," thought Mr. Partridge, "is the Goods."

Physically he was suffering considerable discomfort; but his spirit carolled like a lark. He felt partly like Sherlock Holmes and partly like a knight-errant. All the ingredients of romance were present—a moonlit night, a swiftly-moving vehicle, a damsel in distress; for if Miss Campion were not in distress already, Mr. Partridge had little doubt that she pretty soon would be. In his mind's eye he saw a discreet bachelor apartment, a champagne supper for two, a bedroom door ajar; he saw Lisbeth's face of horror and surprise; he saw himself springing from the lobby just in time to save her honour and restore her to Dormouth Bay. . . .

"We'll have to get a lift on a lorry," thought Mr. Partridge practically, "for there won't be a train till morning."

He raised himself on his knees and peered through the window in the hood. What he saw surprised him.

Lisbeth was apparently asleep, her head tucked down against the man's shoulder; to which contact Charles Lambert seemed perfectly indifferent. He kept his eyes on the road, and both hands on the wheel. He might have been driving his grandmother to a flower show.

Mr. Partridge sank back, puzzled. He remained puzzled. At frequent intervals he heaved himself up again, each time a little more stiffly, and took another look: Miss Campion never stirred, her companion continued to devote his attention exclusively to his driving. He drove extremely well, and they made good time: at twelve-fifteen they were approaching Hammersmith, a quarter of an hour later they were in Trafalgar Square; and there, for the first time, they stopped.

Mr. Partridge looked about to discover why. The traffic light showed green, no policeman raised his hand, the wide roadway was deserted. They had stopped, so far as Mr. Partridge could judge, for no reason at all.

The door opened, and Lisbeth got out. She got out alone. In her hand she carried a small dark hat, which she now pulled on. She was wearing a plain dress and jacket.

"Thanks," said Lisbeth. "Three-thirty."

"Three-thirty," replied the voice of Charles Lambert; and Mr. Partridge had only just time to heave himself out before the car moved off.

2

Lisbeth Campion was walking slowly towards the centre of the Square. If she felt the lack, at that dubious hour, of male protection, she did not show it. The set of her very straight shoulders expressed not so much courage as indifference. Mr. Partridge, on the other hand, could almost hear the clang of his own knightly armour. For a moment his first emotion—rage with the villain who had thus abandoned her—held him rooted to the spot, brandishing, as it were, a drawn sword at the villain's departing car—of which some more civilized instinct prompted him to take the number; then he turned and followed her.

There were few people about, but almost at once a man appeared in Miss Campion's path. Mr. Partridge hurried forward: before he could come up the man had stepped aside and Lisbeth was walking on alone. She circled the base of Nelson's column until she reached the angle facing Pall Mall East; and there she halted, almost invisible against the dark plinth, and dwarfed to insignificance by the great impassive Victorian bulk of the lion couchant above.

Mr. Partridge approached. She continued to stare straight before her.

"Good evening," said Mr. Partridge.

At that Miss Campion turned her head; and he was no longer surprised that the man had so soon been shaken off. Her face in the lamplight was a mask of scorn, and, like a mask, it was blind. Her eyes seemed not to see, but to look through and past him.

And then Mr. Partridge did an absurd yet highly imaginative thing. He stooped, hitched up his trousers, and revealed his socks. The artificial light darkened their scarlet; but there was no mistaking those dapper feet.

"Oh!" said Lisbeth; and the mask dropped. "You're—"

"Mr. Partridge," said Mr. Partridge. "Arthur, the first name. I had the pleasure of taking tea with you and your aunt."

"Oh!" said Lisbeth again. "Then how did you get here?"

"The same way as you did," explained Mr. Partridge. "I been sitting in the back."

Rather to his disappointment, she showed no further curiosity. She simply accepted his presence as the most natural thing in the world. Mr. Partridge received the impression that she was so tired that all her faculties had to be concentrated on one function; and what that function was he had little doubt.

"If you'll tell me who you're looking for," he suggested, "I'll help watch out for 'em."

Miss Campion gave him a long, searching look.

She was trying to remember him; and after all there wasn't much to remember.

"I'm reliable," said Mr. Partridge earnestly. "Whatever you're up to, it's all right with me. But you didn't ought to stand here alone—"

That made her smile.

"I've stood here every night this week," she said, "and I'm still a virgin."

It was now Mr. Partridge who stared—not so much at the freedom of her language as at the implications of the remark.

"You mean—you've been coming up from Dormouth Bay regular?"

She nodded; and for the moment Mr. Partridge asked no more. He was entranced. By day the innocent pleasures of Dormouth Bay, by night this solitary, dangerous vigil—the contrast was superb, unsurpassable! "You never can tell!" thought Mr. Partridge joyfully: and he gazed upon Miss Campion as an amateur of china might gaze upon a piece of old Chelsea, or an amateur of painting upon a Vermeer, or a schoolboy naturalist upon a goat-sucker's egg. His mind flashed back to his first sight of Lisbeth on the terrace of the hotel; indolent and relaxed, she had been like a cat waiting for the night. . . .

"And *he*—that Lambert fellow—has brought you up every time?" asked Mr. Partridge at last.

Lisbeth nodded again.

"Three times. Before that it was—oh, other men. But Charles was the best, because he didn't ask questions. With the others I had to pretend to be going to a night club, or they wouldn't have put me down. But Charles—"

"It's my belief," put in Mr. Partridge, *"he's on the same side of the wall too."

She was very quick. She knew at once what he was talking about.

"The—out-of-bounds side? How did you know that about me?"

"Stands to reason," said Mr. Partridge. "Otherwise you wouldn't be here. Nor me. We'd both be safe in our beds. Mark you, I'm not always outside: it's only when civilization gets a bit too much for me. For what," demanded Mr.

Partridge (warming up to his favourite theme) "is civiliz-ation? It's—"

Lisbeth stepped away from the plinth and tilted her head towards the huge stolid beast above.

"It's *that*," she said. "Can't you see?"

Mr. Partridge nodded appreciatively.

"Law and order," he agreed, "Mayors and Corporations, good plumbing and the bench of Bishops. You can see 'em all in the set of his paws."

Lisbeth continued to stare up.

"Ronny and I used to laugh at him," she stated sombrely, "and now I'm frightened. I'm afraid he'll get back at us."

"He does look a bit broody, since you mention it," agreed Mr. Partridge, "but I daresay that's the light. I've seen him by day as mild as a pussy-cat. Who's Ronny?"

There was a long pause; but the answer, when it came, was explicit.

"Ronny," said Miss Campion, in a very distinct tone, "is my young brother, who has just done six months for peddling cocaine."

It might have been another trick of the light; but above her head the lion seemed to quiver.

3

A more unprejudiced mind than Mr. Partridge's would have been hard to find; but right from the start it struck him as ominous that Ronald Campion's best defence, as put forward by his sister, was that he had been such a fool.

"He thought it was baking-powder," said Lisbeth. "He did really. The magistrate wouldn't believe him, but it was true. Some man got hold of him and offered him two pounds a time for delivering packets to people at night clubs, pretending it was the real thing, and of course anyone but Ronny would have suspected that it was. But Ronny didn't think. He never does. He has no imagination. If he'd ever realized what it meant—what awful things cocaine does to people—he'd have gone straight to the police and told even about the baking-powder. But he just saw the whole thing as a lark. And they caught him, and put him in prison."

Mr. Partridge frowned.

"I'm bound to say it," he pronounced. "They were right."

"Of course they were right," said Lisbeth grimly. "I I hated it, but I wouldn't have stopped Ronny being punished. I've always been firm with him. I stopped him going to the Riviera—"

She broke off, and looked at Mr. Partridge with an air of surprise.

"How funny!" she said. "You don't know a thing about us!"

4

The career of the two young Campions, up to the time of the catastrophe, can best be summarized as the triumph of charm over chattels. It was also a phenomenon such as is possible only in a very large city.

They had no money beyond what they earned, and their earnings were erratic. They had no connections beyond two aunts (of whom Miss Pickering was one) who lived in Sussex, and a third aunt who had indeed married well, but in Australia. The late Mr. Campion had been a school-master, his wife a teacher of music. Both had died young, and in the same year: Lisbeth (aged ten) and Ronny (aged nine) were taken over by the Misses Pickering and passed the rest of their childhood in the pleasant though circum-scribed ways of a very modest country household. In nine years they never went farther afield than Worthing. In London they went everywhere.

They frequented first nights, and were seen at the Savoy afterwards. They danced at whatever club had swung momentarily into fashion, and dined at all the most expensive restaurants. When they returned, in the small hours of the morning, to their two rooms in a Soho slum, it is probable that neither of them ever noticed the contrast between the luxury they had just left and the meanness they came home to. They took it for granted. They moved in the thick of semi-Bohemian, semi-modish society on an income of about six pounds a week; but of course they never paid for themselves. They were so gay, and so decorative, and so young: in short, they were such born guests.

Someone, shortly after their arrival in town, when Lisbeth was nineteen and Ronny a year younger, christened them the Babes in the Wood; and the nickname was appropriate, if one imagined the wood to be no dark and terrifying forest, but an orchard of plums and apricots. Lisbeth, who had a genuine talent for design and who had insisted on spending the last of her patrimony at a London art school, slipped into an apprenticeship with a firm of theatrical designers: she plunged into the world of the theatre like a small bright fish into its natural element. The firm—a very famous firm indeed—gave large stage-cum-society parties, to which apprentices were not usually invited; but Lisbeth was smuggled in, because she was so charming. She charmed, in particular, an elderly actor-manager who needed a secretary, and who was presently surprised to find that he had acquired for that post not Miss Campion but Miss Campion's brother. Ronny didn't do badly; whenever he got into a jam he could always ring up Lisbeth, and he quite effortlessly kept the actor-manager's wife in a good humour. It was Lisbeth, oddly enough, who lost him the job, by refusing to let him be taken by that lady to the Riviera; Ronny, at eighteen, was still fairly docile, and always hated to cause pain, especially to his sister. She got him taken on by her own firm instead, chiefly to answer the telephone; but he was also very good at soothing temperamental actresses whose costumes weren't ready. He earned thirty shillings a week, and Lisbeth was soon earning five pounds, and if they had no home comforts they didn't miss them.

They didn't miss them till first Ronny, and then Lisbeth, went down with influenza. Lisbeth fortunately held out until Ronny was convalescent, but Ronny was not a very good nurse. Their many friends (most of whom did not know their address) made a few enquiries at the firm, and then forgot them. One of the great points about the young Campions was that they were never sick or sorry; sickness and sorrow were things one simply didn't associate with them, and an impression arose that they had gone to Paris. They always fell on their feet . . .

And they did fall or. their feet. Just when things were worst, when Lisbeth was delirious and Ronny at his wits' end, there arrived in London the aunt from Australia. Mrs. Maule got their address from Miss Pickering in Sussex (with whom Ronny had never thought of communicating) and descended on them like a goddess in a Rolls-Royce car. She was a woman with a strong sense of duty, and within two hours of her appearance Lisbeth had been transferred to the spare bedroom of a house in Wilton Place. Ronny naturally came along too, and unobtrusively accommodated himself with a bed in his uncle's dressing-room. He knew already that it was much easier to withhold an invitation than to turn a guest out.

And now began for the young Campions a new and prosperous phase. They had been prosperous, in a sense, before, but this new prosperity was of the solid and respectable sort. The Maules had money. They were come to London to spend it, but they meant to get value; and as soon as Lisbeth had recovered it became obvious that her company would greatly heighten their enjoyment of the town. She knew where to go, she introduced them to all sorts of interesting people, above all, she enjoyed herself so. She was grateful. She made benevolence worth while. "We look upon her," said Mrs. Maule, "quite as our own daughter"; and indeed after two months both uncle and aunt were fully prepared for a legal adoption. But from this Lisbeth for some reason held back; and before the situation grew uncomfortable settled everything by becoming engaged to a Captain in the Black Watch.

The Maules were delighted. They felt so amply repaid. For Hugh Brocard was more than eligible, he was a catch. Among his connections was a Scottish peer, and his mother had inherited a brewery. His character was impeccable, his appearance (particularly in kilts) so magnificent as to take away the breath; and but for the Maules (as they themselves often pointed out) Lisbeth would never have met him. This was probably true: Captain Brocard did not frequent the Bohemian-theatrical circles in which Lisbeth was previously to be found. In any case, such a background would have frightened him; he would have considered it highly disorderly, and disorder was abhorrent to his soul. Lisbeth in Wilton Place, however, was beyond criticism: she was exactly what a young girl should be—charming, and sheltered. Once, in an effort to express the strength and quality of his devotion, he actually quoted Shakespeare to her: he wished he might not beteem the winds of heaven visit her face too roughly. The tears came into Lisbeth's eyes, and that night at dinner they were both so radiant that the Maules, watching, received an extra emotional dividend.

And what of Ronny during this halcyon period?

Ronny was quietly peddling snow.

His position, it must be admitted, was a difficult one. He was not turned out; to do so (as he had foreseen) would have been extremely difficult; but the warm winds of approval, which blew so continuously upon Lisbeth, turned in his quarter to icy blasts. Ronny was puzzled rather than resentful. His uncle had apparently a great idea that he should work, and Ronny, who had long since lost his job with the theatrical firm, showed his goodwill by going cheerfully off to a succession of interviews arranged for him by Mr. Maule with persons in the wool trade. On each occasion he very frankly admitted that he knew nothing about wool, that he had no business experience, and that he could not conscientiously describe himself as either punctual or efficient. There were no offers, but that was obviously not Ronny's fault. The winds blew colder. The Maules tacitly agreed that he was to be given food and shelter; but they refused either to lend or to give him a penny in cash. If he wanted money, he must earn it.

Ronny didn't want much. His friends, when he re-appeared among them, were as hospitable as ever; but now that he went about without Lisbeth he was quite often commissioned to escort a young lady home; and it was awkward not being able to pay the taxi. He tried to borrow from Lisbeth, but Lisbeth had no money either. She didn't need it: she was so absorbed in her role of fiancée that she positively enjoyed asking Hugh for a sixpence to buy violets. Ronny suggested that she should ask for more—for five pounds; Lisbeth thought not. She loved her brother as much as ever, as he was soon to find out, but she was temporarily preoccupied. Ronny somehow did not care to approach Captain Brocard himself, and his attempts at borrowing among his friends were not encouraged.

He had to do something; so he peddled snow.

He thought it was baking-powder. He wanted to think it was baking-powder; but no one can be tried for what goes on in the subconscious. The magistrate simply disbelieved him; Ronny's customers had been chiefly very young girls; and Ronny got *six* months.

5

In Wilton Place it was as though a thunderbolt had fallen. The outraged Maules reeled under the blow—their bitterness being increased by the knowledge that they themselves were partly to blame. For they ought to have got rid of Ronny earlier. They ought to have turned him out by force as soon as his unprofitableness became apparent. By not doing so they had contravened the great principle of their lives; and now they were paying. They suffered severely, but even so it is probable that Captain Brocard suffered more. To a man of his temperament and upbringing Ronny's crime, with its mingling of the sordid and the flashy, was peculiarly horrible. But he behaved perfectly. He had been just about to carry Lisbeth north on a visit to his family, and underwent silent agonies until she herself suggested postponing it. He uttered not a word of reproach to her, and so handled the Maules that they were silent also. The atmosphere of the house in Wilton Place was rather like that of a morgue, but all its inhabitants, save Lisbeth, behaved well.

Lisbeth behaved badly. She was forbidden to go to the trial, and she went. Worse still, she was disorderly in court. As soon as the sentence was pronounced she stood up and called across to Ronny in a loud, clear voice. "I'll be there when you come out, darling!" called Lisbeth; and held up her crossed fingers to show that it was a life-and-death promise such as they had made in childhood; and Ronny, who still looked more bewildered than anything else, grinned back before he was led away.

The incident was reported in several papers, but Captain Brocard never flinched. At heart he was one with the Maules; but he never uttered a word against Ronny in Lisbeth's presence. He never mentioned him. Sometimes when he woke up in the night the prospect of having a criminal for a brother-in-law was so devastating that he had to get up and do dumb-bell exercises to relieve himself; then he would reflect that it was worse for Lisbeth, who was connected with Ronny actually by blood, and his tenderness towards her was renewed. He took her about as much as ever—though showing a preference for the quieter restaurants—and urged her to advance the day of their marriage. But Lisbeth, just as she had done before the prospect of being adopted, held back; and once more fate intervened. Captain Brocard was appointed Military Attaché to a Parliamentary Commission for a nine-months' tour of the Far East.

Before he went he had a long private conversation with Mr. Maule. They understood each other perfectly. Then he marched away (he left the house actually by car, but there was a general impression of bugles) leaving Lisbeth in Wilton Place.

He wrote twice a week, and three dozen roses arrived every Saturday from the Army and Navy Stores.

Lisbeth passed her time, as a fiancée should, in hand-sewing the trousseau: Among her unsuspected gifts was a talent for fine needlework. She had suggested returning to business, but both the Maules and Captain Brocard frowned on this idea. Nothing happened till the day of Ronny's release, when, as she was preparing to go and meet him, her uncle and aunt very kindly explained that since the remission of sentence for good conduct amounted to six weeks, and since Ronny's conduct had been up to standard, his liberation had taken place over a month earlier.

"Who did meet him, then?" asked Lisbeth.

They told her that no one had met him. They added that it was their earnest desire, and the earnest desire of Captain

Brocard, that Ronny should be wiped, as far as his relations were concerned, from the human register.

"But where *is* he?" persisted Lisbeth.

They didn't know. They hoped never to know. They implied that if Ronny had any decency left he would change his name and go for a soldier. His clothes and ten pounds had been sent to him at the prison, but he had been warned off Wilton Place, and off any attempt at communication. In short, every possible step had been taken to safeguard Lisbeth from the disastrous consequences of having Ronny for a brother.

"All you have to do now, dear," explained Mrs. Maule, "is to forget him."

A week later it was discovered that Lisbeth was not occupying her bed at night. The Maules asked no questions, but summoned the surviving Miss Pickering from Sussex to chaperone her niece during a month's holiday at the famous Dormouth Towers Hotel. Lisbeth submitted. Her sojourn in Wilton Place had softened her: she felt that until she had found Ronny again she had no energy to feed or look after herself, and had better let someone else do it. Also she had no money. But her resolve was unweakened. So slight an obstacle as sixty miles of good road could not prevent her from spending her nights, as usual, in Trafalgar Square; and the chief result of the Maule tactics—a result which in turn brought about the most unexpected and far-reaching consequences—was her meeting with Mr. Partridge.

6

"But why," asked Mr. Partridge, when he had received an outline of the foregoing facts, "Trafalgar Square?"

"Because we used to come here," said Lisbeth. "Almost every night, after a party, Ronny and I used to run down here and laugh at the lions. I don't know why, unless it was that we were always too excited to go to bed. It was just one of the things we always did. We were terribly childish."

Mr. Partridge looked at her.

"How old are you now?"

"Twenty-four. Ronny's twenty-three. And—you know how when you're very happy it's fun to think about being very miserable?—we used to swear that if ever we got old and awful we'd come here and drown ourselves, one in each fountain. I wish we hadn't, now. Because Ronny isn't old, but he must be feeling—he must be feeling pretty bad."

She shivered. Mr. Partridge moved close, and patted her clumsily on the back, and felt her shoulders stiffen. The lamplight touched the angle of her jaw and made it steel. Then she took a quick step forward: she had seen, across the square, the figure of a man in evening dress. She began to run.

The man wasn't Ronny. He was too old. But Lisbeth knew him, and he knew Lisbeth. He was not exactly intoxicated, but his state was such that her sudden appearance, at that hour and in that place, caused him no surprise.

"Hello, darling!" he said casually. "I've just seen your brother."

"Where?"

"Oh, in one of the old haunts. Not very tactful, all things considered. You ought to tell him."

"Where?" said Lisbeth again.

"Angel," said the young man reproachfully, "how can I possibly remember? My only sister got married this afternoon."

He began to render, in a pleasing baritone, the march from "Lohengrin." Lisbeth stepped up to him and slapped him sharply on the cheek.

"Where," she asked, for the third time, "did you leave Ronny?"

"At the Blue Shoe," said the young man, suddenly sober. "But all the same—"

Lisbeth did not wait. There was a taxi drifting by, she stopped it and got in.

So did Mr. Partridge.

Chapter 4

1

THE Blue Shoe was very much like all other night clubs, but since Mr. Partridge had never been in one, he looked about with great attention. The lobby, approached from street level by a descending flight of stairs, had a blue carpet and pale walls covered with drawings and caricatures. Mr. Partridge thought he could have done better himself. Within were small tables ranged round a narrow dance-floor, more drawings on the walls, and a band in blue jackets. The band was not playing. On each occupied table stood a bottle of champagne, but most of the clients were drinking lager beer. There were about a dozen of them all told, and all seemed very quiet sort of people.

At one of the tables, alone, sat Ronny Campion.

Mr. Partridge knew him at once because he was so like his sister. He was of the same build, though taller. He had Lisbeth's fair hair and straight nose, and as Lisbeth had lounged that afternoon so Ronny lounged now, one elbow on the table, the other over the back of his chair, his legs asprawl. He was intermittently occupied in drawing profiles on the cloth.

Lisbeth did not, as Mr. Partridge expected, rush to fling herself upon his neck. Instead she lounged across, and leaned over the table, and touched his arm.

She said, "Hello, Ronny."

He jerked up. For a moment he had the exact look of a lost child who finds itself on familiar ground. . . . Then he deliberately composed his features into an expression of dignified resentment. . . . He did not speak.

"I've been," said Lisbeth steadily, "the damnedest, stupidest fool on earth, and if you never speak to me again I'll deoorvo it. But I didn't know, darling, you'd be let out early. I—"

"That's right." His voice was like Lisbeth's too, even when, as now, he was making it bitter. "That's right, darling. Spread it abroad. Shout it from the roof-tops. I've been let out."

At the next table heads turned, then leaned close together. Ronny raised his voice.

"Hasn't this place changed, darling? In the old days I used to get rid of quite a lot of snow here; now you can't sell 'em so much as a dirty picture."

Lisbeth glanced round and did one of her tricks. Or so Mr. Partridge was always to think of them: and indeed, ever since the trickster Merlin was out-tricked by Vivian, tricks and charms have been much the same thing. What Lisbeth did was to produce music, and she got it by smiling at the leader of the band. Instantly the latest *rumba* filled the air, blanketing all conversation with its raucous strains.

"I'm glad I've found you," said Lisbeth, sitting down. Mr. Partridge sat down too. His utility was now at an end, but he was too much interested to go away; and neither of the Campions appeared to object to his presence.

"Why?" asked Ronny pointedly.

"Because I'm alone in London, darling, and you've damn well got to protect me."

He looked at her with suspicion.

"Why didn't you ever write?"

"But I did! Why didn't you? Wasn't it allowed?"

"It was," said Ronny, "and *I* did. I wrote to you each time. But you didn't answer."

Lisbeth's eyes narrowed. She looked suddenly dangerous.

"The letter-box," she said. "Ronny, you know. You know it was always kept locked, and uncle had the key. So I never got anything you sent. And my letters to you—I just put them with the rest on the hall table. I wouldn't have believed that people could be such swine. I'll never speak to them again as long as I live."

Ronny looked at her with what might have been a dawning of hope.

"Aren't you living with them now?"

"Not now," said Lisbeth. "I'm through with them. That's why you've got to come and look after me again."

There was a short silence, Ronny's next remark was unexpected.

"They had awfully good food," he said wistfully. "Are you sure you don't want to go back?"

Lisbeth shook her head. Ronny opened his mouth again, but did not speak. He let out his breath in a long sigh; and the two of them sat looking at each other in silence so long that Mr. Partridge lost patience. They couldn't sit there all night . . .

"Now then!" he said firmly. "Pull yourselves together. What's to do next?"

For the first time Ronny turned and looked at him.

"Who's that?" he asked, with interest. "Another dick?"

"Ronny!" Lisbeth leaned urgently across the table. "Do you mean the police have put detectives onto you again?"

"Not the police, darling. Your fiancé. Hugh. His other emissary tracked me down this afternoon, but I gave him the slip. He hadn't nearly such a good moustache."

"But Hugh," said Lisbeth, "is at Basra!"

"He's not. He's here in London, at his flat. Armed, no doubt, with a horse-whip and a tract. I can be horse-whipped, if I care to call round, any time up to three A.M. to-night."

2

It took a quarter of an hour, and a good deal of both moral and physical force, to get Ronny into a taxi. Lisbeth was radiant. She did not stop to enquire why her fiancé had not let her know of his return, it was enough that he was there, at hand, obviously willing and competent to take all responsibility from her shoulders. It was an attitude which Mr. Partridge highly approved: he liked women to be feminine, and it pleased him to discover that Miss Campion's true character, now revealed, was that of a clinging vine. Her hand flew to her powder-box as her heart evidently flew to Captain Brocard: she made up her lips even while reasoning with her brother. If Hugh had found him a job—and for what other reason should he wish to see him?—all was well: she and Ronny would live together again, free of the Maules, light-hearted as they used to be, until—

"Until you marry him," said Ronny.

"But if he has to go back, darling, that won't be for months! What do I do till then, if you can't support me?"

She drooped back in her chair, looking so appealing, so helpless, that Mr. Partridge's heart melted within him; and as though in sympathy the strains of the rumba were suddenly modulated to the strains of a Viennese waltz. Lisbeth turned and gave the band-leader a smile. It was a smile so exquisitely appropriate, so perfectly expressive of wistfulness, gratitude and friendly understanding, that Mr. Partridge marvelled how she found time to achieve it in the midst of all her other preoccupations; but Lisbeth had turned, smiled, and turned back again to Ronny all within five seconds. Ronny had taken up his pencil again and was starting on another profile; and as Lisbeth watched her expression underwent another rapid change. There was nothing of the clinging vine about her as she reached across the table and half hauled him to his feet.

"Come on, you idiot!" said Lisbeth sharply; and with Mr. Partridge's assistance got Ronny out from behind the table. Between them they steered him across the floor and up the blue stairs. He did not seem to be drunk, but he was obviously too much for any young woman to handle alone; so after pushing him into the cab, Mr. Partridge nipped in too.

3

The flat occupied by Captain Brocard was one of a fine set of apartments in St. James's Street; but there was at that hour no porter on duty, and the progress of Ronny up to the first floor was therefore unobserved. At the door of number 3 Lisbeth stopped and rang—one hand on the bell, the other sleeking her hair; her eyes were bright, her mouth tender, and Mr. Partridge (Ronny leaning heavily on his shoulder) fervently hoped (not for the first time) that the Captain would prove worthy. Mr. Partridge had thought about the Captain a good deal, and now, as the door opened, he involuntarily drew a deep breath and released it in an agitated snort.

The snort, as a rule, is a sound indicative of contempt. The snort emitted by Mr. Partridge was a snort of admiration.

For Hugh Brocard was admirable. No other adjective so justly summed him up. He was splendidly tall, splendidly built, with firm handsome features that were eloquent (though of course in a restrained and gentleman-like way) of every strong and honourable quality. "A tower of strength," thought Mr. Partridge; and as the phrase rang in his mind Lisbeth seemed to drop forward and disappear into those tremendous arms.

"Darling," she said, "when did you get back?"

"Day before yesterday, flying," said Captain Brocard. His voice matched with the rest of him, being at once strong and perfectly controlled. "I rang you up from Basra, and your aunt told me—"

He broke off; over her head his bright blue eyes took in first Ronny, then Mr. Partridge.

"But didn't she tell you I was at Dormouth Bay? Why didn't you ring me up there?"

"I wanted to get everything settled first," said Hugh Brocard, "so that you shouldn't have to worry. I didn't know you and your brother had already . . . come in contact."

His voice was affectionate, but it was also the voice of a man who would stand no nonsense; and Mr. Partridge, feeling that eye still upon him, made haste to look as though he agreed with everything the Captain was about to say. Lisbeth also became aware of her lover's steady gaze, and half turned.

"This," she explained, "is Mr. Partridge. He's been . . . helping."

Captain Brocard nodded, and with one arm still round Lisbeth reached out and opened a door.

"Wait in there, will you?" he directed; and Mr. Partridge, with prompt obedience, conducted Ronny through.

4

The room in which they found themselves was evidently a study, not large, but very comfortably furnished with a desk, bookcases, two easy chairs and a couch. Upon this last Ronny immediately flung himself down and apparently went to sleep. Mr. Partridge took one of the chairs; and there they waited for the best part of an hour.

Mr. Partridge did not mind in the least. He was savouring to the full the extraordinary sensation of sitting in a perfect stranger's flat, sixty miles from home, at two in the morning. He studied his surroundings with passionate interest, taking in the row of silver cups (proofs of excellence in many a manly sport) the pair of foxes' masks (each with date painted beneath) the dust-whisk fashioned from a fox's brush, the doorstop fashioned from an elephant's foot. There seemed no doubt that the Captain had all the correct predatory instincts. Mr. Partridge himself possessed a portion of elephant's tusk, but it was not the spoil, so to speak, of his own bow and spear—he had actually received it in part payment of a debt of five pounds—and these trophies of the chase impressed him greatly. The walls were further adorned by several photographed groups of cricketers, among whom the Captain's superior size made him easily identifiable. Mr. Partridge sighed with satisfaction, and sinking back in his chair gave himself up to a beautiful day-dream in which he too returned from hunting the fox to score a hundred not out before leaving for India to pursue big game. He was just embarking on a very large liner when the door opened and Captain Brocard came in.

He gave a quick look at the dormant Ronny, and with an air of relief addressed himself to Mr. Partridge.

"Miss Campion tells me," he stated, "that you've been very good to her brother."

"It was nothing much," said Mr. Partridge modestly; and indeed it wasn't. He had merely supported young Ronny to the taxi and helped him out again. But Lisbeth had evidently elaborated, for the tone of voice employed by Captain Brocard at once domesticated (as it were) Mr. Partridge as a humble but worthy family friend. He tried as hard as he could to look like an ex-butler, and waited for what was to come next.

"May I take it," continued the Captain, "that if a permanent arrangement is made for Mr. Campion, you would be willing to—er—keep an eye on him for the next few days?"

"You may," said Mr. Partridge.

The permanent arrangement, as outlined by Captain Brocard, was simple but water-tight. It was also traditional: the black sheep was to be transformed into a remittance man. An adequate income (payable weekly and so tied up that it could be neither anticipated nor borrowed upon) awaited him in Canada, where each Saturday for the rest of his life Ronny would be able to enter the Bank at Woodville, Ont., and confidently demand the sum of ten dollars.

"And very handsome too," said Mr. Partridge.

Captain Brocard looked as though he agreed. The money was coming out of his own pocket, and though his income could easily stand it, he felt there were few men who would have done so much, and so promptly, for so peculiarly undeserving an object. He was probably right. He was right about most things.

"And if you'll pardon the liberty," added Mr. Partridge—he rolled the phrase over his tongue: it had a good ex-butlerish ring—"it will be a great weight off Miss Lisbeth's mind."

"That's just it," said Captain Brocard, unbending slightly. "Miss Campion, as you know, is very much attached to her brother. She has a feeling of responsibility for him—"

"Even when they were kiddies," put in Mr. Partridge, "she was always getting him out of scrapes."

The Captain unbent still further.

"And now it's absolutely essential," he said earnestly, "that she should have nothing more to do with him, I don't say the Maules have behaved well, but on that point I thoroughly agree with them. Campion must get out of the country, and stay out. He ought to be able to leave the day after tomorrow. You can keep him till then?"

"With pleasure," said Mr. Partridge. ("Ex-butler it is," he thought. "Ex-butler keeping lodgings . . .")

"Any expenses you've already incurred, of course—"

"Call it two-pound-ten," said Mr. Partridge moderately.

The Captain took out a pig-skin wallet and from it produced a fiver. He was a gentleman all right. Mr. Partridge accepted the note with dignified gratitude, and next found himself charged with an envelope bearing the address of a firm of solicitors in Lincoln's Inn.

"Take him along there," said Captain Brocard, "and Mr. Treweeke will make all arrangements. There'll be no difficulty about his passport. It must seem odd, in a way, my putting all this on to you, but I'm leaving the airport at dawn, and from what Lisbeth tells me—and naturally the fewer people who know of my connection with this business the better—"

He broke off: he looked, for the second time, at the figure on his couch; and his fine brow darkened.

"He ought to have been flogged," said Hugh Brocard curtly.

In Mr. Partridge's imagination a horse-whip whistled. He had a vision of Captain Brocard, in hunting pink, beating down to earth a cowering Ronny—as was only right, for did not the one stand for all that was strong and virtuous, and the other for all that was weak and sinful? And was it not well for Lisbeth that her lot was to be cast with the one, and not with the other?

The mantelpiece clock struck three. Captain Brocard swung round, alert and soldierly.

"I've got to go," he said. "I can't even drive Miss Campion back. She'll stay here the night, and go down in the morning. I'd like you to get *him* off the premises as soon as you can. If you want to communicate with me, write care of the address on that letter. And I'm much obliged to you."

Having thus given his orders like a soldier, and expressed his gratitude like a gentleman, Captain Brocard turned on his heel and marched out to bid his fiancée farewell. To do so he no doubt adopted a softer style, but he did not linger. Duty called. Mr. Partridge had hardly resumed his own non-buttling personality when a door slammed, a door opened, and Lisbeth Campion came quietly in.

5

Her face was white with fatigue, yet bright with a soft candlelight radiance; and her expression changed as a candle flickers. She looked proud and happy, as a girl should who has just been kissed by her lover; she looked a little forlorn, as a girl should when that lover has just departed for Iraq; and she also looked extremely determined—for which last expression Mr. Partridge could find no reason at all.

"Isn't he splendid?" she demanded; and the question, though spoken so softly, for fear of waking her brother, was a paean of triumphant praise.

"Splendid!" echoed Mr. Partridge, beaming back.

"The minute the Maules told him what brutes they'd been he got leave and flew all the way back from Basra! Just because he knew I'd be worrying! There isn't another man in the Army who'd have done it!"

Mr. Partridge was conscious of a slight jar. The statement struck him as unnecessarily precise: "in the world" would surely have been more natural? Then he reflected that to Captain Brocard the Army doubtless was the world, and to Lisbeth also, since she was about to marry into it. . . .

"He's thought of everything," praised Mr. Partridge. "By the way, who did you tell him *I* was?"

Lisbeth giggled.

"I said you'd married our old nurse and kept lodgings in Baker Street—and that that was where Ronny went when he came out. To lie low and look for work. I thought it would show he was trying to turn over a new leaf."

"So it would," agreed Mr. Partridge dubiously, "if he had."

"And so he *would* have," retorted Lisbeth, "if he'd thought of it. I mean if you had married Nurse, and did keep lodgings, and if Ronny'd remembered the address, he'd most likely have gone there. So it wasn't really a lie. And anyway I had to tell it, because I wanted Hugh to get a good impression. He never thought much of the poor lamb, even before—and that's what makes it all so wonderful, because Hugh hated the whole business worse than anyone. He was afraid it might upset his Colonel. And now to do all this for us—!"

"We're to see Mr. Treweeke tomorrow," said Mr. Partridge, with importance. "To get the tickets, I expect, and so on."

"Oh!" said Lisbeth, suddenly frowning. "I wonder if they're bought already? Would the steamship people take them back?"

"They take 'em back on the boat," explained Mr. Partridge. "Till then your brother hangs on to them."

"But Ronny," said Lisbeth, "won't be on any boat."

Mr. Partridge looked puzzled.

"Then how's he going to get to Canada?"

"Ronny isn't *going* to Canada," said Lisbeth, patiently.

6

Mr. Partridge gaped. He had gone through a lot since leaving Dormouth Bay, and though his adventures had been highly enjoyable, they had also exhausted him. For a moment he wondered whether fatigue had affected his hearing.

"But I thought," he recapitulated, "you said it was all so wonderful—"

"So it is! It's wonderful of Hugh to have taken so much trouble, and to have been so marvellously generous, and

I'm adoring him for it every minute. But he doesn't understand Ronny."

Mr. Partridge looked towards the couch. Ronny Campion still slept. He slept silently, peacefully, and—or so felt Mr. Partridge, with a rush of annoyance—deliberately. He was deliberately absenting himself from the tiresomeness of life. He had already avoided, by sleep, what would certainly have been a most unpleasant interview with Captain Brocard. When other people had taken thought for him, and racked their brains for him, and at last settled something for him—then he would perhaps wake up. But certainly not before.

"Ronny's weak," stated Lisbeth. "I've no illusions about him. If he goes to Canada he'll be ruined. He'll hate it, he'll be bored, he'll have two pounds a week to drink on. If it was wicked to sell cocaine, it would be just as wicked to send Ronny like that to Canada. Ronny couldn't imagine, and Hugh can't imagine either. Of course I pretended to be pleased—I was pleased, terrifically, because Hugh had . . . had gone to his limit for me; but as for doing what he says, that's just nonsense."

"And what isn't nonsense?" enquired Mr. Partridge sceptically.

"Keeping Ronny here with me. I can get him on his feet again. I've six months to do it in, and then Ronny will be all right and I can marry Hugh."

She spoke with such earnestness of conviction that Mr. Partridge nearly groaned. But he saw his duty. He saw it all too plainly. For the first time in his life he found himself in complete agreement with the conventional point of view.

"Listen to me, my dear," he said heavily. "I'm an old man, I've seen a thing or two, and in a general way I'm all for the under dog and the outsider. But your brother's too much of a handful altogether. He's no job for a young girl like you. Let him go to Canada, write him a nice letter once a month, and you'll have done your bit."

Lisbeth looked at him.

"Ronny is not," she said steadily, "rubbish to be thrown away."

In Mr. Partridge's opinion that was almost precisely what the young man was; but he knew better than to say so. He tried an argument less personal. "How d'you think you'll live?"

"Ronny shall support me," said Lisbeth lightly. "It will be very good for him."

She crossed to the desk, found a piece of unheaded paper, and sat down to write. From her manner it was plain that she considered the discussion at an end. Mr. Partridge fidgeted about the room, and finally came to a halt under one of the cricket-groups.

"Your auntie and uncle—" he began.

"I'm through with them," said Lisbeth promptly. "And they'll be through with me. But I'm writing to Aunt Mildred— Miss Pickering—at the Dormouth Towers. Are you going back now?"

"Yes," said Mr. Partridge. He had no idea how the journey, at that hour, was to be accomplished; he knew only that if Miss Campion wanted him to get back he would. A thought struck him.

"What about that Lambeth chap? Won't he wait?"

"Oh, no," said Lisbeth, with assurance. "He knows that if I'm not there something's happened. He'll just go back. But I'm afraid you've missed him."

"I'll manage somehow," said Mr. Partridge stoutly.

"Then will you put this through the hotel letterbox? So that Aunt Mildred will get it at breakfast as though I'd left it last night? I'm asking her to send my clothes and things here, which she will, if she thinks I'm with Hugh."

Mr. Partridge took the letter and nodded. . . . There was a vague plan forming at the back of his mind.

"And you write to me," he said, "at Peters Library, Cliff Street, and tell me your address. I could maybe lend you five bob, a week or so, just till you're properly fixed."

"You're a lamb," said Lisbeth, smiling at him. It was a delightful smile, appreciative, friendly, even affectionate. Mr. Partridge wished he didn't remember how she had smiled at the leader of the band. He knew that as soon as the door closed behind him she would have forgotten his existence.

"Good-bye," said Mr. Partridge.

"Good-bye," said Lisbeth. "I wish I could tell you—"

On the couch Ronny stirred and opened his eyes: a subconscious instinct must have told him that the coast was clear. Lisbeth at once turned.

"Good-bye," said Mr. Partridge again.

The door closed.

7

For the first time since their reunion the young Campions were alone.

Lisbeth curled herself up in one of the big chairs, Ronny continued to recline on the couch; for some moments they did not even look at each other, but there flashed between them that silent signal exchanged all the world over by children when their elders have left the room. The silence was companionable and unembarrassed. Lisbeth spoke first.

"Do you remember," she asked idly, "that place—down at the Aunts'—where the blackberry hedge was so thick there was a sort of tunnel inside?"

Ronny nodded.

"Where we found the dead rabbit. I felt sick, and you buried it." He reached for a cushion, and made his shoulders more comfortable. "As a matter of fact, I've thought about it quite a lot lately. It was a—a place to get into . . ."

Lisbeth curled herself round still farther, and leaned her head against the back of the chair, so that she could watch Ronny's face without raising her eyelids. It was a delicate business, this probing; but she had to find out the extent of the damage. She kept her tone light.

"Was it rotten, darling?"

"Awful!" said Ronny, with fervour. But he did not sound repressed, as though the horror had gone too deep for words; he sounded quite simply and healthily cross about it. "Awful!" he repeated energetically. "I was never so bored in my life. All male nurses—"

"What nurses?"

"In the hospital, of course. I wrote you a letter about it. The very first thing I did in jug was to break my ankle falling down their beastly stairs. Didn't you notice my limp?"

"No, I didn't," said Lisbeth, forgetting, for the moment, to be tactful. "I thought you were tight. Do you mean to say you were in hospital all the time?"

"All the time, darling," agreed Ronny. "Five bloody months. . . ."

Lisbeth sank back and relaxed. It was all right. The iron hadn't entered in. It had barely grazed the surface. And how like Ronny—she giggled, very faintly, for she was very tired—to duck so simply and effectively out of the whole thing! She needn't have worried, she ought to have known him better. She did not indeed suspect her brother of deliberately crocking himself, it was simply that given Ronny, and given the circumstances, a broken ankle was the natural answer. . . .

"Do that some more," ordered Ronny drowsily. "It's a silly noise, but I've missed it."

Lisbeth laughed again; but he did not hear. He was already asleep. She got up, and found in the next room a big bathrobe, and tucked it over him. Then she kicked off her shoes and made herself as comfortable as possible in the chair. The future was extremely doubtful, and for some minutes, before sleep overtook her also, Lisbeth considered it gravely. Her view of the situation was extremely clear. Wash out the Maules; wash out, for six months, Hugh Brocard; wash out—here she paused, but she knew their world—the legion of their loving friends. "Alone in London!" thought Lisbeth wryly. Well, they had been alone in London before, and they had come out on top, so they presumably could do it again. But that was the bright side. Before, they had been merely unknown; now they were more or less notorious. Ronny hadn't a chance of any job that required a reference. Lisbeth looked at her brother, sleeping so neatly and enjoyably, and with complete realism reflected that it would be almost impossible for him to re-embark on a criminal career, since the police would certainly be keeping an eye on him.

She made a knot in her handkerchief, to remind herself to point this circumstance out to him first thing in the morning. On the other hand, he could capitalize, so to speak, his criminality, and get himself taken up by some philanthropic individual or institution: the actor-manager's wife, for example, would quite likely still be willing to save Ronny's soul by taking him to the Riviera. . . .

Lisbeth sighed. The iron hadn't entered in far enough. In her sleepy brain she first visualized it as an actual poker that could be rammed down his throat as a backbone; then, more rationally, as a good stiff job of work. "I've got to be as hard as nails with him," she thought. "I've got to be a tyrant and a brute"; and she set her jaw in what she judged to be an expression of unmitigated ferocity.

Ronny opened one eye and smiled at her. He had a delightful smile, candid and good-humoured.

"The little mother," he commented. "Aren't you going to sing me to sleep?"

"I'm going to wait until you're properly awake," retorted Lisbeth, "and then I'm going to swear at you."

8

Mr. Partridge got back to Dormouth Bay by hopping two lorries, the first bound for Norbury, the second for Brighton, and then by walking a mile and a half over the spur of the downs. He was not particularly tired: both drivers had been taciturn, after the manner of their kind, and he had got in nearly two hours' sleep. The air was pleasant, smelling of hay and honeysuckle; larks sang overhead, and the turf made easy going. But Mr. Partridge scarcely enjoyed his walk. He was leaving behind the first genuine adventure that had ever come his way; he was leaving town for country, London for Dormouth Bay, and he could see, at that moment, no compensations. Skylarks sang. Mr. Partridge did not think of them as blithe spirits, but simply as birds he could hear any day of the week all through summer. The honeysuckle was sweet; Mr. Partridge looked at it with passing approval, and reflected sardonically that it was a pity he wasn't a bee. It struck him that nature had been consistently overrated.

His thoughts turned back to the young Campions, and in melancholy reaction he now asked himself whether even they were worth regretting. Their story was after all common enough: you could read it—or one very like it—in the police court news of any paper. He had simply been, for a few hours, on the inside, and that—ah, there you had it!—that was why it had all been so enthralling. Anything was enthralling, if you knew the inside. You saw a woman in the bus fumble for a coin: an incident too ordinary for notice—unless you could know that the Queen Victoria penny she slipped back had been given her in 1870 by her only lover who had subsequently been lost at sea off the coast of Ecuador. . . . "You never can tell!" thought Mr. Partridge, with a lift of the heart. Then his spirits sank again. For you didn't often get inside. You could make up tales about the passers-by on the promenade, but it was a thousand to one against ever finding out the truth. They were like houses known from the outside. And it was hard, when a door had for once opened, to step back again onto the common pavement.

"She'll never do it," thought Mr. Partridge. But the memory of Captain Brocard was comforting. At the end of six months, if Lisbeth didn't get flu again and die of it, and if Ronny didn't let her in for another and a worse scandal, her prosperity was sure. Too many ifs, though, and nothing to set against them, so far as Mr. Partridge could see, but the incongruous strength of Miss Campion's jaw. He fingered her letter, now slightly dog-eared in his pocket, and for a moment considered tearing it up, going to Miss Pickering with the whole story, calling in the Maules, and cabling the Captain, so that they could all descend together—like a host of righteousness or a ton of bricks—upon Lisbeth's idiotic schemes.

"It's the Best Course," thought Mr. Partridge sententiously.

But he did not take it. He did not take it for the simple reason that if he did Lisbeth would never forgive him. Since he was never likely to see her again, the objection was frivolous; but on the unbalanced character of Mr. Partridge it had effect. He would deliver the letter as agreed, and then make his way home, and open up his library, and settle down once more to the cosy, the familiar, the safe routine of life at Dormouth Bay.

He topped the last ridge, and there the town lay below him. The red roofs of its houses rayed out in orderly spokes from the Post Office, the Aquarium, the Municipal Hall. It had the lowest death-rate in Great Britain, and no illegitimate births. It was a beauty-spot and a moral all in one.

Sulkily, Mr. Partridge descended.

CHAPTER 5

1

LISBETH was twenty-four, Ronny a year younger: they both slept soundly and peacefully for the next ten hours. Even at one o'clock they did not wake, but were aroused by a prolonged ringing at the door of Captain Brocard's flat.

Lisbeth opened her eyes, automatically reached for her vanity case, and within fifty seconds was alert and presentable. Ronny took longer to come to the surface; he was still yawning and tousled as his sister reached the lobby. The bell rang again, and they both stiffened.

"Who is it?" whispered Ronny.

Lisbeth stepped forward and raised a hand to the lock. That whisper had decided her. They must begin as they meant to go on, and if they began by whispering and being afraid to open doors, life wouldn't be worth living.

"It's probably the manager come to turn us out," she said firmly. "Do something to your hair, darling, you look like the morning after the week before."

She hesitated nevertheless a moment longer: she had an odd feeling that the opening of that door marked a definite step in both their lives. It would open on the next six months, at the end of which, if all went well, there would be happiness and security for herself with Hugh, happiness and security (though of a less defined nature) for the regenerated Ronny. And if all didn't go well—"But it will!" thought Lisbeth defiantly. "So whatever's coming, we'll take it."

She opened the door.

It wasn't the manager. It was Mr. Partridge.

2

He carried a small suit-case. At his feet lay a large bundle done up in a table-cloth, a cuckoo-clock and an elephant's tusk. He had the air of being surrounded by all his worldly goods; as indeed he was.

"Good morning," said Mr. Partridge. "I'm glad to find you still here, I thought p'raps you might be gone."

"We've only just woken up," explained Lisbeth. "Come in and sit down."

But Mr. Partridge stood his ground. His manner lacked its usual aplomb. Even his shoes were slightly dusty.

"I delivered your letter all right," he continued. "Put it through the box at half-past seven. Your auntie must have got it with her breakfast."

Lisbeth thanked him warmly. It was difficult to keep up a social conversation whilst resolutely ignoring a large bundle, a cuckoo-clock and an elephant's tusk; but since their owner persisted in treating them as invisible, politeness constrained her to follow suit. Ronny, however, gaping over her shoulder, was less punctilious.

"What on earth's all that?" he demanded simply.

Mr. Partridge fixed his eyes on Lisbeth.

"There's been," he said heavily, "a bit of trouble. Mind that clock, young man; the cuckoo's loose."

"Trouble?" prompted Lisbeth sympathetically. (Was it unlucky to open that door and find trouble outside? Ridiculous!)

"At the library," went on Mr. Partridge, evidently struggling with a sense of grievance. "Though I'd locked up all right. No one could get in. Which, in a manner of speaking, was the whole Cause."

The allusiveness of his style made him a little difficult to follow: but the fact finally emerged that on the previous day an agent of the library's owners had called three times. On each occasion Mr. Partridge was of course absent; on each occasion (by a series of most unlucky coincidences) a baffled subscriber had been actually clamouring on the step; and when, that morning, the agent paid his last and successful call, it was merely to give Mr. Partridge the sack.

"I call it a damned shame," said Ronny vigorously.

But Mr. Partridge was a fair man. Sympathy, and the unloading of his heart, had assuaged his sense of grievance.

"I don't know," he said, "Looking at it from their point of view, I daresay they thought they had a right. Not but what there isn't too much reading anyway—specially among females. There was one young woman would have taken a book out twice a day, if I'd let her. I practically saved her eyesight."

He paused, and looked anxiously at Lisbeth. It seemed to strike him for the first time that he had perhaps mistaken his functions as librarian. He had taken too broad, too human a view. But Miss Campion was smiling back with complete approval. She understood. If she remembered what he had said about the five bob, she gave no sign. She appeared even glad to see him.

"So we're all in the same boat," said Lisbeth lightly.

Mr. Partridge nodded. He picked up his bundle, Lisbeth (taking care) picked up the cuckoo-clock, Ronny picked up the elephant's tusk, and by common consent they all moved back into the study. There was no need for speech. As simply and casually as children acquire a stray dog, so the young Campions had acquired Mr. Partridge: and like an old, sagacious Airedale, who knows he is in for a hell of a life but lets himself be acquired all the same, Mr. Partridge followed them.

"Breakfast," said Lisbeth practically.

She picked up the telephone, and from her conversation it was apparent that the person at the other end, though considerably surprised, remembered Miss Campion, felt a high regard for Miss Campion, and was willing to supply her with three breakfasts at one o'clock in Captain Brocard's rooms.

"What will you have?" asked Lisbeth over her shoulder.

"Everything," said Ronny. "God knows when we'll eat again."

Lisbeth ordered bacon and eggs, bacon and sausages, bacon and kidneys, toast, rolls, coffee, honey and marmalade. Mr. Partridge was pleased to see that she had proper ideas about food; from her appearance she might have been living on one of those diets he read about in the papers— grapes and a rusk, varied by orange-juice or steamed fish. With the breakfast arrived the manager, a middle-aged Scot who greeted Lisbeth with great cordiality, but who remarked that the sub-letting of Captain Brocard's flat had already been arranged, and that the new tenant was expected on either that or the following day. Lisbeth said she quite understood, and Ronny rather unnecessarily added that the Captain seemed to have left a good many personal possessions still in evidence. He looked, as he spoke, at the row of silver cups; and the manager, following his glance, at once replied that an inventory had already been made. He then produced a telegram addressed to Captain Brocard, and asked Lisbeth whether she would take the responsibility of dealing with it. Lisbeth replied in the affirmative, and the slightly constrained little interview then came to an end.

"I don't," said Ronny, helping himself to bacon, "care for that bloke's manner. It's a wonder how Brocard put up with him."

Neither Lisbeth nor Mr. Partridge answered—though one at least of them could have pointed out that the manner to which Ronny objected was one which the Captain had probably never himself encountered. Lisbeth opened the telegram.

"What's it about?" asked Mr. Partridge inquisitively.

She passed it over. It had been handed in at Dormouth Bay, and neatly epitomized the mingled simplicity and wariness of Miss Pickering's character. "IS LISBETH WITH YOU?" that lady had wired. "PLEASE CONFIRM IF BOXES REALLY REQUIRED. TRUST IN YOUR GOOD SENSE BUT DO MAULES KNOW KINDEST REGARDS MILDRED PICKERING."

Now Mr. Partridge had received only two telegrams in all his life—one informing him that his wife had not been involved in a railway accident, the other announcing the arrest of his mother-in-law for assaulting a policeman—and naturally regarded them with great respect; he was therefore much surprised when Lisbeth, after but a moment's consideration, picked up the telephone and quite calmly dictated a reply.

"Pickering, Dormouth Towers Hotel, Dormouth Bay," said Lisbeth. *"'Send luggage here leave all to me wish us luck love from both Brocard.'"* Then she hung up the receiver and in exactly the same tone of voice asked Mr. Partridge whether he took his coffee black or white.

"White," said Mr. Partridge.

Over the rim of his cup he looked at her with something like apprehension. She was evidently quite unscrupulous. She was also a clinging vine, a steely-jawed Amazon, and—at that exact moment—a hungry schoolgirl sitting down to a good feed. "You never can tell," thought Mr. Partridge. He took a large helping of bacon and egg. You couldn't always tell even about eggs; but these happened to be excellent.

3

"The first thing to do," began Lisbeth briskly, as soon as the meal was over, "is to find somewhere to live."

"Ah," said Mr. Partridge.

Ronny said nothing, but gazed wistfully about the room. It was all very handsome. The couch and chairs were of the best quality, deeply sprung and upholstered in solid leather. One of the bookcases incorporated a wireless-gramophone, the other a cabinet which probably contained cigars. . . .

"No, darling," said Lisbeth gently.

"Why not? It's all rot about its being let."

"That's what I mean, darling."

Ronny considered this a moment, and then nodded.

"I know," he said intelligently. "Fear of pollution. Me. And speaking of pollution—hadn't we better all have baths?"

Rather to Mr. Partridge's astonishment, Lisbeth seemed to think this a good idea. Mr. Partridge himself took baths regularly, every Saturday night, and considered himself a very clean man; but this notion of breaking off a serious discussion merely to wash struck him as frivolous in the extreme. It was also, after so large a meal, highly dangerous.

"Not for me, thank you," he said firmly. "I shaved at home. But I wouldn't mind dabbling my feet."

He got up, and went across to his bundle, and unloosed its knots; and at once the chaste grey carpet was incarnadined by a bulging, collapsing pyramid of scarlet wool.

"Good God!" exclaimed Ronny. "Whose are those?"

"Mine," said Mr. Partridge modestly. "My socks. A hundred and fifty-two pairs."

"Good God!" said Ronny again. "Let's start a gent's outfitters!"

It was only a joke, of course, but both he and Lisbeth stared so speculatively at the pile that Mr. Partridge involuntarily placed himself before it in a position of defence.

"I daresay," continued Ronny, "Brocard's left some shirts . . ."

Lisbeth shook her head.

"No good, darling. We can't start any shop, we haven't the capital."

Mr. Partridge coughed. He personally, as it happened, possessed at that moment more capital than ever in his life before.

"I've got five pounds," said Mr. Partridge; and with some ceremony produced and displayed the clean and crackling note. Lisbeth looked at it admiringly.

"We could live on that for a week," she said. "A week at least. Only it seems rather a shame—"

"Not at all," said Mr. Partridge quickly. "Call it the kitty, and share and share alike."

Their gratitude, considering the circumstances in which the note had been acquired, was a little embarrassing; but he felt it wiser not to divulge its source. Unscrupulous as Lisbeth had shown herself in the use of the Captain's name, the Captain's apartment, and (potentially) the Captain's shirts, Mr. Partridge suspected that she might develop finer feelings with regard to the Captain's cash. He himself was more logical. Moreover, if he didn't look out, he would have young Ronny making off with his socks and selling them for the price of a drink. . . .

"Look here!" exclaimed young Ronny, turning to his sister. "What about your engagement ring? It must be worth pots."

"It's in the safe at the Dormouth Towers."

"But you can get it out. We could pop it for a couple of hundred at least, and live like Dukes." Lisbeth was silent.

"Anyway, you can't just leave it about," argued Ronny. "It's so careless."

"Aunt Mildred will look after it for me," said Lisbeth calmly.

There was a moment's silence, during which the two young Campions appeared to read each other's thoughts with extreme clarity. Then Lisbeth turned back to Mr. Partridge.

"Do you know London?" she asked.

"Do I know London!" repeated Mr. Partridge. "Why, I lived here man and boy, bar four years in France, till the day I was married. If you're thinking about lodgings, there's places round the Edgware Road—"

"Or Bloomsbury," put in Ronny, recovering his spirits.

"Or Notting Hill—" added Lisbeth.

They looked at each other with sudden pleasure. They had five pounds, and the city of London to live in. The Campions were very young; Mr. Partridge (as he told himself) was an old fool. He had never felt happier in his life.

"We'll house-hunt this afternoon," said Lisbeth, "and send round here for my stuff afterwards. Because I think they'll be glad to see us go."

As though to confirm her words, there entered at that moment a porter in uniform carrying a large canvas bag and a handful of chamois leather. Without a word, and with some ostentation, he wrapped up and bore off all the silver cups, the silver pen-tray, and the silver calendar.

"We'd better have those baths straight away," said Ronny Campion.

He had, where his own comforts were concerned, a certain amount of practical sense.

CHAPTER 6

1

THE district in which the Campions (and Mr. Partridge) found a home was not disreputable. It was simply broadminded. It lived and let live. It was also peculiarly urbane. Landladies (who required a week's money in advance, but who never asked for references) and tenants (who locked up their correspondence but always passed the time of day) ceased, within its purlieus, to be natural enemies, and worked in alliance against such common foes as duns and gas-inspectors. They lent and borrowed not only money but household goods; they were always ready to swear to complete ignorance of each other's whereabouts. The whole district, in fact, was lawless rather as Mr. Partridge was lawless: in a quiet way. It was certainly not criminal. It now and then got into trouble, but its troubles were only those of normal human beings living on incomes inadequate to complete respectability.

The apartment for which Lisbeth and Mr. Partridge paid down their pound advance consisted of the top floor of number 7 Marsham Street, in the neighbourhood of Paddington Station. The ground floor was occupied by a small grocer (T. Cubitt) who lived on the one above, the second by a family of well-to-do but slightly Bohemian pastry-cooks. The three Walkers—a father and two sons—were at the top of their profession: they were employed in one of the great Park Lane hotels, and could toss off a basket of marzipan fruit, or an ice-pudding in the shape of an aeroplane, as easily and casually as the average confectioner tosses off a doughnut. It was their great regret that they did not work in France—and this not from any lack of patriotism, but simply because, being artists, they desired recognition for their work. There was a centrepiece of old

Mr. Walker's, made for a Coronation banquet, which in Paris would almost certainly have won him the Legion d'Honneur; his phlegmatic countrymen merely consumed the whole (thus paying indeed a certain brutish tribute, for the confection, representing Windsor Castle, was on a large scale) and passed on to the savoury without the least idea of recommending Mr. Walker for an O.B.E. He was a man who took himself very seriously: in his early days he once got religion, and experimented for a time with a charlotte russe which when cut would reveal on each portion the words "Prepare to meet thy God." (The project never matured, but Sidney, the eldest son, made quite a lot of money out of a sort of peppermint-rock displaying the legend "What-ho!") The Bohemianism of the Walkers consisted chiefly in keeping, as a result of their West-End associations, very late hours; they seldom went to bed before two, and were said to spend fabulous sums on cherry brandy. The proximity of three such affluent and raffish characters naturally threw T. Cubitt (grocer) somewhat in the shade, and it was long before Lisbeth and Mr. Partridge found out, for example, that he had been an ex-Rechabite since the age of ten. In the meantime his chief attraction was his telephone.

Both the Campions appeared to consider this extremely important; from the way they talked (thought Mr. Partridge) one would have imagined that a telephone was as essential to life as drinking-water. "We ought to have one ourselves," said Ronny seriously. "It's the one thing worth paying money for. And even if we can use T. Cubitt's, it means twopence a time—in cash."

"But we get incoming calls free," pointed out Lisbeth. "He can easily shout up the stairs. Run down and try." So Ronny solemnly descended to the ground floor and uttered a variety of yodels which brought T. Cubitt out at his side-door and Sidney Walker out on to the intermediate landing. Both looked at Ronny with some sternness; then both looked up and saw Lisbeth's head over the banister, and no rebuke followed. "It's all right," called Lisbeth, "we're the new tenants." The grocer, a man of few words, merely said "Ah," but Mr. Walker stood his ground. He was a man in the early forties, short and heavy-shouldered, with dreamy brown eyes which slowly turned to follow Ronny's upward progress like the eyes of a cow watching a train. "Fine day," observed Ronny, over his shoulder; "Not very," replied Mr. Walker; his gaze, reaching and resting on Lisbeth, became slightly more vaccine than before; then he slowly backed into his own territory to invent (though this of course transpired later) a new variety of *Coupe Jacques*.

The top-floor suite consisted of three rooms, one medium-sized, one smaller, and one little more than a cupboard. The first contained a table, four chairs, a cupboard and a divan-bed, the second a divan-bed, a small cooker, a sink and a geyser-supplied bath, the third a divan-bed and some hooks. Divan-beds were in fact the feature of the place, and the main reason why Lisbeth and Mr. Partridge had rented it. It was decided that Ronny should have the one in the kitchen, Mr. Partridge the one in the cupboard, and Lisbeth the one in the sitting-room. The sitting-room wasn't bad, though curiously piebald as to its woodwork: a previous tenant had evidently started repainting, and given up half-way through, for half the skirting-board was pea-green and half an involuntary off-white, and there was a pot of pea-green paint still on the landing. But the walls were a pleasant faded yellow, and the furniture of plain deal stained dark brown. The sitting-room wasn't bad at all, and when that evening they all three sat down to supper in it, the scene struck Mr. Partridge as not only intimate, but gay. He and Lisbeth had spent half an hour at Woolworth's, buying bright blue china, pots and pans, and a variety of hooks, rails and other household gadgets which Mr. Partridge proposed to put up next day. Lisbeth had also laid out seven shillings on a dozen yards of checked cotton, for tablecloths, curtains and bed-covers; it was red-and-white, blue-and-white, white-and-orange, for she didn't want, she explained, a colour-scheme, she just wanted colour. The curtains were as yet merely tacked over the windows, the covers as yet unhemmed; but it was abundantly clear that the completed effect would be very colourful indeed. Mr. Partridge, looking about, felt rather as though he were living in a harlequin's house.

"You must have spent," observed Ronny, "a hell of a lot." He had not been out shopping himself, he had passed the evening lying on his bed. Neither Lisbeth nor Mr. Partridge ever discovered exactly how he had spent his time since being released, but he evidently needed to make up on sleep.

"Only a pound," said Lisbeth quickly, "with the sausages. A cheerful home keeps up the morale. And we'll all look for jobs to-morrow."

"I suppose you'll try your theatrical show again?" Lisbeth shook her head.

"No, darling. They got someone else ages ago."

"But you were such a roaring success there—"

"No, darling," said Lisbeth.

There was a slightly awkward pause. Mr. Partridge again received the impression that the young Campions were carrying on their conversation in silence. But since he had been waiting for an opening himself, he had no scruples about interrupting them.

"I know what *I*'d like to do," he said, "and that's start a night club. I've been thinking about it ever since we went to that Shoes place, and I've some very good ideas."

"Such as?" enquired Ronny.

"Ratting," said Mr. Partridge unexpectedly. "There's nothing livelier than ratting. There must be old warehouses down by the docks just as full of rats as they can stand—and I daresay we could get the use of one for almost naught. We'd provide the terriers, d'you see, the customers hire them by the evening—"

"I don't *think*," said Lisbeth gently, "that the women would really care for it. Not in evening dress. And it's the women who keep night clubs going."

Mr. Partridge looked hopefully across at Ronny, but Ronny gave him no support either. Mr. Partridge sighed.

"In any case," said Ronny blandly, "you haven't taken Lisbeth's point. I'm to be kept away from the old crowd and the gay lights. Isn't that so, darling?"

"Yes," said Lisbeth.

"Honest toil," declaimed Ronny, "is now our watchword. All right. I'm reformed already, but anything you say goes. What would you like me to be?"

"A postman," said Lisbeth thoughtfully. "It's an open-air life, with regular pay, and you wouldn't be dull because you would get off with all the housemaids."

To Mr. Partridge's surprise, Ronny at once agreed.

"I'll start to-morrow, darling. I'll get up early, and go round to the G.P.O., and find out the drill. If they can't make me a postman I daresay they'd have me as a messenger boy. 'Do the task that's nearest, though it's dull the whiles, helping, when you meet them, lame dogs over stiles.'" He broke off; his animation left him. "Do you suppose," asked Ronny anxiously, "they'll mind about my limp?"

Mr. Partridge pushed back his chair and began to clear the table. Ronny helped. He showed an almost pathetic willingness to make himself useful in spite of his disability. He washed up, and sang while he did so. During the remainder of the evening he held tin-tacks and screws while Mr. Partridge put up a rail, and offered to read aloud to Lisbeth (from an old copy of *Tit-Bits* found in the cupboard) while she tacked hems. He behaved like a ray of sunlight crossed with a Boy Scout. But there was no further talk of making him a postman.

2

Mr. Partridge passed a bad night. This was due neither to the liver sausage he had eaten for supper, nor (as would have been quite reasonable) to any fears for the future, but simply to the badness of his bed. It was a shocking bed. It creaked loudly at the least movement. The mattress was also bad: it had previously been slept on (decided Mr. Partridge, after consideration) by two large dogs; for there was a deep circular hollow at either end and a ridge in the middle. Fierce dogs they must have been, too: they had torn great rents in the ticking, through which hard gobbets of flock worked out and granulated the under-sheet. Mr. Partridge writhed uneasily, then turned on his front and crouched like a sphinx, his elbows in one hollow, his knees in the other. But nature had not designed him as a sphinx: he had not—as Dr. Johnson remarked of his host's bull-dog—that quick transition from the thickness of the forepart to the tenuity behind.

Mr. Partridge rolled over again and sat up. He knew what he wanted: he wanted his socks. They made a splendid padding, and judiciously arranged would bring the surface of the bed to a uniform level. But he had left the whole pile in the sitting-room, now Miss Campion's bed-chamber, and his sense of decorum prevented him going after them. He listened intently: not a sound was to be heard save the unnaturally loud ticking of his cuckoo-clock, also in the sitting-room. He could hear it because his door, for purposes of ventilation, had been left wide. For a moment he wondered whether he should go and stop it, in case it kept Lisbeth awake—such an act would excuse his entry, and he could get hold of his socks at the same time; but Lisbeth's complete silence seemed to indicate that she possessed the same powers of sleep as her brother. They could both sleep through anything. Mr. Partridge coiled himself down in the upper hollow and resentfully began to count sheep.

He had, or so it seemed to him, but just dozed off when he was reawakened by a loud rapping. He did not answer, but the next moment someone came in.

"Tea," said Ronny.

He had a cup of tea in his hand. He was fully dressed. The tea was for Mr. Partridge. He had already, he explained, taken tea to Lisbeth. He had also prepared the bathroom. He had been up very nearly an hour.

"What time is it now?" asked Mr. Partridge.

"Seven o'clock," replied Ronny pointedly. "Shall I tell Lisbeth you'll have the bath before her, or after?"

"After," said Mr. Partridge.

He sucked up his tea, put the cup on the floor, and once more coiled round the ridge. He had perhaps been ungracious, but at his age he needed his sleep.

Almost immediately the door opened again. Mr. Partridge lay doggo.

"Your bath's running," announced Ronny cheerfully.

And here it may be recorded that his association with the young Campions produced on Mr. Partridge one lasting and irrelevant result. He formed, under their influence, the habit of bathing every day: thus showing his freedom from prejudice, his adaptability, and the strength (or so he believed) of his constitution. "It's a great change," he used to say at first. "For a man of my years, I'm not sure it isn't dangerous. It thins the blood." But he persisted nevertheless, and in time so assimilated the Campion prejudices as to speak disrespectfully of Saturday-nighters. But this of course was much later; his first bath in Marsham Street, what with the lack of privacy—Ronny kept coming in and out, and Lisbeth talked to him through the open door—and the erratic behaviour of the geyser, was more of an ordeal than a pleasure. Mr. Partridge emerged clean but slightly ruffled, and with a feeling of being unusually susceptible to draughts.

The day, which was to inaugurate the reformation of Ronny by turning him into a sister-supporting world's worker, produced one outstanding event. Lisbeth got a job.

As soon as her luggage arrived (it reached Captain Brocard's flat that morning, and was sent on by taxi, as soon as Lisbeth telephoned her new address, by the only-too-willing manager)—as soon as her luggage arrived, she attired herself in a grey flannel coat and skirt, took three shillings off Mr. Partridge, and went out. That was about four in the afternoon. When she came back at six, she had a job.

The name of the firm which was to employ her struck Mr. Partridge as very curious indeed. It was called Wanted Women; and it was a direct result of the declining birth-rate and the Suffragette movement. Under Victoria the Good, even under Edward the Peacemaker, it would have been unthinkable; for in those days there was still an adequate supply of active single women ready to run about and perform extra tasks for the more fortunate married. (Miss Pickering, taking charge of her sister's two children, and being dispatched with Lisbeth to Dormouth Bay, was a good example.) But since then times had changed: the ranks of these useful creatures had been thinned: some had entered the professions, some preferred to work for (and be paid by) strangers, some had simply not been born. Wanted Women stepped into the breach. It would supply, on the shortest notice, a competent gentlewoman to supervise spring-cleaning, take children to school, show country-cousins the town, meet trains, exercise dogs. The shades of a thousand Victorian aunts must have been constantly wringing their hands at this intrusion of hired help into the family circle; but Wanted Women was prosperous and busy. Its Principal was also shrewd. She was so shrewd that when Lisbeth, in answer to the usual request for a clergyman's reference, frankly detailed Ronny's exploits, she did two things. She took down Lisbeth's address (and T. Cubitt's telephone number) without further ado, and added in the adjoining column a couple of cryptic signs. They stood, translated, for "Good in emergencies, no male employers . . ."

Mr. Partridge (a Victorian himself) was both startled and impressed. Ronny was merely startled.

"You'll hate it," he prophesied. "You'll do nothing but look after sick brats."

"Not sick, only convalescent," retorted Lisbeth. "That's one of the rules. And I get ten shillings a day, or two bob an hour, and extra at night. And I've got one job for to-morrow already—reading French to an old lady in Bayswater. It's money for jam."

"Money for bread, more like," said Mr. Partridge uneasily. He and Ronny, after scrutinizing the advertisement columns of the daily papers, had also been out trying their luck. Ronny had applied for one post (as secretary to a Bridge Club), Mr. Partridge for six—as house-porter (twice), baker's roundsman, boot-and-shoe salesman (twice) and store detective. He tried for this last mainly because Ronny had taken him for a dick, and because hope springs eternal in the human breast, and his failure, owing to complete lack of qualifications, did not depress him. His five other failures did. He had been told in each case simply that he was too old.

That evening he went downstairs and privately looked through T. Cubitt's telephone-book to see if there were anything called Wanted Men. There was not. The unmarried Victorian uncle, unlike the unmarried Victorian aunt, had played but little part in the nation's domestic economy: his passing left a gap outside the stage-door rather than a gap in the kitchen or nursery. Mr. Partridge closed the book and went back to his daily papers.

On the three succeeding days he was told that he was too old seventeen times.

3

Ronny, on the other hand, seemed to be too young: at any rate he was equally unsuccessful. There was no doubt that his limp, which became very pronounced after the least exertion, lessened his chances, and his incurable honesty in disclaiming all experience and all business ability probably lessened them still further. But Lisbeth was apparently just the right age, and was soon almost fully employed. The Bayswater lady had asked for her regularly, three afternoons a week; she made quite a corner in packing—Wanted Women, receiving after each of her expeditions in this line a complimentary 'phone call, thought it due to the expertness with which Miss Campion packed; but it was not; it was due to her practice of warmly admiring each garment put in—and she had spent two most profitable evenings sitting with a small boy while his parents went to the theatre. The variety of the work, its constant challenge to her wit and efficiency, suited her down to the ground. She was always gay, and never tired. In her spare moments she vamped T. Cubitt, with the result that he readily took messages for her on the grocery telephone. She also vamped Mr. Partridge, though he did not recognize the process as such, by requiring him to conduct her every morning to either the bus-stop or tube-station. Mr. Partridge liked going to the tube-station best: it took five minutes longer.

"I wonder," he remarked suddenly, on one of these occasions, "whether were being shadowed."

Lisbeth looked surprised.

"Who by?"

"Agents," said Mr. Partridge.

"But whose?"

"Well, there's your auntie and uncle," said Mr. Partridge thoughtfully, "and Miss Pickering, and that lawyer chap we never went to see—Treweeke, his name was—and I suppose some of 'em must be looking for you."

Lisbeth shook her head.

"Mr. Treweeke won't take action. I've met him. His instructions were to wait till Ronny turned up, and he'll just go on waiting. I'm sure he won't write to Hugh, because of course he doesn't want Hugh to have anything to do with us. He treats Hugh like a schoolboy." She paused to reflect. "I daresay Aunt Mildred gives us an occasional thought, but that's all. She's used to not hearing. And the Maules never want to see hair or hide of us again. Anyway, I think they must have gone back to Australia, because I passed the house, and it was to let."

"It still seems rum," persisted Mr. Partridge, "you dropping clean out of a world, so to speak, and no one wondering."

"That's London. But I expect they're wondering about *you*, darling, at Dormouth Bay."

"I'll lay they are," agreed Mr. Partridge complacently. "But then I was always a bit of a mystery to 'em. They hadn't the minds to take me in."

He had cast off Dormouth Bay, and without regret. But he was not happy.

He had begun to fret. He did what he could: he kept the flat in order, went out shopping, and made Ronny take his fair turn at washing up. He and Ronny were seeing too much of each other—or at any rate Mr. Partridge was seeing too much of Ronny. They were not precisely on bad terms, but their conversations as a rule were limited to a series of detached remarks from the one acknowledged by a series of snorts from the other. It was therefore all the more surprising that the one exception proved of great interest to both, and, as regarded Mr. Partridge, of far-reaching effect.

It occurred on a Saturday afternoon. Lisbeth and Mr. Partridge had lunched early, the former being engaged to meet two children on the 1.30 to Victoria, and Ronny did not appear till she had left. (The day was very warm, so that he could sit on a bench in the Park, and watch the passers-by, without tiring his leg.)

He was in very good spirits: he announced himself by tapping on the door.

"Who's there?" called Mr. Partridge.

"Obadiah," replied Ronny, entering with a cheerful smile.

"Obadiah?" repeated Mr. Partridge.

"Obadiah'd *love* to!" said Ronny.

Mr. Partridge turned the witticism over in his mind, grasped the point, and didn't think much of it. It was simply a leg-pull, and he resented having his leg pulled by whipper-snappers. At that moment, in fact, his resentment against Ronny altogether—against his smile, his amiability, his general air of being sure of a welcome—came suddenly to a head.

"Back for your dinner?" enquired Mr. Partridge sardonically. "We've left all the best bits."

"Good," said Ronny, with simple pleasure. Then he looked at Mr. Partridge again, and appeared to be struck by a surprising notion.

"I say!"

"Well?"

"Don't you like me?"

It was a hot day, and Mr. Partridge, in the midst of his morning's shopping, had turned aside to apply for a post as fishmonger's assistant; only to be told, as usual, that he was too old. At lunch with Lisbeth he had unobtrusively eaten as little as possible, and now felt hungry. He could see no reason for concealing the truth.

"No," said Mr. Partridge.

Ronny put a piece of corned beef in his mouth and chewed it thoughtfully.

"Why not?"

"Because you're a good-for-naught," said Mr. Partridge, with conviction. "You have to be kept and cosseted and looked after as though you were a pet dog. You let your sister work for you, and never do a hand's turn, and sit there eating corned beef like a blooming Duke. You make me tired."

Ronny continued to munch, and to fix Mr. Partridge with his extraordinarily candid gaze. He was not abashed, but neither was he annoyed.

"It wasn't I," he pointed out, "who came and hooked on to Lisbeth. It was Lisbeth who came and hooked on to me."

"I know," admitted Mr. Partridge impatiently. "That was her foolishness. That's what women are like. That's why they want protecting, so to speak, from themselves. And it's the man's place to protect 'em. You ought never to have let her do it."

Ronny shook his head.

"You don't know Lisbeth. Once she got on my trail she'd have followed me to the North Pole. If I were to go out into the night this minute, she'd be after me again."

There was so much truth in this that Mr. Partridge could not answer it. Ronny present was a nuisance; Ronny absent would be an even greater one. He was a fair problem. . . .

"The fact is," continued Ronny, as though following this thought, "I'm superfluous. I'm not one of those great hefty fellows who can mend roads, I haven't much brain, and

I'm not particularly well educated; and now I've got a sort of tin can tied to my tail as well. It's no wonder I can't get a job, with all this unemployment about. I *oughtn't* to get a job. I ought to be tucked into a nice lethal chamber with an asbestos wreath."

"Why asbestos?" asked Mr. Partridge, interested in spite of himself.

"So that it could be used again for the next candidate, The classic British mixture of sentiment with economy. I'm thinking of it, of course," explained Ronny, pushing back his chair and giving the project his full attention, "as a Government job. A new branch of the Civil Service—Undesirable Cremations. Or—making it a private matter—I could just put my head in the gas oven and turn on the tap. But that would upset Lisbeth."

"You're right there," agreed Mr. Partridge. "And I must say I shouldn't care for it myself."

This concession appeared to cheer Ronny up. He reached for a piece of bread-and-butter, spread an excessive quantity of jam on it, and made himself a sandwich. He had many innocent tastes. He was innocent—as Mr. Partridge dimly realized—fundamentally: as innocent as a lamb in a field, or a bird in the hedge, or a snow-drop in a wood. It was rather his misfortune than his fault that he could not live on grass or worms or dew, but needed corned beef and bread, to say nothing of overcoats and bedding . . .

"You ought to have been a bulb," said Mr. Partridge, thoughtfully. "Or some kind of a vegetable."

"A forked radish," agreed Ronny. "But what can I do?"

"You can at least make yourself useful," said Mr. Partridge. "You can wash up."

Ronny at once began to clear the table. He moved very neatly and handily.

"You could do that every day," continued Mr. Partridge. "You could do the whole work of this place, easy."

And then from the mouth of the forked radish, of the lamb, of the snow-drop, fell a shattering home-truth.

"And leave you without an occupation?" said Ronny cheerfully. "The fact is, we're overstaffed."

4

Mr. Partridge put on his hat and went out. He hurried, but his step was not light. One of the Walkers on the stairs, T. Cubitt, from the shop, greeted him affably; Mr. Partridge did not reply. The bright sunshine without, the pleased Saturday-afternoon faces of the passers-by, gave him no pleasure. They rather jarred. His mood was that of a wet Sunday night.

"Overstaffed," repeated Mr. Partridge aloud. It was a phrase of doom. It meant, in nine cases out of ten, the loss of one's job; and though it did not carry, in his own case, exactly that significance, it carried one very near it. It meant that he wasn't wanted. He was useful, indeed, but his utility simply left Ronny idle. If Lisbeth worked, and Ronny ran the flat, the position would be in a way paradoxical, but not economically unsound. A fleeting doubt crossed Mr. Partridge's mind: *would* Ronny run the flat, with anything like competence, if there were no one to keep an eye on him? "Pah!" thought Mr. Partridge. "I'm making excuses, Because I'm too old to get a job myself."

He had reached, he did not quite know how, an island in the middle of Oxford Street. On either side the traffic hemmed him in. He swore at it with such violence that a lady standing alongside started apprehensively away. "Never fear," Mr. Partridge told her bitterly. "*I* shan't harm you. I'm too old." The lady started again, and Mr. Partridge laughed a cynical laugh. He waited no longer, but plunged through the traffic, and felt his coat brush the side of an omnibus. The experience was sobering; his fury left him; he continued down Oxford Street at rather less than his usual pace.

Since it was Saturday afternoon, all the large shops were shut, and the pavements were unusually clear. Mr. Partridge loitered along, looking automatically at the windows, but without really taking in anything he saw. It was the merest chance (or else it was fate) that made him pause outside the Bonnie Scotland Tea Rooms; for the place was not particularly attractive. But Mr. Partridge paused, looked, and there in the window, propped against a plate of scones, saw a small notice. The Bonnie Scotland wanted a commissionaire.

He went in.

5

The lady who received him was spare, elderly, and bore a vague resemblance to Miss Pickering, Mr. Partridge would have bet anything up to half-a-crown that she did raffia-work in her spare time.

"Good afternoon," said Mr. Partridge. "I see you're wanting a commissionaire."

The lady looked slightly embarrassed.

"Not *exactly*," she explained. "At least, I'm not sure that's the right description. I just want someone to stand outside and hold *that*" she indicated, leaning against the wall, a sort of banner consisting of a two-dimensional wooden thistle on the end of a long pole. The thistle was painted in its natural colourings, with the addition of the words: "Bonnie Scotland, Lunch 1/6, Teas and Light Refreshments." Mr. Partridge looked at the thing without enthusiasm.

"How much?" he asked.

"One-and-six a day—with your meals. Lunch and tea, and a snack in the evening."

Mr. Partridge thought. Such a job, and he knew it, was the rock-bottom of respectable employment. It was like being a sandwich-man. But he would get his food, and the money clear, which meant nearly ten bob a week towards the rent. He would be able to give Lisbeth ten bob every Friday, and cost next to nothing for keep. . . .

"*And* uniform," added the lady persuasively.

Mr. Partridge flinched.

"What uniform?"

"Kilts," said the lady.

There was a long mirror at the back of the room. Mr. Partridge gazed at his oval reflection and tried to imagine himself in the garb of a Highland chief. He could imagine most things, but not that.

"I'm sure," said the lady, "you'd look *very* nice." She sounded quite anxious to engage him, as indeed she was: he was by far the most respectable applicant she had yet had. "You could wear your own jacket, and there's a tam-o'-shanter, and stockings."

"What colour stockings?" asked Mr. Partridge.

"Red," said the lady.

That settled it. The finger of fate, dipped in a ruddy dye-pot, unmistakably pointed. Mr. Partridge could have wished it pointed in some other direction, but after his experiences of the last week, after his conversation with Ronny, he dared not ignore it. He promised to appear at ten o'clock the following morning, and the lady offered him, along with his wrapped-up accoutrements, a piece of very good gingerbread. Mr. Partridge munched it thoughtfully, one eye on the thistle sign-board. The green of its foliage was just about the same colour as the pot of paint they had found in the flat.

"Wants brightening up," said Mr. Partridge. "You let me take it away with me, and I've a friend who'll do it for half-a-crown."

CHAPTER 7

1

IT WAS an anxious moment for Mr. Partridge when he first issued from the door of number 7 Marsham Street clad in his Highland regalia. The kilt (or so Lisbeth assured him) was by no means unbecoming; but it felt uncommonly draughty, though Mr. Partridge had so far departed from Highland tradition as to put on a pair of pants. Through the grocery window he could see T. Cubitt's and T. Cubitt's assistant, and the young lady in the Cash, all turning their heads to take a look at him: from his rear came a sudden sound of bagpipes, proceeding, he suspected, from T. Cubitt's boy. Mr. Partridge did not look round. His tam-o'-shanter, worn askew, made a sort of one-eye blinker, which he turned ostrich-like upon the street as he hastened on keeping close to the wall. His self-consciousness, while it lasted, was acute: but it did not last long. He turned two corners, reached Edgware Road, and at once became anonymous. The soothing indifference of London going about its business was a shelter and a balm.

Few people so much as glanced at him, and as his confidence returned an unexpected change came over his demeanour. Mr. Partridge stepped out: it might almost be said that he swaggered. The swing of his kilt put a swing into his stride: he thrust out his chest, and by a firm compression of the lips made his moustache bristle. He felt fine. His newly-painted standard, carried like a lance at rest, clove a passage through the morning crowds. Mr. Partridge could have wished it to bear a more martial legend; but he remembered, and drew comfort from, a scrap of poetry about another fellow whose banner had something odd about it. "Excelsior!" thought Mr. Partridge; and marched up to his post in good spirits and smack on time.

It may be said at once that as standard-bearer-cum-commissionaire Mr. Partridge made good. He had at first considerable trouble with his feet, which by the end of the day became so swollen that he could hardly hobble home; but this was only until he got his shooting-stick. He got it for a shilling, in the Caledonian Market, and sat upon it proudly during business hours. There were a few difficulties: a policeman objected to his being seated on the pavement; Mr. Partridge pointed out that he was not sitting, but leaning, and demanded to know by what law a man was forbidden to lean on his stick in the public street. The policeman very wisely decided that the use of shooting-sticks in Oxford Street was not likely to become wide-spread, and that the matter might be dropped. Miss Macbeth (his employer) also objected, on aesthetic grounds: she thought it didn't look well. Mr. Partridge explained that he had bought the stick with one eye indeed to his own benefit, but with the other to hers: he hoped by means of his shooting-stick to remind passers-by so forcibly of the Scottish moors—so to fill their ears, as it were, with the cry of the bonnie grouse— that they would feel an overwhelming desire for a cup of bonnie Scottish tea. Miss Macbeth gave in. One didn't really see much of the stick, since Mr. Partridge always draped his kilt neatly over it.

The strain on his feet thus relieved, he began actually to enjoy himself. There was always plenty to look at: people often asked him the way, and he got into some very interesting conversations. He gave ladies advice on the best place to shop, and was always ready to look after their dogs for them while they did so. Dog-tending, in fact, developed into quite a side-line: he sometimes had as many as three or four leashed about his standard, and made as much as a shilling a day in tips. Miss Macbeth at first looked askance, but Mr. Partridge argued very plausibly that since many of the dogs were Scotch terriers, they served as additional publicity; and he swore never to have any truck with either French bull-dogs or Irish wolf-hounds. (The district, so far as he knew, contained none: but the promise showed good feeling.) Miss Macbeth gave in. She even acquired, under her employee's persuasions, a small enamel trough marked "DRINK PUPPY DRINK." Mr. Partridge was establishing himself, and though the Bonnie Scotland was by no means a night club, for the moment at least his ambition slept.

2

The household in Marsham Street was now on a fairly sure footing; it did not for that reason become dull. Indeed, Mr. Partridge was sometimes puzzled: he and Lisbeth were undoubtedly engaged on a work of reformation—a process which in Mr. Partridge's experience usually entailed an atmosphere of strenuous gloom: the atmosphere of the Marsham Street flat was light, casual, and frivolous. There were evenings when the high spirits of its inhabitants over-flowed in song; social evenings when an off-duty Walker and T. Cubitt's assistant came up for a game of rummy, or simply for conversation. They were very interesting. The assistant had a secret ambition to own a Derby winner, and was full of good tips for training racehorses; the Walkers all had secret sorrows. Mr. Partridge's private (and unlikely) explanation was that they had all been jilted by film-stars: there was no doubt that any reference to the screen at once threw them into a profound melancholy. As companions they were rather fascinating than gay, but they were also such thorough men of the world that Mr. Partridge never ceased to take pleasure in their company.

Ronny enjoyed these parties too. In fact Mr. Partridge often wondered whether, for a reformee, he weren't enjoying himself too much all round. The work of the flat was now supposed to be entirely his, but as usual he had ducked out of it: T. Cubitt's Cash, a young lady of amiable and domestic temperament, having formed the habit of slipping up in her lunch hour to sweep, dust, and wash the breakfast-things. (Mr. Partridge found this out one pouring wet day when Miss Macbeth humanely dismissed him at half-past twelve: on reaching Marsham Street he found the Cash engaged at the sink while Ronny entertained her with stories of high life. Her demeanour was that of a person completely at home; and Ronny, under the subsequent cross-examination, freely admitted that she came up every day. He had no further explanation save that she seemed to like doing it. He also borrowed half-a-crown to buy her a box of chocolates.) Something, felt Mr. Partridge, had gone wrong.

Lisbeth's avowed plan had been to awaken Ronny's sense of responsibility by throwing upon him the entire burden of her support, and what had happened?

Lisbeth was working on an average nine hours a day, and Ronny was still as irresponsible as a canary. The explanation, of course, was that Miss Campion's natural efficiency had simply got the upper hand; and when Mr. Partridge thought back to Ronny's naïf self-analysis, he could not but admit that this was probably just as well. The deaths from starvation of Lisbeth and himself would no doubt have had a very rousing effect on the young man's conscience; but Mr. Partridge wanted to live. He was enjoying life, in these days, very much indeed.

He had a job—humble, but by no means unpleasant. The society of Lisbeth (even when he had to check her for swearing) was a constant delight. The impromptu quality of Ronny's housekeeping did not offend him. He was getting two good meals a day at the Bonnie Scotland, and the meals he took in the flat, on Sundays, were equally satisfying though in a different way. The first course was always so homely, the second, supplied by the Walkers, so exotic. The Walker standards were very high, and they evidently took a large view of their perquisites: an unsuccessful bombe (carried home in an ice-pail swathed in newspaper), the wing of a sugar swan, half a marzipan flower-basket—such and suchlike were the delicacies involuntarily supplied to the Campion table by the hotel in Park Lane. The Walkers would take no denial; they had always (explained Sidney casually) plenty for themselves; and Mr. Partridge for some time attributed their generosity partly to temperamental open-handedness, partly to the natural love of scrounging, and partly to artistic pride. There presently occurred, however, an incident which, upsetting all these preconceptions, also upset Mr. Partridge.

Returning one night from his post outside the Bonnie Scotland, he observed T. Cubitt coming down the top flight of stairs. This was highly unusual. The grocer as a rule kept strictly to his own territory; not even Lisbeth had been able to break down his reserve, and though he was most punctilious and neighbourly about delivering her 'phone messages, he always sent them up either by the assistant or the errand-boy.

" 'Evening," said Mr. Partridge.

" 'Evening," replied T. Cubitt.

"I expect there's no one in," said Mr. Partridge.

"Ah," said T. Cubitt.

"But if you'd care to come back and wait—"

The grocer merely shook his head (though courteously) and without any explanation of his presence passed straight on. Mr. Partridge continued up, and outside the door found a small parcel wrapped in white paper. On the top was written "With compliments," and inside was a jar of calves-foot jelly.

3

It was this incident which led Mr. Partridge, that evening, to a careful observation of Lisbeth's appearance. He had not noticed it before, but she had undoubtedly changed very much since leaving Dormouth Bay. In the first place, she had lost her tan; her skin was no longer honey-coloured, but creamy, so that her fine soft hair looked darker, a deep instead of a pale gold. Aesthetically Mr. Partridge rather approved the change: if Lisbeth's eyes had been blue instead of grey, and her cheeks pink instead of pale, she would, in his opinion, have been very pretty indeed. But it wasn't her looks he was bothering about, it was her health; and though you couldn't call her actually skinny, she looked about as big round the middle as a stalk of asparagus—

"What's the matter?" asked Lisbeth, pausing hat in hand before the mirror.

"You feeling quite well?" asked Mr. Partridge anxiously.

"Of course I'm quite well. I'm always well. Why?"

Mr. Partridge produced the jar.

"From old Cubitt," he said. "Left outside the door. Like leaving, as you might say, crumbs for the birds. And there's all that sweet stuff we get from the Walkers. It's my belief they think you don't get enough to eat through supporting a fat old man like me." Lisbeth spun round and stared at him.

"Darling! What an insane idea!"

"It's not," said Mr. Partridge unhappily. All his old misgivings were back in force; the happiness of the last weeks, he felt, had been but a hollow thing. "It's not," he repeated. "You keep this place going—"

"I don't! You pay half the rent, and you have all your meals at that awful little place and you stick to that awful job and never complain, and you clean my shoes for me, and what I should do without you I can't imagine!"

Her fury, as much as her affection, was grateful. Mr. Partridge felt slightly better. He sat down. Lisbeth came and stood over him and took him by the shoulders.

"Do I *look* starved?"

"You're very thin . . ."

"I'm always thin, thank heaven. If I weren't I should have to diet."

"How much do you weigh?"

"Seven and a half stone. It's too much."

"Old Cubitt—" began Mr. Partridge again.

"Mr. Cubitt is an admirer. The jelly's probably the most expensive thing in his shop, and that's why he sent it. If it had been roses, you wouldn't have thought there was anything queer in that?"

"Yes, I should," said Mr. Partridge. "A chap of his age—" He paused; he had a feeling that he was being ridden off. He wasn't discussing the morals of elderly grocers. . . .

"And Mr. Walker is an admirer too," went on Lisbeth shamelessly. "*All* the Walkers. But I can't put marzipan fruit under my pillow, so we have to eat it."

She was smiling now, she was at once demure and impertinent, and Mr. Partridge knew that he had only to grin back, and they would be in for one of their rich hilarious evenings—Lisbeth chattering nineteen to the dozen, laughing at all his jokes, making him laugh in turn. The prospect was tempting; but Mr. Partridge had been too thoroughly put out. There was something else on his mind, something about which he had too long kept silence.

"And then," he began heavily, "there's Ronny."

At once Lisbeth's expression changed again. It became one of polite but slightly bored attention.

"What about him?"

"I'm not sure, my dear, you're doing the right thing." Mr. Partridge hesitated: he was on dangerous ground. "We started out, if you remember, with the idea of making him work for his living and yours too. He does a bit up here, I'll admit, but what's the good of it? It's not giving him regular habits even. He needs a hard, steady job—with a taskmaster. He needs some one who'll bawl him out when he does wrong, and dock his pay when he's late. That, mark you—" Mr. Partridge was getting into quite a rhetorical stride—"is what he *needs*; but if you tell me he'd never stick it, I'll agree. It's no use asking pigs to fly. But what I do say is this: till he gets a proper something to do—by which I mean something he's got to finish before he's paid for it—there's no hope. Now I've said my say, and I hope you'll take it as meant."

There was a short silence. Mr. Partridge watched Lisbeth's face anxiously. But she did not seem angry, only thoughtful.

"You're right, of course," she said at last, "And I've never forgotten, really, about Ronny's job. It's simply that I haven't had time to get round to it."

"There you are!" exclaimed Mr. Partridge. "And so long as someone else works hard enough to keep him in smokes, Ronny won't bother. If you ask my opinion of him—"

"I know it already," said Lisbeth calmly. "It's also the opinion of Mr. Cubitt and the Walkers and Hugh and—and I suppose every man who's ever met him. And I can see what you all mean. I'm not sentimental about Ronny. He's in many ways—" her voice was dry—"a born gigolo. But he's also my brother."

"And if that's not sentimental," said Mr. Partridge, "I don't know what is."

Lisbeth stiffened. He had brought against her, though unwittingly, the one charge of all others which her generation most resented.

"I'm not," she retorted. "I'm being purely selfish. I simply don't choose to have a relation I'm ashamed of. I more or less brought Ronny up, and it's offensive to my pride if he turns out a rotter. I daresay it's hard on Ronny, making him go against all his natural instincts, but that's his lookout. If he wants to be a gigolo he can damn well fight for it; and he's got to fight me."

Mr. Partridge examined this statement for some moments, and being a man of strong common sense, found it slightly bewildering. He suspected sophistry. That they were in any sense being hard on Ronny was of course ridiculous. . . .

"I'm a complete egoist," continued Lisbeth. "Haven't you noticed?"

"I can't say I have," said Mr. Partridge.

"Well, I am. I like to be indispensable to people, and to be made a fuss of, and generally to rule the roost."

"So would everyone else," pointed out Mr. Partridge, "only they can't pull it off."

"Because they haven't such strong egos. I've got an ego like an elephant."

Mr. Partridge suddenly grinned.

"There's a pair of my socks want mending. You might do 'em before you go to bed."

"I will," said Lisbeth promptly. "But it's only to show how beautifully I darn—which you'd never expect from my useless and decorative appearance."

She reached for the sewing-basket, and sat down cross-legged on the floor, and pushed her hair up from her ears. Even in that ungraceful position her appearance, as she had said, was extremely decorative. She was wearing a black frock and pale stockings: the heap of scarlet wool in her lap, the twist of gold on the top of her head, made two perfect-ly-placed patches of colour. She also looked so extremely juvenile and so gently domestic—her occupation always influenced her appearance—that Mr. Partridge returned momentarily to the attack.

"We ought to have let him go to Canada," he said; "he's not worth the trouble—"

"He is."

"Tell me one good quality he's got!" challenged Mr. Partridge.

"He would make," said Lisbeth thoughtfully, "a very good father."

Mr. Partridge gaped.

"How d'you work that out? If young Ronny ever raises a family, it'll be the rate-payer who supports 'em. . . ."

"Oh, I wasn't thinking of his *supporting* them," Lisbeth explained. "But my father was an exceptionally good man. I can remember him myself, and I've met people who knew him. He was very unselfish, and hard-working, and yet light-hearted. And my mother was sweet. Well, they say qualities often skip a generation . . ."

This excursion into genetics startled Mr. Partridge so much that he simply ignored it altogether and stuck to the immediate point.

"Anyway, you'll *never* find him a job," he said.

"I shall," said Lisbeth.

The next day, she did.

4

She practically invented it. There was in the main street at the end of the road a drapery establishment, large, cheap, and thriving, but whose old-fashioned name—the London Bazaar—was matched by the old-fashioned character of its window-dressing. Each article bore a card with the price

and one uninspired adjective—"Smart," "Hard-wearing,"
or—more rarely—"Chic." On this stronghold of conserva-
tism Lisbeth, after a morning's preparation, launched her
attack. She penetrated as far as the junior partner (aged no
more than fifty-five) and proposed to supply him with a new
type of show-card at the moderate rate of two shillings per
dozen. The examples she brought with her illustrated ladies'
underwear, and the junior partner could not deny that they
would prove a great attraction. Lisbeth further pointed out
that, unlike those supplied (in insufficient quantity) by the
manufacturers, her cards all bore in a prominent position
the name of the London Bazaar. The junior partner, who
knew a good thing when he saw it, and who had prolonged
the interview merely for the pleasure of conversing with
Miss Campion, allowed himself to be convinced, and even
agreed to supply the materials. He then offered Lisbeth a
cup of tea, and showed no objection to walking as far as
Oxford Street, where she knew, she told him, a very good
place called the Bonnie Scotland. There they had two cups
of tea apiece, and complimented the proprietress—or rather
Lisbeth did—on the picturesque appearance of her commissionaire. Time flew so fast that the junior partner was forced
to take a taxi back; and it had flown so pleasantly that he
gave the commissionaire sixpence. It had been, from everyone's point of view, a most successful afternoon.

"What have *you* been up to?" demanded Mr. Partridge
suspiciously.

Lisbeth stood on the curb beside him, and brought out
her cards, and explained that Ronny was going to earn
at least twenty-five shillings a week in the service of the
London Bazaar. It would take him, she calculated, nearly
two months to reach the first saturation point, by which
time the original cards would have become soiled and due

for replacement. She had found him, in short, not only a job, but a life work. . . .

"But can he," asked Mr. Partridge, "draw?"

"He can shade," replied Lisbeth. "He can go over the outlines with ink, and blob them in with wash. It's quite easy."

"But who'll draw 'em first?" persisted Mr. Partridge.

"I shall," said Lisbeth.

Chapter 8

1

RONNY took to his new occupation with great docility. He even enjoyed it, he said, and when Mr. Partridge came home the following night produced no less than a dozen completed cards—six displaying each a pair of stockinged legs, crossed at the knee, one toe pointed, the other kicking in the air, and six showing more intimate garments still. Mr. Partridge was quite struck.

"You've got a real gift for it," he said. "Not up to your sister's of course; but some of that shading's very neat."

Ronny pushed back a lock of hair—his hair didn't usually fall in his eyes, but his whole appearance, since that morning, had taken on a subtly artistic character—and remarked modestly that he thought there was something to be said for the combinations. They had feeling. It was very difficult, he implied, to get feeling into combinations; and Mr. Partridge, nodding intelligently, agreed that they often washed hard.

"That's the best, of course," added Ronny, pushing forward a brassière.

"Very lifelike," said Mr. Partridge.

To tell the truth, the brassière rather shocked him. He felt dimly that it was an odd way of reforming a young man to set him drawing ladies' underclothes. It might put ideas into his head. But Ronny, contemplating his handi-work, seemed moved only by impersonal and artistic pride. "Things have changed," thought Mr. Partridge; and rather to his own astonishment decided that they had changed for the better. There was less . . . sniggering . . .

Still in a reflective mood, he went out to get a drink. One of his first acts, as soon as his tips had begun to provide spending-money, naturally had been to find himself a nice little pub: there was one most conveniently situated at the corner of Marsham Street, called The London Apprentice, where the type of conversation—wide-ranging and prop-erly serious—was just such as he enjoyed. Its doyen was a chauffeur in the service of a Member of Parliament, so that any political discussion was unusually well-informed: the regulars also included the valet of a theatrical knight, a butler from Porchester Terrace, and the proprietor of a small local cinema. It says much for Mr. Partridge's person-ality and *savoir-faire* that his presence in so distinguished a company was found not unacceptable, for the nature of his own employment, owing to his kilted progress twice daily along Marsham Street, could not be concealed, and it was definitely low; but the sedate affability of his manners, backed by casually-dropped hints of past glories, won over even the chauffeur. There was a general impression that he had once owned a book-shop, and lost it by fire, and been done out of his insurance money by the lawyers. A connec-tion with literature (in the retail branch) was not low at all, but highly respectable, and much sympathy was expressed for Mr. Partridge's loss. He was considered lucky to have escaped with his life. . . .

2

The saloon bar was for once nearly empty; but Mr. Partridge did not mind. He got his half-pint, and took it to a quiet corner, and went on thinking about the vicissitudes of human life. Things changed, there was no doubt of it. They changed not only in general, but in particular. Ronny's attitude towards female underwear was part of something big; his personal escapade was something small, which had nevertheless brought about two more small changes in altering the circumstances of his sister and of Mr. Partridge. Mr. Partridge closed his eyes and saw great waves of the sea specked by particles of foam: the waves thundered on like wars and revolutions, and on their surface the foam-flakes shifted, separating, coalescing, drawing each other this way and that . . . The image was bewildering; he opened his eyes, and took another sup of bitter, and began reflecting more particularly on the surprising fact that he was sitting there drinking it at all. He felt perfectly at home. He felt perfectly at home, also, in the queer harlequin's house down the road—and so, apparently, did Lisbeth and Ronny; and yet where had all three of them come from? From prison, from the lap of luxury, from a twopenny library at Dormouth Bay. "But p'raps we're the sort that would be at home anywhere," mused Mr. Partridge. "At any rate in this world . . ."

He must have spoken aloud; a tall thin fellow at the bar—a stranger—turned round and grinned at him.

"But not in the next, eh?"

Mr. Partridge came out of his cloud. He was always ready to be sociable.

"That I can't say," he agreed. "Crowns and harps, now—they've clean gone out, and the same with hell-fire; but I'm blessed if I know what we're supposed to expect instead."

"Oneness," said the stranger. "Oneness with the principle of the universe. Doesn't that appeal to you?"

"It might if I knew what it meant," said Mr. Partridge cautiously.

"It means understanding why the tides follow the moon, and why Bill Jones beats his wife. And everything in between."

"That I *should* like," said Mr. Partridge, with enthusiasm. "That would be worth putting sixpence in the plate for. In fact, it almost seems—if you follow my meaning—a bit too much of a bargain . . ."

"Ah," said the stranger, "but suppose when you knew it all it was no longer interesting?"

"It wouldn't be uninteresting to me," retorted Mr. Partridge stoutly. But he was conscious of a slight discomfort. The stranger had approached; his long, very bony face was now only six inches from Mr. Partridge's own. "Doing his Ancient Mariner stuff," thought Mr. Partridge. "Be touching me for a drink, like as not." This rational explanation slightly fortified him.

"If you want my view," proceeded the stranger, "I'm all for oblivion. In the meantime, I agree that we ought to make ourselves as much at home here as possible."

He grinned again, so suddenly and disarmingly that Mr. Partridge was encouraged to continue the conversation.

"*I* feel at home all right," he said. "That's what I was pondering on. I'm living in a sort of harlequin's house—"

"Whose house?"

"Harlequin's," repeated Mr. Partridge, feeling rather foolish. "That's just a sort of name I gave it because it's all so patchy. All different colours—"

But the stranger was no longer listening. He banged the table so violently that Mr. Partridge's glass quivered.

"Of course!" he cried. "That's it! The whole world's a harlequin's house! Run by a malicious, irresponsible devil . . . a giant's child playing with soldiers. That explains everything. The idiocy of wars, killing off the best first. The idiocy of governments. The idiocy of the City. The patchiness, you called it—fools raking in the rewards, wise men starving . . . slums round a palace . . . the conquest of the air, the panic of a raid . . ."

Mr. Partridge saved his beer and quickly finished it. He got up to go.

"What about the other half?" asked the stranger, in more normal tones.

"Not for me, thanks," said Mr. Partridge.

"I'm not really mad, you know. I'm remarkably sane."

"So'm I," said Mr. Partridge, edging towards the door. "At any rate as yet. But if ever I go off my rocker, I'll come and look you up."

3

The air of Marsham Street had a pleasant evening freshness. A good solid bus came lumbering up, a good solid policeman brought it to a standstill, a girl carrying a child—the girl wasn't so solid, but the child was—scurried across the road and gave the policeman a smile. "That's more like," thought Mr. Partridge: woman and child, law and order, and a bit of sex thrown in. "*Much* more like," thought Mr. Partridge. He felt oddly relieved.

Another girl, profiting by the hold-up, dropped lightly from the bus. It was Lisbeth, back from one of her jobs. She came running up, fresh as a daisy, and slipped her hand through Mr. Partridge's arm.

"What an evening!" she exclaimed. "Don't let's go straight in, let's walk as far as the Park."

"What about your supper?" objected Mr. Partridge.

"I'll have it later. I'm not hungry. The children had buns and cocoa, and so did I."

"You live too much on scraps," said Mr. Partridge: but he fell into step beside her very willingly. Lisbeth chattered on, relating, with a wealth of probably fictitious detail, the stratagems by which she had kept four exhibitionist brats from breaking in on their parents' cocktail party. So far as Mr. Partridge could gather there had been a pitched battle at the head of the stairs, and another outside the drawing-room door; but Lisbeth had very cleverly persuaded all four to play at dentists, and bound up their jaws with handkerchieves, so that the fight was waged in silence. She was very good, she added, at tying knots. . . .

They turned into the Park, admired the flower-beds and the fountains, and looked at the view down the Serpentine. The tranquil water reflected the tranquil trees. Ducks swam quietly about with a businesslike air. A pair of lovers paused to look at each other and sigh, and then walked on.

"I've just had," said Mr. Partridge, "a most peculiar talk. Most peculiar indeed."

"What about?" asked Lisbeth.

"The hereafter," said Mr. Partridge. "I picked up a fellow in the Apprentice—or rather *he* picked me up—who said some very extraordinary things. He said the only thing worth having after you're dead is just naught. And he said the whole world here is run by a sort of great devilish harlequin just to make trouble. What d'you think?"

"I think it's nonsense," said Lisbeth serenely.

"So do I," said Mr. Partridge. "But he was so upsetting, I'm quite glad to have someone agree with me."

They gazed at the water in silence, and then Lisbeth spoke again.

"It may be right about the harlequin, though. Look at the way things change—so suddenly, and for such queer reasons. Like transformation scenes. But I don't believe he's devilish. He's got too much sense of humour. And I don't believe he's the top."

"Nor do I," said Mr. Partridge.

4

For the next few evenings, however, he omitted his customary visit to The London Apprentice and stayed at home instead. On the Tuesday and Wednesday Lisbeth was in too, but Thursday brought one of her sitting-with-a-child jobs, so Ronny and Mr. Partridge had the flat to themselves. It was very quiet, for the former was working at his cards, and did not care even to have pieces read out of the paper to him. There was an interesting bit of news, too, about a jewel robbery at the Dormouth Towers Hotel, where a famous actress had been robbed of her famous emeralds; and Mr. Partridge would have liked to expatiate, and marvel, and propound theories; but Ronny, who did not know the place, refused to take an interest. Mr. Partridge finished the sports page, fidgeted round the room a bit, and came to a halt by the littered table.

Ronny worked on; he dipped his brush in the wash, and twirled it neatly to a fine point, and drew a beautiful florid curve that was a lady's calf. More lightly, he indicated the shin, and put in a bit of fancy work round the toes. It was fascinating. For some moments longer Mr. Partridge watched intently, while a second pair of legs sprang to elegant life; and then he made his great mistake.

"Let me have a go," said Mr. Partridge.

Ronny hesitated.

"It's pretty tricky . . ."

"I'll take care," promised Mr. Partridge.

He drew up another chair, and seized the brush. He screwed up his eyes, and breathed heavily. The wash proved more unmanageable than one would expect, but by going over the first stroke a good many times he achieved at last a properly clean edge.

"How's that?" he demanded.

"A bit buxom," said Ronny critically.

"And that's what's wanted," retorted Mr. Partridge. "The ones you do may be very neat, but they're too skinny. Pass me another card."

The second card took longer, for in spite of his warm defence Mr. Partridge had not been altogether satisfied; but this time Ronny was lavish in his praise.

"You do 'em almost as well as me," he said enthusiastically. "I bet you've studied drawing?"

"It just comes natural," said Mr. Partridge.

He bent over the table again, completely absorbed. It was now Ronny's turn to fidget. As Mr. Partridge had done, he wandered round the room, came back to the table; but he did not stay there.

"I'm out of cigarettes," he said. "I'll just go along and get some."

"Ah," said Mr. Partridge; and worked on.

5

Ronny went quietly out. There was a slot machine just down the street, and another round the corner. He went on to the latter, and found he had neither a sixpence nor a shilling. To get change he entered a pub—not the Apprentice, but the larger and gaudier Bull. Here he rapidly got into conversation with the barmaid, and with an artist named Jimmy, with whom he had a long discussion of surréalisme. The clientèle of the Bull was far more mixed, and far less solid, than that of the Apprentice. The artist introduced Ronny to a journalist, the journalist produced a girl who taught dancing, and between them they made up a very pleasant little party. Jimmy and the journalist drank a great quantity of beer, the girl drank whisky-and-splash, and Ronny had a gin-and-lime. They stayed till closing time, by which hour they had all become too fond of each other to separate; so they went on to the journalist's rooms, where a great deal more beer was drunk, though not by Ronny. Soon after midnight the girl wanted to go home, and Ronny escorted her. On the door-step she told him that she was afraid to go to sleep because of a man on the same landing who always tried her door. "Jam a chair under the handle," said Ronny practically. The girl (who seemed to him a little slow-witted) asked him to come up and do it for her; which, as Ronny pointed out, would be simply silly, since he would have to open the door again to get out himself. The night air then striking fresh, he bade her a rapid though affectionate adieu, and walked briskly home.

He hadn't bought any cigarettes, but he had passed a most pleasant and innocent evening.

CHAPTER 9

1

ON THE next Tuesday night Lisbeth and Mr. Partridge went to a ball.

The experience was novel to both of them: to Mr. Partridge because he had never been to such a thing before, to Lisbeth because she was not going as a guest. She was going to earn fifteen shillings as a substitute palmist, and she got the job—so strangely are human affairs interwoven—owing to the illness of one of His Majesty's Judges. Lord Morecombe, in Switzerland, took a turn for the worse; his daughter, the Honourable Mrs. Cory, was summoned to his side; and Wanted Women received an urgent call for a fortuneteller—"Someone," explained Mrs. Cory over the 'phone, "who has an evening dress." The ball, in aid of charity, was being held at one of the great semi-country houses still to be found near Regent's Park; in its garden sideshows of all kinds would provide extra amusement for the guests and extra receipts for the funds. Wanted Women had no fortune-teller on their books, but since a hasty enquiry assured them that all sideshows, save the roundabout, were to be in amateur hands, they had no hesitation in sending Miss Campion. They felt she could get away with it.

Mr. Partridge went to take care of Lisbeth. He never liked the idea of her going out at night alone, and they both felt it was as yet too early to expose Ronny to any social excitement. They didn't tell him about it: he was suffering from a slight cold, and willingly let Lisbeth send him to bed with a hot-water-bottle and a detective story. (Lisbeth encouraged detective stories; they all had such moral endings.)

"We'll be catching colds ourselves, like as not," commented Mr. Partridge gloomily. The sky promised rain, and he had taken the unusual step of setting out for a ball with a spare pair of socks in his mackintosh pocket. Lisbeth, on the other hand, wore no more than a velvet tippet over her long pale frock: she was doing her best to look inconspicuous, but Mr. Partridge's heart swelled with pride as he helped her on to the 'bus. The conductor also assisted: Lisbeth was handed in with as much ceremony as is accorded to Duchesses entering their Daimlers. She was enjoying herself already; the bus lurched, tipping her into the lap of an elderly butcher, and at once the butcher began to enjoy himself also. He made room for her beside him, an ex-stoker moved up and made room for Mr. Partridge, and Lisbeth's wide skirts fanned out over their laps, and every male passenger looked at Mr. Partridge and envied him his luck. "Buckingham Palace?" enquired the conductor humorously; and Mr. Partridge, not to be outdone, replied that they would have two tuppennies to Windsor Castle. This simple exchange gave general pleasure: the ex-stoker was suddenly moved to announce that he had just won five bob on a ten to one shot, and by an extraordinary coincidence the butcher had only a month earlier won the same amount at Chepstow. The company congratulated them warmly. Bonhomie prevailed. When Mr. Partridge and Lisbeth got out it was like breaking up a party.

They found the house, and were directed straight through to the grounds, where Lisbeth's tent inconspicuously lurked at the back of a coconut-shy. Mr. Partridge regarded it with disfavour. He considered it a bad pitch, and said so.

"We shan't take five bob," he complained. "We're right off the track. Like me to stand out in front and do a bit of barking for you?"

Lisbeth thought not. She had acquired, that afternoon, a sixpenny book on palmistry, but was still liable to lose her way between the mount of Venus and the mount of Jupiter. Mr. Partridge, who considered palmistry *vieux jeu*, wanted her to cut out the whole thing and give spirit messages instead: he was perfectly willing to be a spirit voice himself, speaking hollowly from the other side of the canvas. They were still arguing this point when the first client appeared in the shape of a fashionable young lady who demanded Mrs. Cory, and who, when Lisbeth explained that Mrs. Cory was not coming, at once turned to go out again. But Mr. Partridge was having no nonsense; he blocked the doorway and fixed her with a menacing eye while Lisbeth hastily prophesied a sea voyage and a handsome stranger. "But I don't *want* my fortune told!" protested the young lady. "I just wanted to speak to Marion!"

"It'll be half-a-crown all the same," retorted Mr. Partridge. "Don't argue." . . . He was wearing his cap over one eye, and a muffler twisted tightly round his throat; the lady cast him a slightly nervous glance, handed over the half-crown, and hurried out.

Her report could not have been favourable: no other clients followed. And yet the grounds were filling up; from the coconut-shies, from the rifle ranges, came sounds of gaiety; the blaring music of the roundabout was answered by softer strains from the house. At first Lisbeth sat inside the tent, and Mr. Partridge (regretful for his shooting-stick) stood sentry at the door; but after a while he came in and they had a quiet game of two-handed rummy. It wasn't very exciting. All the excitement was outside.

"After all," said Lisbeth cheerfully, "we're not here to enjoy ourselves."

Mr. Partridge looked dubious. She was right in a way, but they weren't taking a penny, and there were evidently grand goings-on all about. He felt he was missing something, and it was a feeling he could not bear.

"Tell you what," he said, "we'll just nip out and have a peek."

Lisbeth hesitated; and Mr. Partridge, watching her, jumped to the wrong conclusion.

"If you're afraid of being recognized," he admitted, "p'raps we'd better not."

"Oh, no!" said Lisbeth. "None of our crowd ever came to this sort of thing. Only suppose someone wants to have their fortune told?"

That was an easy one. Mr. Partridge took out a pencil and wrote in bold black strokes across the centre of the tablecloth.

They would be Back Shortly.

2

There were fairy lamps in the trees, there were lights before all the booths, light streamed from the windows of the house; and the combined effect was of the footlights of a theatre. The garden was now thronged, but to Mr. Partridge he and Lisbeth were the only real people there. This was perhaps because no one took any notice of them, and as they slipped this way and that through the crowd they instinctively took on the liberties of spectators at a play—freely commenting, bidding each other observe this perfectly-cast dowager, or that mistaken ingenue. "Look!" cried Lisbeth. "See there!" responded Mr. Partridge: they clung arm in arm, and went where the drift took them, and sometimes Mr. Partridge had to stand rigid, his moustache not an inch from a lady's bare back, and sometimes they were alone in a bubble of space; but always they moved in a narrowing circle, for the gaiety had a heart, whose beats made brazen music; and the voice of Calliope drew them to the roundabout.

"Oh, *see!*" cried Lisbeth.

It was a fantastic and an enchanting sight; for as the horses leapt by in an endless cavalcade the skirts of their lady-riders made waves of silk, of thin muslin, of shining brocade; and the riders themselves, sweeping high through the air, were translated by light and motion into the bright, inhuman creatures of a dream. They were Valkyries, they were queens out a-hawking; some reclined along their mounts like sea nymphs on the horses of Neptune; there was a woman—or a flower—whose stiff pale satin skirt blew out in the shape of a Convolvulus; a girl in a crinoline flew by like the ghost of the young Victoria; a girl, still younger, stood up in the saddle, her dress whipped to wings, and laughed like Victory. For perhaps two minutes the vision lasted; then the horses came to rest, the nymphs, the queens slid down into the arms of their squires, and at that human contact lost their immortality.

"That was worth crossing the road for," said Mr. Partridge, with satisfaction.

"It was—beautiful," stated Lisbeth softly.

Something in her tone made him feel in his pocket.

"How much does it cost?"

Lisbeth sighed.

"A shilling—"

"What, just for one ride?" demanded Mr. Partridge, dropping the coins back. "You could get six for that, up on Hampstead Heath." Then he looked at her again, and felt for a milled edge, and pulled the shilling out. It meant three half-pints, and one ride lasted only about four minutes. Three half-pints would last nearly three hours; you could spend a whole evening, in a nice pub, on three half-pints . . .

"Nip up," said Mr. Partridge.

Lisbeth pressed his arm.

"I ought to be telling fortunes . . ."

"No one wants 'em," pointed out Mr. Partridge. "If they do, they can have 'em from me. Up you get!"

He waited just long enough to see her settled on a prancing steed, and made his way back to the tent as the first drops of rain began to fall.

3

In his hot-water-bottle-warmed bed Ronny Campion, who had gone to sleep in the middle of his detective story, woke up and heard the cuckoo cry twelve. He was feeling much better. He felt practically cured. He wanted company, and shouted for Lisbeth to come and talk to him.

When there was no response, he got up and went to investigate. The unmade-up couch of his sister, the empty bed of Mr. Partridge, explained their silence only by their absence. Ronny sat down on the edge of the table and lit one of Mr. Partridge's cigarettes. A pile of cards lay ready for the morning; he toyed for a moment with the idea of setting to work there and then, and astounding Lisbeth on her return by a picture of midnight industry. Then he thought it might look rather ostentatious. Besides, if she were out, as he supposed, on one of her infant-tending jobs, she might not come home till three or four, and as he had only just recovered from a cold he felt he ought not to sit up so late. The light wasn't good, either. On the other hand, he was by no means sleepy enough to go back to bed, and though there was the detective story to finish, he remembered having heard that to read in a supine position was very bad for the eyes. He had to take care of his eyesight, because of all those cards waiting to be done in the morning.

The flat was so still that he could hear the ticking of the clock. It was also chilly, but when he tried to light the fire there wasn't any gas. Ronny began to feel worried—not so much on his own account as on Lisbeth's: she had looked after his cold so carefully, it would be terribly hard on her if he had a relapse. And yet there was nothing that brought on a relapse (after a cold) so much as depression, and he was beginning to feel very depressed indeed. The silence, the low temperature, even the smallness of the room, were getting him down. Lisbeth had undoubtedly been thoughtless—she might at least have seen that Mr. Partridge stayed in—but he bore her no grudge; all he wanted now was to save her from the results of her heedlessness.

In the end, the most sensible plan seemed to be to get into his evening clothes, and borrow ten shillings rent-money; and make a beeline for the West End.

4

The rain that beat down on Ronny's taxi beat down with equal force, and with more resonance, upon the roof of Mr. Partridge's tent. It had been beating down for an hour, during which time Mr. Partridge had taken but one half-crown, off a middle-aged lady to whom he gave a spirit message from William Shakespeare. She did not seem convinced by it: she happened to be a London University don; and Mr. Partridge, sensing a lack of response, determined to stick in future to dark strangers and overseas travel. But no other customers appeared; it had set in for a proper wet night; not a sound came from any of the booths, only the roundabout music (unanswered now by any music from the house) still played on, and only the roundabout lights, when Mr. Partridge peered out, showed strong enough to thrust back the dark. He began to feel uneasy; Lisbeth had not come back, and she had had money for only one ride. The thought crossed his mind that someone might have taken her home in a car—he knew how liable she was to such accidents; but he could not believe that she would have left him thus marooned. In the end he put on his mackintosh, turned up the collar, and plunged out to look for her.

The scene was desolate. An empty garden in the rain is a fit subject for poets, full of romantic pathos; this one was not empty, but full of flapping wet canvas. It looked derelict. The fairy-lamps in the trees tossed like the lights of a lost fishing-fleet; the riderless horses of the roundabout fled before the wind as though from a lost battle. Mr. Partridge approached them nevertheless; they were at least brightly visible in a storm-shrouded world; and as he drew near he saw that they had carried away from the field two survivors.

On one horse rode Lisbeth, her eyes half-closed, her head thrown back, her skirts streaming out into the rain; and on the steed directly behind, ever pursuing, yet never (owing to mechanical reasons) gaining an inch on her, rode a young man in tails.

Against the revolving lights the rain fell like harp-strings, oblique and silver; Mr. Partridge gaped through them, hardly able to believe his eyes. For a moment, as the riders flashed by for the second time, he was caught by poetry: the lovely leaping motion, the fluid fantastic shapes of Lisbeth's blown skirt, the taut contrasting line of her twined arms; then common sense returned, and in a loud voice he shouted to the thing to stop.

Whether in obedience to his summons or not, the horses slackened speed. Calliope stilled her voice. Mr. Partridge ran round over the wet grass and caught at the hem of Lisbeth's dress. He meant to give her a good scolding, but when she slid off almost into his arms she looked so extremely white (and no wonder) that he hadn't the heart.

"Going to be sick?" asked Mr. Partridge kindly.

Lisbeth shook her head. She had the Kilmeny look, as though she had just come back out of another world, and had left half her wits behind her.

"If you've been on all this time," said Mr. Partridge, "I don't wonder you're addled. And your frock's all wet—"

He looked round, worried. It occurred to him that the last bus had probably gone, and that they would have to walk home. At this moment, however, the young man (who had been having a word with Calliope's priest) tentatively approached.

"Pardon me," he said, "but if I might have the honour of driving you home—"

Mr. Partridge looked at him, and saw that he was already far gone. His eyes, when they dwelt on Lisbeth, were submissive and adoring. Even when they dwelt on Mr. Partridge they remained respectful. "If she'd got a mongrel dog," thought that gentleman grimly, "he'd been down in the mud for it to wipe its paws on . . ."

Lisbeth turned to Mr. Partridge and slipped her hand through his arm—thus showing, very properly, that she was not unchaperoned.

"I'm dropping," she said. "We live in Paddington. And—thank you for making it go on."

"Calliopes," said the young man earnestly, "are my passion."

Mr. Partridge felt almost sure this was a lie: the young man's face was faintly green. But love, temporarily at any rate, had conquered nausea; he was able to drive, and in the car Mr. Partridge made Lisbeth take off her thin slippers and put on his spare pair of socks. The young man also insisted on lending her his scarf, and when they reached Marsham Street omitted to ask for it back. But he reckoned without Mr. Partridge, who was on the lookout for just such a gambit.

"It's on the seat," said Mr. Partridge, putting his head back through the window. "Don't trouble to get out. And we're much obliged to you."

The young man made a motion to open the door, but Mr. Partridge had his knee under the handle. He kept it there till he heard Lisbeth's key turn in the lock; and then he nipped after her, and hustled her inside, and swiftly closed the door. Lisbeth contemplated it with an expression of doubt.

"We weren't very polite?" she suggested.

"When you're saving a chap from drowning," retorted Mr. Partridge cryptically, "you don't bother about manners."

And he gently pushed her upstairs.

CHAPTER 10

1

RONNY did not come home with the milk, he came home with the morning paper, and he brought with him a present for Lisbeth. It was a long silken doll, which in the limpness of its legs, as well as in its air of innocent folly, bore a striking resemblance to Ronny himself.

"Darling, it's lovely!" exclaimed Lisbeth, setting the creature up on the breakfast table. "Where did you get it?"

"Oh, at a new place," said Ronny vaguely. "I picked up some people at the Café Royal and went along with them. I hope you didn't worry, darling, but if only we had a 'phone of our own I could have rung up."

"I never gave you a thought," said Lisbeth—which was a lie, as Mr. Partridge knew, for he had heard her moving about twice in the night.

"And as a matter of fact," added Ronny, "it's absolutely cured my cold."

This, on the other hand, was true. It was unjust, but there it was. The stern morality of detective fiction had been flouted by Ronny's hormones.

"And that," finished Ronny virtuously, "is really why I went out."

Neither Lisbeth nor Mr. Partridge made any further comment, but in the minds of both was the same thought: Ronny had tasted blood. He was getting into his pyjamas just as Mr. Partridge was getting into his kilt. The breakfast things were still on the table.

"It's all right," said Lisbeth, following Mr. Partridge's glance. "I've nothing to do this morning."

Mr. Partridge grunted. It didn't strike him as right at all. It struck him as topsy-turvy. He put on his tam-o'-shanter at a fierce angle, and clumped heavily downstairs.

2

When he got home again the flat (looking remarkably spruce) was empty, but there was a note from Lisbeth propped on the mantel: it said that she had gone out on a job, and asked Mr. Partridge to keep an eye on Ronny and be sure that he finished two dozen cards, because a message had come through requiring them by nine next morning. With love from Lisbeth.

Mr. Partridge grunted. The love part was all right, but where was Ronny? You couldn't keep an eye on a person who wasn't there—and even if he were, Mr. Partridge had begun to feel that the power of the human eye was overestimated. It might still work with lions. It didn't work with Ronny.

His mind filled with quite pleasant thoughts of lion-hunting, he went into his room, and changed his clothes, and extracted from under the bed a book he was reading called *Piebald, the Broncho King*. Lisbeth had borrowed it for him from T. Cubitt's boy; she had read it herself, so they could have interesting discussions about all the characters, and Mr. Partridge was hastening to finish it to see whether he shared her opinion of the dénouement. He took it back to the sitting-room and prepared to enjoy himself.

But he could not. Whichever way he sat, he always saw, out of the corner of his eye, the pile of untouched cards. The cuckoo cried nine, and then half-past, but still Ronny did not appear. He was probably out, thought Mr. Partridge with bitterness, curing his headache. A draught stirred the curtains: Lisbeth's note, which he had left on the mantel, fluttered down with a sound like a despairing sigh. Mr. Partridge sighed also. Then he got up, and fetched the inks and the brushes, and set the cards out on the table, and sat down to work.

3

At the sound of a footstep without he did not look up: he intended that Ronny should receive the full rebuke of his vicarious industry. He bowed his head still closer over the table, and laboured on.

There was a tapping on the door. Mr. Partridge did not answer. He knew that if he said "Who's there?" Ronny would reply "Obadiah," and Mr. Partridge felt that if Ronny announced himself as Obadiah once again he, Mr. Partridge, would hit him, Ronny, over the head with the elephant's tusk. He did not want to do this because it would spoil the effect of his silent and dignified reproach. So he took no notice, even when the tapping was renewed, and when at last the door opened, and a young man who was not Ronny came in, it was some seconds before Mr. Partridge noticed the difference.

"Good evening," said the young man, tentatively.

He wore dress clothes, and his appearance was familiar: he was the young man on the roundabout, who had brought Lisbeth and Mr. Partridge home the previous night. In his hand he carried a small round package, and the appearance of that was familiar also.

"Calves-foot jelly?" said Mr. Partridge at once.

The young man looked startled.

"It is," he admitted. "How did you know?"

"Second lot we've had this week," said Mr. Partridge. "Goes on the top left-hand shelf."

He nodded towards the cupboard; the young man opened it, and ranged his jar alongside two others. Mr. Partridge resumed work.

"I guess you don't recall me," stated the young man. "My name's Lester Hamilton, and I met you and Miss Campion at the dance last night."

Mr. Partridge knew this already, but he was in an unsocial mood. He had the stage all set for the discomfiture of Ronny, and the presence of a stranger—particularly of a stranger in tails—would ruin all. He knew Ronny's susceptibility: white tie would call to white tie, white waistcoat to white waistcoat, the atmosphere of honest toil would give place to the atmosphere of a night club. However, he bore the visitor no real grudge—in fact he rather liked the look of him; so with the double object of saving his own time and the young man's trouble, Mr. Partridge at once gave the necessary information.

"She's engaged to be married," he said baldly.

Immediately—just as he had known it would—an expression of despair passed over Mr. Hamilton's face. But he stood his ground.

"Even so," he said, "I hope there's no objection to my paying a call?"

"Not a mite," agreed Mr. Partridge, "except that she's not here, and I'm busy, and it's getting on for eleven."

Mr. Hamilton flushed.

"I know," he said. "I got the jelly a whole lot earlier—in fact I got it first thing this morning—and sort of lost my nerve. And then I went to a dinner party, and couldn't leave off thinking about her—" He broke off, all his diffidence gone, and fixed Mr. Partridge with a stern eye. "Have you any idea," he demanded fiercely, "how much she weighs?"

"Seven and a half stone," replied Mr. Partridge.

"What's that in pounds?"

"How should *I* know?" demanded Mr. Partridge, with irritation. "She's not a salmon. And if you're thinking she doesn't get enough to eat—"

"Think! I know it!" interrupted Mr. Hamilton. "I lifted her on to that horse, and there's just nothing of her!" He glared round the room: through the open door into the kitchen he could see Ronny's bed wedged between the cooker and the bath. "My God!" he ejaculated. "She *lives* here!"

Mr. Partridge had had just about enough. He laid down his brush and spoke his mind.

"Now, you listen to me for a bit," he commanded. "I won't say anything about your manners, because, knowing your complaint, I don't hold you responsible. But this I will say: we're not starving—not by any means. We do very nicely. If I don't chuck your jellied eels back in your face, it's just to save your foolish feelings and not make you look a bigger booby than you are. *I* know what manners are, if some people don't. Miss Campion's got me, and she's got her brother, and she's got her fiancé, who happens to be in foreign parts, and she doesn't want no one else. Speaking personally, I'd go without my beer for her; but I will not sit here and be insulted by a got-up young whipper-snapper with the milk on his mouth."

There was a short silence. Then the young man slowly approached the table. His gibus lay on the floor, but he gave the impression of standing hat in hand.

"I guess I ought to apologize," he stated. "I—got carried away by my feelings. I'd no business to talk that way, and I apologize for it."

"Granted," said Mr. Partridge—but still with reserve.

"It's just," continued the young man, "that I'd do anything on earth for Miss Campion. I wouldn't try to horn in, but if her fiancé, as you say, is abroad, perhaps I might be useful. You know, just to wait about for her . . ."

Mr. Partridge hesitated. The obvious sincerity of this foolhardy proposal spoke to his heart; more important, there was something about the young man's bearing that spoke to his head. Lester Hamilton had an indefinable air of solvency and competence. It was nothing to do with his clothes; Ronny, in similar attire, looked just as immaculate, but no one would ever offer a guinea for the contents of his pockets. "Makes good wages and earns 'em," thought Mr. Partridge, looking at his visitor. "Knows how to get on . . ." And aloud he said slowly, "The best thing you—or anyone else—can do for Miss Campion is to get her brother a job."

The young man at once looked alert and businesslike.

"What does he do?"

"At the moment," said Mr. Partridge thoughtfully, "he's painting ladies' stockings. At the moment, he's painting all these stockings here, ready for delivery to-morrow morning at nine A.M."

"But—" said the young man.

"And if you're going to stay here talking and disturbing me," finished Mr. Partridge, "you might as well lend a hand."

The young man was a good sport. Without a moment's hesitation he at once drew up another chair and reached to the pile of cards.

"Don't touch the lingerie," warned Mr. Partridge, "because that wants doing special. And the great thing with stockings is to get a good bold line down the calf. Don't be afraid to lay it on."

They worked for a while in silence. Lester Hamilton laid it on as he was told, and displayed quite a pretty technique in his handling of the instep. He worked even faster than Mr. Partridge: he worked with a kind of fury. Every now and then he glanced across at the lingerie-pile, till Mr. Partridge, divining his ambition, thought it kinder to check it at once.

"Even when we're through with the stockings," he pointed out, "we shan't touch those. If Ronny can't do them, Miss Campion will."

"Where is she?"

"Out on a job—minding kids, I expect. She does anything like that."

The young man drew a line so full and bold that it covered an entire stocking.

"Now see what you've done!" rebuked his overseer. "We'll have to label 'em 'Mourning.' If your hand's shaky, you'd better give over."

But Mr. Hamilton worked on. The clock struck twelve.

"For instance," he said abruptly, "if I knew where Miss Campion was now, I could go and meet her."

"For the matter of that, so could I," said Mr. Partridge. "You were up pretty late last night."

This was true; Mr. Partridge was feeling tired; but before he had time to deny it, the door opened and Lisbeth came in.

4

Looking back on the incident afterwards, Mr. Partridge decided that he must have been very tired indeed; for he could never remember exactly how Lisbeth had greeted Mr. Hamilton, nor how Mr. Hamilton had explained either his presence or his occupation. It was all somehow—and this applied to Mr. Hamilton's subsequent activities as well— taken for granted. He did not stay long: Lisbeth checked over the cards, found the tale complete, and with an entire lack of ceremony began to make up her bed. She praised their workmanship, and at the same time plumped her pillow. There was not even (so far as Mr. Partridge could recollect) any formal exchange of good nights: the young man merely nodded casually from the doorway, Lisbeth, over her shoulder, nodded back, and then the door closed, very quietly, and there was a sound of quiet footsteps retreating downstairs. . . . For a moment Mr. Partridge wondered whether he had been dreaming; the finished pile of cards told him that he had not. He looked at Lisbeth, now engaged in brushing her hair, and the intimacy of the scene suddenly struck him with a renewed sense of strangeness. Did she feel the strangeness too, or did she really accept everything—including the odd harlequin room, the cards with the ladies' stockings, and his own presence at her toilet—without a second thought?

"What's she thinking about now?" wondered Mr. Partridge.

She was thinking about men.

"Lisbeth thinks of nothing but men"; the remark had been made, by various female acquaintances, often enough;

there was truth in it, but it was also, in its common, superficial sense, unjust. For Lisbeth had to think about men.
They imposed themselves on her thoughts. They mixed
themselves so inextricably in her life. She had to think
about Ronny—about him, and for him; he needed as much
attention as a month-old baby. She had to think about Mr.
Partridge, who had so gallantly thrown in his lot with hers,
thereby putting her under an obligation. She had to think
about the Walkers, who had at one period, with the greatest
delicacy, supplied more food than Mr. Partridge ever knew
of. She had to think about T. Cubitt, who let them use his
telephone. There was also, or there soon would be, Lester
Hamilton . . .

"Do you ever," asked Mr. Partridge suddenly, "think
about the Captain?"

Lisbeth suspended her brush with a look of surprise.

"About Hugh? Of course. I write to him every week."

It was Mr. Partridge's turn to be startled.

"What ever about? Us here?"

"Oh, no!" said Lisbeth quickly. "That would simply upset
him. I write about how the town looks, and the things we
used to do together, and what shows are on—"

"But you don't go to any shows!"

"I read about them in the paper. And about all the new
books. I write *pages*."

Mr. Partridge regarded her uneasily. He had always
suspected her mental powers to be great, but the ability to
write pages per week, to an adoring fiancé, without touching on a single essential of one's daily life, struck him as
something altogether out of the ordinary.

"Where does he think you're living?"

"Here. Only of course he doesn't know what it's like,
because he's never set foot out of Mayfair. And I *think*, he

thinks Aunt Mildred's with me. And that she's better off than she is . . ."

"In fact," said Mr. Partridge thoughtfully, "it's all a pack of lies."

"Oh, no, it isn't! There isn't a single lie anywhere. About Aunt Mildred, for instance, I said something like: 'Aunt Mildred makes a perfect chaperone, and though she adores the country is quite happy in town.' Which is all perfectly true."

Mr. Partridge looked at her.

"You know as well as I do," he said, "you might just as well lie straight out. It would be just the same, and less trouble."

Lisbeth, with her frank and candid gaze, looked back at Mr. Partridge.

"But not nearly," she pointed out, "so much fun."

5

Mr. Partridge gave it up. For the next two days he regarded her as a heartless baggage. On the third morning, chancing to enter the sitting-room while Lisbeth bathed, his eye fell on a corner of pasteboard sticking from beneath the pillow of her unmade bed. It was the corner of a photograph of Captain Brocard.

Mr. Partridge gave it up again.

CHAPTER 11

1

THE following Monday was the first day of the autumn sales, and the Oxford Street pavements were so crowded that Mr. Partridge was regretfully forced to abandon his shooting-stick; he would have had to place it dangerously near the edge of the curb. He was thrust off several times as it was: some of the eager ladies who jostled about him would have been capable, in Mr. Partridge's opinion, of thrusting aside a bus. But in general he regarded them with benevolent detachment. It was a slack time for dog-tending, since most women, when bent on serious hand-to-hand shopping, left their animals at home, and he was able to give all his attention to the passers-by. A good many faces were familiar, but there was also a large contingent of strangers—women drawn from remote suburbs, from the country even, by the lure of first-day bargains. Many of these hunted in couples, but the more determined and efficient worked alone. Mr. Partridge followed their fortunes—for they passed and repassed—with great sympathy; sometimes they went into a shop wearing one hat and came out wearing another; sometimes they stood in doorways matching stockings or gloves by daylight; all their faces wore the same look of eager yet disciplined concentration. Mr. Partridge thought that the faces of locusts going into action (supposing their features to be sufficiently mobile) probably looked much the same. . . .

There was one lady, however, whose expression was different. That was chiefly why Mr. Partridge noticed her, for her angular and countrified figure was in no way remarkable. But she was looking at Mr. Partridge as though he were a person, and not merely an obstacle in her path. She was looking at him, moreover, with the obvious intention of catching his eye. Mr. Partridge, always ready for social intercourse, allowed his eye to be caught; and a second later had realized his mistake.

The lady was Miss Pickering.

"Good gracious!" cried Miss Pickering. "It's Mr. Partridge!"

2

Mr. Partridge clutched his standard and stiffened. For the moment he was luckily too much astonished to speak, and by the time Miss Pickering addressed him anew he had had time to take in the situation and recover his wits.

"Mr. Partridge!" cried Miss Pickering again.

"Hoots!" replied Mr. Partridge—cannily.

Mildred Pickering scrutinized him once more and appeared to hesitate.

"It surely *is*," she persisted, "Mr. Partridge? From Dormouth Bay?"

Mr. Partridge shook his bonnet.

"The name, leddy, is M'Tavish. If ye think ye ken me, ye're makin' a wee bit error."

All about them the stream of shoppers pressed in a steady flow. A parcel-laden matron, catching Miss Pickering in the back with a mop-handle, nearly sent her into the gutter. Mr. Partridge upped with his standard and shoved her back.

"Ye'd better be movin' on," he said severely. "There's a gey press o' folk the morn."

And then, all at once—and just as his Scottishness was fully established—Mr. Partridge was struck by a sudden thought. *She didn't know.* He had been so fearful of betraying Lisbeth, so conscious of his own part in her flight, that not till that moment did he realize Miss Pickering's complete ignorance of his complicity. So far as she knew, he had seen Lisbeth but once, on the hotel terrace. "Of all the old gabies!" thought Mr. Partridge—referring to himself. Apprehension gave place to curiosity; there were a dozen things he wanted to know, and Miss Pickering was already on the point of moving (as he had bade her) on. . . .

"Stop!" cried Mr. Partridge, in his normal voice. He reached out his ever-useful weapon and barred her path. She turned round.

"It's me, all right," said Mr. Partridge sheepishly.

But Miss Pickering was by now thoroughly flustered.

"Are you *sure*?" she asked dubiously.

"Sure as eggs," said Mr. Partridge.

"Then why—" her eye was not unnaturally resentful—"did you say you weren't?"

"Because I'm incognito," explained Mr. Partridge. "Being Scotch is part of my job—only I hadn't the heart to deceive you any longer. I hope I see you well?"

"Oh, very," replied Miss Pickering. Her manner became more cordial: looking again at the kilt, at the stockings, at the tam-o'-shanter hat, she felt a wave of sympathy for their wearer. "And you?"

"Braw," said Mr. Partridge. "Were you much longer at the Towers?"

(This was one of the things he wanted to know. He and Lisbeth had both hoped, when discussing the subject, that Miss Pickering had stayed on blowing the Maule money till it was all gone; but Lisbeth at least was not sanguine, and she proved right.)

"Only till the end of the week," said Miss Pickering. "However, I was quite set up."

"And how," proceeded Mr. Partridge, "is the young lady I met at tea? Your niece, I believe?"

The answer surprised him.

"Married," said Miss Pickering.

3

The confidence of this statement (which Miss Pickering fully believed) was due to two causes: to her simplicity, and to the fact that she had been in her youth a great devourer of romantic fiction. Her simplicity led her to accept the pseudo-Brocard telegram at its face value; for three days after Lisbeth's departure she had stayed on quite happily at the Dormouth Towers, hoping for further news by every post, but not being really disappointed when no news came. Lisbeth was always bad at letter-writing, and the fact that she was with her fiancé stilled all fears. Miss Pickering had met Hugh Brocard only once, but that solitary occasion had sufficed to establish him in her eyes as the Impeccable Male. There was, however, one point that bothered her: she had not dared pack Lisbeth's engagement ring, which was still in the hotel safe. On the third day she telephoned Captain Brocard's flat, and to her astonishment learnt that he was abroad; though further enquiry (to her relief) elicited the fact that he had been in London for two days, the second of which dates coincided with that of Lisbeth's disappearance. Miss Pickering then telephoned the Maules, and from the outraged lady of the house gathered no more than that Captain Brocard had rung up and had been positively insulting. Mrs. Maule did not explain that his call had been made from Iraq, and Miss Pickering, whose only datum was the telegram, naturally assumed that it had been made in London, after his reunion with Lisbeth; and instinctively took the young people's side. When Mrs. Maule added that henceforward she and Mr. Maule washed their hands of them, Miss Pickering with unusual spirit retorted that they would probably do very well by themselves; and added that she would make up her accounts, return the balance in hand, and leave Dormouth Bay at once. She had never liked the Maules, whom she considered purse-proud, and the conversation was both brief and acrimonious.

Miss Pickering left. She did so quite happily, for it was here that the influence of romantic fiction came into play. In all the novels of her youth the heroine, however black things might look against her—and often, about Chapter Thirty, they looked very black indeed—regularly turned out to have been safely married all along; so that Miss Pickering knew better than to be taken in (where heroines were concerned) by the appearances of guilt. Lisbeth was in the position of a heroine. Miss Pickering felt quite sure that she was by now also Mrs. Hugh Brocard, on her way to the East.

There remained the engagement ring. Sewn up in pink flannel, and tucked inside Miss Pickering's stays, it travelled down to Sussex and the next day found lodgment in the safe of a Horsham bank. Its insured value was five hundred pounds. Miss Pickering's income was an annuity of a hundred and fifty a year, augmented to about a hundred and sixty by raffia- and barbolawork, and she had never been able to afford proper treatment for her rheumatism. But whenever the dear Brocards came back—whether in five, ten or twenty years—the ring would still be there.

4

"And now I must get on with my shopping," added Miss Pickering. "It's been quite a surprise, hasn't it?"

"You're right there," agreed Mr. Partridge. "I've never been more surprised in my life . . ."

"Have you left Dormouth Bay for good?"

Mr. Partridge nodded.

"It was too cramping," he said. "I left, as you might say, by chance—" He broke off: the circumstances of his first trip suddenly returned. "What became," he asked, "of that fellow Lambert? Tall, dark chap?"

"Oh," said Miss Pickering, *"he* was still there when I left. And I must say I didn't like him. There was probably no harm in the man, but he used to look at me in such a queer way. And he made, just as I was leaving, such a queer remark. He said: 'I don't know which of you has surprised me most.'"

"I can see what he meant," said Mr. Partridge thoughtfully.

With mutual expressions of regard they parted. Miss Pickering went on to buy a pair of sheets, Mr. Partridge remained (inevitably) where he was. The rest of the day seemed long; he was impatient to get home and tell Lisbeth— not so much with the idea of relieving her mind, as because it would be a pity if she chose that afternoon to write to her aunt from a London address.

5

Lisbeth had not written. She listened to Mr. Partridge's account with more amusement than anything else, and showed no astonishment at learning of her own marriage.

"It's just what Aunt Mildred *would* think," she pointed out. "Don't you remember the telegram?"

"I remember the bit about 'Leave all to me,'" said Mr. Partridge.

"Then you've forgotten the most important part."

"And what was that?"

"'Wish us luck'," quoted Lisbeth. "The 'us' really meant Ronny and me, of course; but I expect she thought it meant me and Hugh."

"I expect she did," agreed Mr. Partridge.

They were interrupted, at this moment, by the appearance of the young man Hamilton, who had apparently turned up for the purpose of walking with Lisbeth down Marsham Street and putting her on her bus. Or at any rate that was all he did do. Mr. Partridge accompanied them; he was on his way to The London Apprentice, but when the vehicle arrived an obscure instinct prompted him to nip on too, at the same time giving the young man such a glance as rooted him to the curb. Lisbeth turned to wave, and then as she sat down looked enquiringly at her unexpected escort.

"Don't you like him?" she asked.

"He's all right," admitted Mr. Partridge.

"Weren't you going to the pub?"

"I thought I'd just put you on your way," said Mr. Partridge. "I'll have a pennyworth and get off at Marble Arch. It'll be a nice walk back."

Lisbeth smiled at him, but did not answer. She opened her bag and took out a small booklet on the rules of bezique: she was going to spend two hours with a bedridden old lady whose companion was on holiday, but from her air of happy expectancy one would never have guessed it. . . .

"He's got," observed Mr. Partridge suddenly, "a funny way of talking. Like what you hear on the movies—though not so violent."

"That's because he's American, darling. And don't call him a Colonial, because they don't like it."

"Why not?" asked Mr. Partridge, surprised. "There was Colonials next to us in the trenches, and some of 'em weren't bad at all. If you *are* a Colonial, why not admit it?"

"Because they're not," explained Lisbeth patiently. "Not now."

Mr. Partridge ruminated in silence till they reached the Marble Arch. He was a fair-minded man.

"After all," he observed, as he rose to get out, "we can't all be British. He mustn't fret."

"I'll tell him," promised Lisbeth.

6

It was fortunate that Mr. Partridge had reasoned himself into a tolerant mood, for he was destined, during the days that followed, to see a great deal of the peculiar young man who was not a Colonial and who was engaged—another peculiarity—in the film industry. To Mr. Partridge, as to many others of the same habit of mind, the films were a sort of natural phenomenon, like the weather. Like the weather, they were always with one, and like the weather, they changed. He occasionally read in the picture papers about the goings-on of film-stars, but of the vast technical and administrative organization behind them he had no idea. A natural scepticism led him to discount the tales which sometimes came to his ears of huge sums of money, and months of time, expended on a single production: he judged by the finished product, and never got away from the notion that a film had taken exactly the same time to photograph as it did to run. It was so obvious that the players had all learnt their lines beforehand. Nor could the most extravagant of backgrounds—Versailles or Constantinople—impress him, as he had also a theory that they were all painted on. It was therefore a great tribute to Lester Hamilton's personality, and also to his powers of exposition, that after a week or two's acquaintance Mr. Partridge began to regard a career in the film industry as something quite promising. Young Hamilton was at the moment attached to the Story Department, but had hopes of becoming a Director. Mr. Partridge knew about Directors—railways had them, also Banks: there was something very respectable in the sound.

"Trustworthy," thought Mr. Partridge. That was how the American struck him, in spite (for of course Mr. Partridge could not believe quite all) of his tall tales. He was trustworthy. He would never get out of bounds. The other side of the wall would never lure him; and it was odd to think, in this connection, of Lisbeth's own ultramural excursions. That business of the telegram, for instance; had she told young Hamilton of that? There was no reason to suppose it, except that they gave an impression of being completely in each other's confidence. And yet some of Lisbeth's confidences must surely have set askew, if they did not tip off altogether, the halo with which that upright young man had so obviously endowed her. . . .

As far as Mr. Partridge could judge, her halo, in Lester Hamilton's eyes, was still intact.

Almost every day he appeared in Marsham Street, if only for a few minutes. (He was both busy and industrious, and never neglected his duties.) His visits had always a practical object—to take Lisbeth to her next engagement, or to lend a hand with the showcards. He managed to relieve Mr. Partridge of nearly all escort duty, and specialized in fetching Lisbeth home if she had been working late at night; but in accordance with a rule which he had evidently laid down for himself, he never took her out for mere pleasure. Mr. Partridge connected this trait with a phrase from their first conversation: he was not trying to horn in. He was just making himself useful, out of sheer disinterested humanity; and Lisbeth had apparently no objection to providing an outlet for his benevolence.

Mr. Partridge, however, was too old a bird to be caught with chaff, and for a while he watched them narrowly: then their complete casualness with each other, the matter-of-fact way in which they arranged to dove-tail (so to speak) their separate activities, gradually reassured him. They were a queer pair. Mr. Partridge once overheard (the door was ajar, and he had no extravagant scruples) their first conversation after Hamilton had been absent for three days.

"You're back," said Lisbeth.

"I got in at six," said Hamilton. "I spent the morning going round the studios, and in the afternoon there was a conference, and then I had a drink with a fellow and came back in his car. On Monday I was in town, at the office till five, and then I went to a cocktail party and afterwards to dinner and the theatre with some people from home. Yesterday was when I went down to Denham. I stayed the night with one of the directors."

"On Monday," began Lisbeth, in turn, "I had a job in the morning taking a child to the dentist, and another in the afternoon helping shut up a house. Yesterday was a blank, so I did a lot of washing and mending, and then we all went to a flick. Today I've been minding an antique shop for a woman who's ill, and I sold a fender-stool for three pounds ten."

That was all, for Hamilton had to go off again at once: he just made his report, and received Lisbeth's, and went. No wonder Mr. Partridge was reassured. And there were other signs too which helped to set his mind at rest: for instance, Lisbeth had the fashionable, foolish (but to Mr. Partridge pleasant) habit of addressing anyone she felt at all friendly to as "darling"; but she never so addressed Mr. Hamilton. She called him Lester, and he, after a time, took to calling her Lisbeth; though they rarely used each other's names at all. The photograph of Hugh Brocard was given a permanent place on the mantelpiece in the sitting-room; whether Lisbeth still transferred it at night to its other place beneath her pillow Mr. Partridge did not know, but the sight of that handsome and honourable countenance presiding, as it were, over their household gave him a feeling of security. They were all under the Captain's eye.

"Fine-looking chap, ain't he?" observed Mr. Partridge, the first time he caught Hamilton's glance resting on this ikon. Lisbeth was not in the room. "Pity it's not full-length, or you'd see his height. Over six foot."

"So I should judge," said Mr. Hamilton. "You're acquainted with him, then?"

"Not exactly *acquainted*," admitted Mr. Partridge reluctantly. "In fact, I've only seen him once, but we had a long talk." He hesitated: it struck him that there were several points on which the young man would be better for a little enlightenment. "It's all," said Mr. Partridge, "a bit of a queer do . . ."

"Yes?"

"The Captain being abroad, he can't look after things. Though he tried, mark you: he flew all the way home in an aeroplane just to put 'em right. And he thought he had. He thinks so still. He thinks young Ronny's safe in Canada, and that Miss Campion's living safe and comfortable with her aunt. If he knew what was really going on he'd—well, I don't know *what* he wouldn't do." Involuntarily, Mr. Partridge blenched; the thought of Captain Brocard's potent and justified wrath was terrible as an army with banners. "It 'ud be worse than the Somme," said Mr. Partridge, with feeling.

The young man was evidently impressed; but he was not yet fully enlightened.

"I don't quite get you," he stated. "If all these arrangements were made—"

"Ah!" said Mr. Partridge. "Now we're coming to it. They were made all right, and very liberal too: only Miss Campion didn't seem to take to them. She's got her own ideas about things—and especially about her brother. She had a great idea of keeping him here with her, and making him work for a living, and generally reforming him. You know what women are: reforming someone's meat and drink to 'em. If ever you want a good wife, just take to the bottle and watch 'em flock."

Mr. Hamilton considered the photograph again. It appeared to give him food for thought.

"When is he due home?"

"In two months' time. That's another two months* reforming. We've been at it nearly four already, and as far as I can see we haven't made a pennyworth of difference. He ought," said Mr. Partridge thoughtfully, "to go round looking for fires: young Ronny, I mean, not the Captain. He ought to find a few fires, and rush through the smoke, and rescue an old lady or two. If he did something like that, I believe it would count just as much with the Captain as holding down a job at two quid a week. He's a gentleman, is the Captain. I'd take my orders from him any day."

Lester Hamilton grinned.

"But you didn't," he pointed out. "As far as I can see, you're abetting Miss Campion for all you're worth."

Mr. Partridge slowly grinned back.

"She's got a way with her," he said simply. "I'm an old fool; but then I know it."

After this conversation they became quite friends, and spent many an evening together tinting ladies' stockings— for Mr. Hamilton settled down to the work as to the manner born. Lisbeth even trusted him with the lingerie, and now and then he in turn would let Mr. Partridge have something easy, such as bloomers, to try his hand on. He never let Mr. Partridge do a brassière, but this was not from selfishness, but from artistic conscience. They worked together so well that Ronny for the first time in his life was holding down a job with perfect ease.

CHAPTER 12

1

IT WAS just about this time that Lisbeth encountered the first set-back in the course of her new career.

She had been summoned to arrange the flowers for a large dinner party and reception at a house in Belgrave Square. It was just such a job as most appealed to her: the masses of white lilies and red carnations were extraordinarily beautiful; and the jars and vases which were to contain them were all firmly based and of sufficient capacity. "Someone in this house has sense," thought Lisbeth, surveying the array: and began on the dinner-table.

The vases for the dinner-table were of Waterford glass. The cloth was a plain white damask. Lisbeth used carnations only, massing them in formal splendour in one great central bowl. Their colour blazed like a heavenly fire; the glass and silver, even the surface of the cloth, picked up faint ruddy tones; stately yet warm, the scarlet at once dominated and lit the entire room. . . .

"This is not," said a voice from the doorway, "a Lord Mayor's Banquet."

Lisbeth looked round, and saw a girl of about her own age dressed in a long dark house-coat that exquisitely fitted her slim and exquisite figure. She had a pale brown skin, touched with colour on the cheekbones, very dark hair, and remarkably beautiful hands.

"No?" said Lisbeth politely.

"No," said the girl. "Use the lilies, please."

"Oh!" said Lisbeth, with an air of enlightenment. "It's a lying-in-state?"

For answer the girl simply advanced to the table and began removing the carnations from the Waterford bowl. She handled them very neatly, whisking them out one by one so that not a drop of water fell upon the cloth. Lisbeth immediately stepped into the adjoining cloak-room, where the flowers were waiting in their boxes, and began to arrange a sheaf of lilies in a large white vase with "staircase" written all over it.

"Mix them, please," ordered the girl over her shoulder.

Lisbeth took no notice. The girl, her hands full of carnations, appeared in the doorway.

"Who," she enquired tartly, "is in charge here?"

"I am," said Lisbeth. "I'm employed to do the flowers, and I'm damn well going to do them. And I don't like being interfered with."

"Nor do I," retorted the girl. "And I always do the flowers myself. I don't know why my mother sent for you."

"I expect," suggested Lisbeth, "she thinks you ought to be resting before the party."

The knowledge that this interfering young woman was the daughter of the house (and therefore Miss Clough) set her mind completely at rest. Miss Clough would shortly have to go and dress. . . . Lisbeth finished the vase at leisure and stepped back to admire the effect.

"You never, I suppose, consider your employer's wishes?"

"Oh, yes," said Lisbeth amiably. "If Mrs. Clough comes and gives me instructions, of course I'll do my best to carry them out. But I haven't seen her."

The girl frowned.

"She *is* resting. She's done nothing all day—"

Moved perhaps by some filial instinct, Miss Clough broke off; but already the atmosphere had changed. Lisbeth nodded. Beneath their antagonism flashed a spark of sympathy. They were antagonistic because they were alike: they were the new generation, ruthless, efficient, and impatient. . . .

"Have you many relations?" asked Miss Clough suddenly.

"Only one that counts. A brother."

"Is he like you?"

"No," said Lisbeth promptly. "He's a young idiot."

"Do you live together?"

Lisbeth nodded.

"He must," observed Miss Clough, "have a hell of a life."

She picked up a box of lilies and went back to the dining-room. Lisbeth, one eye on the clock, filled the remaining vases with water. Somewhere in the hall a telephone rang. A butler appeared and summoned Miss Clough to answer it. While she was gone Lisbeth's first act was naturally to go and take a look at the dining-table, and she was forced to admit that Miss Clough had worked both well and speedily.

The big lily-heads were beautifully arrayed: they rose like a silver fountain. But the effect was not what Lisbeth had intended; it was cold. She glanced at the clock again, and carried her own white armful out to the foot of the stairs. Miss Clough, returning, caught her in the act; but it was at once plain that Miss Clough's mind was no longer on flowers. She was furious, and her fury had to find words.

"Man short," she said briefly. "Half-past six, and a man rings up to say he's definitely got influenza. If you have influenza at half-past six, you've had it at half-past five. I never heard such nonsense."

"Did you tell him so?" enquired Lisbeth, with interest.

"I was going to, but he pretended to be cut off. It's infuriating. I can't start phoning round the town at this hour."

Lisbeth looked at her speculatively.

"You must know dozens of men?"

"I do. But three-quarters of them will be engaged already—and I don't care to be refused." She became suddenly thoughtful. "What about your organization? Can't they supply a presentable guest at half-a-crown an hour?"

"Three-and-six," corrected Lisbeth. "Evenings count as over-time. But we don't provide escorts."

"Damn," said Miss Clough. She too turned to the clock, which now showed twenty to seven. Then she swung round on her heel with a look of resolution.

"Has your brother a tail-suit?"

"He has," admitted Lisbeth. "A relic of our brighter days."

"Then send him along."

Her calm assumption that Ronny, unlike the majority of her own friends, could not possibly have a previous engagement, was naïf. Of course he had not, but Lisbeth shook her head.

"I'm afraid that's impossible. You see, he's infectious."

"Not influenza again!"

"I mean morally," explained Lisbeth. "He's Ronald Campion. He's just done six months for being mixed up with a cocaine gang."

Miss Clough at once looked interested.

"I read the case," she said. "He seemed to me to have been more a fool than anything else."

"Oh, he is," agreed Lisbeth warmly. "He's probably the greatest fool on earth. But you obviously can't have him here."

"Why not? No one who's coming will even have heard of him. They're not the sort who frequent night clubs—or read the police news."

"In any case," added Lisbeth priggishly, "I don't let Ronny go to parties. It's bad for his morale."

There was no doubt that Miss Clough had a great sympathy for the oppressed. Her eyes flashed.

"I can see exactly what's happening," she exclaimed. "You're making him feel a criminal and a pariah, and probably imagine you're reforming him. . . . But that's not the point. You said three-and-six an hour: from eight till eleven's three hours, which comes to—to ten-and-six, and I suppose as you're doing this sort of job you want the money. You've no right to stop him earning what he can."

Lisbeth appeared to consider. The argument appeared to have effect.

"Very well," she said reluctantly. "The butler can give it him in a plain envelope . . ."

"And tell him," continued Miss Clough, now throwing herself into the scheme with what was evidently her accustomed energy, "to get here at eight sharp, and I'll be in the drawing-room. Does he know anything about the Crimean War?"

"As much as most young men."

"Well, my father wrote a book on it. Now I suppose I must dress, and you'd better go straight back. The maids can finish the flowers. I'll tell Peters."

"If that's the butler," said Lisbeth firmly, "I expect he's got a plain envelope for me too."

Miss Clough did not wait to see the envelope change hands, but went straight upstairs; and Lisbeth was thus able to finish her job to her liking, and make what alterations she wished, without interruption. She had to hurry, but she reached Marsham Street by seven-fifteen (just in time to stop Ronny from eating a now superfluous supper), explained the situation, and hustled him into his dress clothes. While he shaved, and she put the buttons in his white waistcoat, she also impressed on his mind two useful facts: that both the Balaclava helmet and the Cardigan waistcoat originated in the Crimea. Ronny, who in early youth had once recited "The Charge of the Light Brigade," hoped he would be able to work in something about that too; but Lisbeth had an idea that in the eyes of a military historian that glorious page had become somewhat tarnished, and discouraged him. He went off, however, in very good spirits, and left Lisbeth (in spite of her chequered experiences) in very good spirits too.

2

The same evening, as it happened, saw Mr. Partridge in better spirits than either of them. On his return home he found the flat empty, for Ronny was in Belgrave Square and Lisbeth had gone out on one of her jobs. Mr. Partridge changed his kilt for a pair of trousers, and set off again for The London Apprentice. But he never got there, for on the second landing he encountered old Mr. Walker; and from this accident there developed one of the most memorable episodes of Mr. Partridge's life.

"Evening," said old Walker.

He was a fine sight. He wore a boldly-checked tweed overcoat, which increased his bulk by about fifteen per cent., a royal blue scarf, and a bowler hat. In his button-hole was a dark red carnation, and on his shoes were spats.

"Evening," replied Mr. Partridge; and looked at his friend admiringly. "Where are you off to?"

"My Club," pronounced Mr. Walker.

"'Strewth!" said Mr. Partridge. He was a true Englishman; his feeling for clubs came halfway between his feeling for the Royal family and his feeling for the Established Church. The fact that old Walker was a clubman did not really surprise him—old Walker was in his eyes capable of anything—but all at once the checked overcoat looked several sizes larger, the scarf took on a brighter blue, the carnation a deeper red. . . .

"Little place in Shepherd's Market," added Mr. Walker casually. "The Drummond."

He paused, and cast a searching eye over Mr. Partridge's apparel. As always, the latter looked very clean, scrupulously neat, and—about the feet—positively dapper.

"Like to come along?" enquired Mr. Walker.

"You bet!" said Mr. Partridge.

The route from Marsham Street to Shepherd's Market led by Mr. Walker's place of employment—the New Park Lane Hotel—and as they rounded its imposing front Mr. Partridge gained a new light on his friend's spacious and unconventional character.

"How many evenings do you get off?" he asked curiously.

"As many as I want," replied Mr. Walker. "I just take 'em."

Mr. Partridge stared.

"But—"

"It's my temperament," stated Mr. Walker calmly. "I'm an artist. And because I'm an artist, they daren't sack me."

Mr. Partridge was too much impressed to comment.

"Sidney and Oswald," pursued his companion, "*they* have to watch their P's and Q's. They favour their mother. I'm different. I do things that are talked about. My Windsor Castle, now—d'you know what the French Ambassador said about that? *'Ce tour de Vindsor, M'soo, c'est un tour de force.'* He was overheard by the Toast-master—a fellow speaking French himself. And I've done better things than that: my Venus and Cupid took three Firsts at Olympia. It was a sensation."

"It must have been a snorter," murmured Mr. Partridge.

"It was," said Mr. Walker.

He relapsed into silence. As he strode majestically along he was evidently reviewing with the mind's eye, perhaps tasting with the mind's tongue, a long succession of masterpieces. Mr. Partridge, trotting alongside, did not speak either; he knew better than to disturb the meditations of an artist. But his heart swelled with pride as he reverently steered his companion through the traffic: he felt that his first entry into Clubland could not have been made under better auspices.

The premises occupied by the Drummond were modestly situated over a tobacconist's; the clubroom itself was small, and so thickly lined with cases of stuffed fish as to give the impression of an aquarium; but the company gathered there amply supplied any dignity or poise lacking to its surroundings. It was essentially the same sort of company as gathered at The London Apprentice, but on a higher level: the two butlers came not from Porchester Terrace, but from Belgrave Square; of the two chauffeurs one drove a Duke, the other a Marchioness. Old Walker himself was of course *hors concours*—he made more money than any of them, and called no man sir—but if he had no equals he at least had associates, and Mr. Partridge, plunged into the cream of the assembly, found himself talking to an elderly

Yorkshireman who (according to Mr. Walker) was the best judge of soft fruit in London. Covent Garden, it appeared, trembled at his approach. Rather to Mr. Partridge's surprise, this celebrity conversed chiefly about greyhound racing, drawing unfavourable comparisons between the long dogs and the whippets of his native heath; but even so he was very informative. He also stood Mr. Partridge a double Scotch. So did Mr. Walker. So did His Grace's chauffeur. It was glorious.

There was only one thing that troubled him: a sense of his own unworthiness. When he remembered the Bonnie Scotland, when he saw himself standing outside it, the lowest creature of the restaurant trade, his breath came fast. Even in the Apprentice, his calling had been against him—but here, in the Drummond, it would surely be enough to have him thrown out. . . .

"But they don't know," thought Mr. Partridge, "and old Walker won't tell 'em. Not for his own sake he won't . . ."

He looked across at his sponsor, and felt a pang of apprehension. The bottle of cherry brandy (kept specially in stock for Mr. Walker's use) was almost empty. Mr. Walker's eye was bright but vague. It was rather like the eyes of the stuffed fish, and even they, to Mr. Partridge's uneasy imagination, seemed to be regarding him with suspicion. Suppose someone asked him his trade? Did a question rise, even then, to the Yorkshireman's lips?

There was only one thing to do, and Mr. Partridge did it. He got in first.

"When I had my bookshop in the Haymarket—" began Mr. Partridge casually.

After that, the evening was more glorious than ever.

3

The results of Ronny's first essay as a hired man were not exactly what might have been expected. He returned home, however, in good order at eleven-fifteen, so that Lisbeth did not have to sit up for him, as she was fully prepared to do. She was extremely curious.

"How did you get on, darling?"

"No cocktails," said Ronny, "but grand food. I sat between Helena and an old Frenchwoman—"

"Who," asked Lisbeth, "is Helena?"

"Miss Clough, of course. I think she's rather intelligent. We had quite a long talk about you, darling. Helena said you were one of the most attractive people she'd ever seen."

"She's intelligent, all right," said Lisbeth placidly. "Any comments on the dinner-table?"

Ronny looked slightly abashed.

"There was one, darling, and I'm afraid I made rather a bloomer. The old French bird—she was quite charming, really—looked at that great splash of carnations in the middle and said *'Magnifique! Hein?'* and I meant to say, 'A sight for sore eyes, *hein?'*—though what made me try to translate a thing like that in French I can't imagine—and what I *did* say was *'Bon pour les aveugles, hein?,'*—which of course is quite different. And naturally Helena overheard. But she was awfully sweet about it."

"I bet she was," said Lisbeth.

Ronny stooped and unlaced his pumps, and pattered across to his kitchen-bedroom. On the threshold he paused. The air was full of fragrance, and the sink was full of carnations.

"I say!" called Ronny. "Where did these come from? They're just like the ones at the Cloughs."

"Aren't they?" agreed Lisbeth. "I got them for you to take along tomorrow, when you pay your bread-and-butter call."

Ronny hesitated.

"Isn't that rather old-world, darling?"

"Good manners," said his sister sententiously, "are never out of fashion."

"But they might think I'd come back for my plain envelope. . . ."

Lisbeth stared at him.

"Do you mean to tell me you never got it?"

"Well," said Ronny uneasily, "the butler chap offered it me all right—when I was getting my hat; but I felt such a fool—I mean, I'd got on so well with those Balaclavas and Cardigans, I didn't like to spoil the effect. So I just, so to speak, waved it away. You're not wild, are you?"

"No," said Lisbeth, sitting down on the edge of his bed. "I'm not wild. And you can certainly pay your call."

"Right," agreed Ronny amiably, putting his nose down to sniff. "These *are* like the Cloughs', though—exactly the same tone. Did they come from the same place?"

"As a matter of fact," said Lisbeth, "they did . . ."

4

And now there began for Ronny a new era, so that it seemed even to Mr. Partridge that the long-awaited reformation was at last under way. In the first place he had been reintroduced, as it were, into respectable society; and in the second, Lester Hamilton found him a job.

It wasn't much of a job. His duties consisted chiefly in answering the telephone. (There must have been a sort of affinity between Ronny and the switch-board: when anyone was actually driven to employ him, they always said "Let him answer the telephone.") Ronny now answered the telephone in the outermost office of the suite occupied by Mr. Hamilton's own corporation. He also sorted letters (but without opening them) and distributed them to their appropriate recipients, and untied knots in the string off parcels. He was not the office boy, because there already was one—a youth named Gordon who studied German in his spare time. This scholarly lad was Ronny's chief companion; and Lisbeth, who had viewed her brother's entry into the glamorous world of the films with something like dismay, was soon reassured by his growing knowledge of irregular verbs.

He had to be at the office at 9:30 A.M., and he stayed there till six. The united efforts of Lisbeth and Mr. Partridge got him off each morning, and he arrived home, a tired business man, at 6:15. For once he was sticking to a job with extraordinary doggedness, and with apparent content; and Lisbeth (always a realist where Ronny was concerned) felt considerable surprise; until one morning, finding herself free at the lunch hour, she met Ronny outside his place of toil and proposed to eat with him.

"Grand," said Ronny. "Here's a bus."

"But where are we going?"

"To the Green Parrot."

"But that's only just down the street!"

"I know," said Ronny. "But I don't want to keep Helena waiting."

5

Miss Clough, already seated at a table for two, presented her usual immaculate and attractive appearance. She greeted Lisbeth with every sign of pleasure, and at once moved to a table for three.

"There's Hamburg steak," she told Ronny, "and chicken rissoles. I think the steak's more sustaining."

Ronny at once ordered it. So did Miss Clough. Lisbeth had a Japanese salad. Ronny looked at it, when it came, with a slight wistfulness, but also with detachment. He evidently had no idea of eating anything but Hamburg steak.

"Brain-work," observed Miss Clough, "is just as exhausting as manual labour."

"What work?" asked Lisbeth incautiously.

"Brain-work," repeated Miss Clough. She turned to Ronny. "Did you have a hard morning?"

"Fair," said Ronny, with an air of understatement. "Very heavy mail. And there's a trade show next Friday."

He sighed, and took a mouthful of steak. Miss Clough watched him maternally; and Lisbeth, looking from one to the other, decided that they really believed it all. They really believed that Ronny was an over-worked and indispensable prop of the film industry, who without a large lunch might faint at his desk during the afternoon. Then she glanced at Miss Clough again, and wondered. Miss Clough looked very intelligent. Her small, exquisitely cut face was not the face of a pretty fool. Lisbeth caught her eye, and half expected a wink; but the gaze of Miss Clough was perfectly straight, perfectly friendly, and perfectly non-committal.

The meal proceeded very agreeably. It seemed to be tacitly understood that Ronny was not to do much talking: he was to be entertained, and relaxed; but Miss Clough enquired after Lisbeth's activities, showing an amiable interest, and referred casually to her own. She apparently spent most of her time taking courses—a course in art, a course in domestic economy, a course in German literature. Ronny knew all about them. From one of his remarks it transpired that the German literature was an innovation: Miss Clough's original choice had been French, and Lisbeth wondered whether the change had been made in order that Ronny might hold his own with Gordon the office boy. Miss Clough was obviously very thorough.

At a quarter to two they separated so that Ronny should be able to walk back to his office breathing the fresh air. Helena Clough paid for her own lunch (since Ronny did not demur, the point had evidently been long ago settled) and tactfully turned right, whereas the Campions turned to the left. At least, Lisbeth thought it was tact, but even she could not be quite sure: Miss Clough was bound for a two o'clock lecture at University College, and she was not the sort of person to let one course interfere with another.

"What I like about her especially," remarked Ronny, "is that she never gets sentimental."

"No?" said Lisbeth.

"No. She's just a damned good pal. And what makes it more unusual is that I suppose some people would consider her very good-looking."

"I think she's beautiful," said Lisbeth sincerely.

"She's got a good figure," admitted Ronny, "and nice eyes. And I like the way she does her hair. Neat. But of course she's not the sort of girl a fellow falls in love with."

"No?" said Lisbeth again.

"She's a bit hard. I mean, one can't imagine her ever needing protection. In a way it would be awful if she did, because she'd feel it so. She isn't like other girls. What did you say?"

"I didn't say anything, darling . . ."

"I thought you said something about classics. Helena doesn't study classics. She studies German literature, and art, and—"

"And domestic economy," finished Lisbeth.

6

The domestic economy of the flat was now in the hands of an elderly lady named Mrs. Stagg, whom Ronny naturally referred to as the Doe, and who did not mind this appellation. She did not mind anything Ronny either said or did, for he was the image (she affirmed) of her favourite nephew who had come to a bad end. But Ronny wasn't coming to a bad end.

He was working steadily, and lunching with Helena, and he had even bought a bowler hat. This new head-gear made an extraordinary change in his appearance, and also, it seemed, in his character: he might laugh and joke throughout breakfast, he might resist, with passive ingenuity, all Lisbeth's efforts to get him out of the house, but once the bowler was upon his head his whole personality altered: he became serious, businesslike, slightly pompous. He walked down Marsham Street with the air of a man about to set the wheels of industry efficiently turning.

"Thinks a lot of himself, doesn't he?" observed Mr. Partridge. "Reminds me of the first time I wore pants."

"He's doing very well," said Lisbeth.

"All right for the present," admitted Mr. Partridge. "He's got a job and he hasn't been sacked. But there's no future in it that I can see."

"Ah," said Lisbeth. "But you haven't had lunch at the Green Parrot."

Since Mr. Partridge could make neither head nor tail of this remark, he said nothing. He was often rather silent in these days, for in a way the reformation of Ronny produced an odd flatness. It took away the raison d'être of the Marsham Street household. They were all three in steady work, and their triple wages put them beyond the reach of care. It seemed almost too good to last. . . .

"And it won't last," said Mr. Partridge prophetically.

"What won't, darling?"

"Well, the peace and plenty. I've got a feeling we're all waiting for something."

"Of course we are," said Lisbeth, with a smile. "We're waiting for Hugh."

"When's he due back?"

"In just a month," said Lisbeth; and her smile faded.

CHAPTER 13

1

A WEEK passed, then two weeks; Ronny continued to behave like a cross between a cherub and a captain of industry. But Mr. Partridge watched him warily, experiencing all the tremors of a gardener before a flower-show. Ronny was his prize marrow, his Table Decoration, his bunch of grapes weighing six pounds. The sensation of flatness left him; as the return of the Captain drew daily nearer, so did Mr. Partridge's anxiety increase. He had noted that fading of Lisbeth's smile, and put it down to emotions similar to his own: she was worried, and he didn't blame her. They had nursed Ronny along, avoiding all major catastrophes, for nearly six months: a fall from grace in the last fortnight would be hard to bear. . . .

In the meantime, everything (on the surface) was much as usual. The Bonnie Scotland, if it did not exactly thrive, at any rate continued to make ends meet, and Mr. Partridge had become one of the sights of Oxford Street. Children out with their nurses insisted on paying him a visit just as they insisted on paying a visit to Peter Pan. Lisbeth continued to run about town like a Spirit of Service, and Lester Hamilton continued to run about after her. They saw each other daily, but only in tubes or buses: the London Transport Board was their constant chaperone. Once, by an odd chance, Mr. Partridge actually found himself seated behind them on top of a No. 27: and this odd chance, owing to the odder happenings that followed, stuck in Mr. Partridge's memory as one of the outstanding events of that last month.

He had picked up the bus at Oxford Circus, after an excursion to a darts match with the M.P.'s chauffeur; the hour was late, about ten-thirty, and as he sat down, and recognized Lisbeth's back immediately before him, he was suddenly reminded of the ride up from Dormouth Bay. On this occasion, however, Lisbeth's head was not tucked down against her companion's shoulder. "Nice straight back . . ." thought Mr. Partridge appreciatively; and turned to ask for a penny ticket.

He asked for it quite loudly, so that Lisbeth should hear, and turn round, and be surprised to see him; but she didn't. Her head never moved, nor did the head of Lester Hamilton. They both continued to sit staring straight before them— which, since they had the front seat, was only natural: there was always plenty to see from the top seat in front on a 27. Mr. Partridge considered poking his own head forward and surprising them that way; but he was too tired himself to think of a suitable witticism. He sat back and relaxed. His day in Oxford Street had been animated by a dogfight, and the excitement of the darts match had further exhausted him. At the next stop an enormous lady in a musquash coat took the vacant half of his seat; she took more than half, she took nearly two-thirds; but the furry warmth of her was so grateful that Mr. Partridge did not protest. He just went under. He closed his eyes. Very soon, he slept.

When he woke up again it was with a vague sense of having gone too far, and though Lisbeth was still seated in front of him, he made an attempt to look out of the window. It was an attempt only, for the glass was misted over, and his arms were pinioned—one against the side of the bus, the other against the lady. Mr. Partridge wriggled.

"'M I squashing you?" asked the lady kindly.

"Not at all," said Mr. Partridge.

After that he naturally could not wriggle any more. Anyway, Lisbeth knew where to get off, and would see him as she passed out. He sank back into the fur.

"I generally do," added the lady, with an air of impartiality.

This time Mr. Partridge did not answer; being once more asleep.

2

His slumber was deep and peaceful, and very warm. His dreams were of friendly bears. Old Walker came into them too—old Walker offering a bear cherry brandy. Then the bear went off, saying it was a teetotaller, and presently Mr. Partridge's sleep was the cold, uneasy sort that ends in waking with a jerk. Mr. Partridge so woke. It took him a moment to remember where he was, to recognize Lisbeth's head still before him, to realize that the lady was gone from his side—that the bus top, save for Lisbeth, Hamilton and himself, was in fact empty. "Hi!" cried Mr. Partridge; and as the pair in front turned round he rubbed furiously on the glass and stared out. He saw water, and trees, and a line of parapet. . . .

"Where the dickens are we?" demanded Mr. Partridge. "Blessed if it doesn't seem like Richmond Bridge!"

"It is," said Lisbeth. She looked surprised right enough; she looked bewildered; but Mr. Partridge had an odd feeling that it wasn't the sight of himself, nor yet the sight of Richmond Bridge, that had set her gaping. She looked as though she too had just come out of a dream.

"Then what are we doing on it?" demanded Mr. Partridge. "Have you been asleep too?"

It was all odd together; as Lisbeth turned her head, Mr. Partridge for an instant quite thought that he had been mistaken, and that her companion was not Hamilton but

Ronny; to no one save her brother had he ever before seen her direct that speaking look. The silent conversation of the young Campions had always been a source of surprise to him; now, it seemed, Lester Hamilton had picked up the same language. Mr. Partridge felt a pang of jealousy.

"I thought," he observed, addressing the young man, "you were supposed to be fetching her home?"

"I was—" began Mr. Hamilton.

"And I s'pose," continued Mr. Partridge, "you'd forgot the address, and thought you'd try Richmond?"

Before this terrific irony the young man naturally quailed. Lisbeth spoke for him.

"He was, darling. But I felt I wanted a nice long bus ride. I don't often have a treat."

Mr. Partridge glanced at her suspiciously. A treat! If she wanted a treat, why didn't she go to the pictures? But before he could ask this pertinent question, Lester Hamilton interposed with another.

"Hadn't we," asked Lester Hamilton, "better get off? Lisbeth's tired."

"I should just think she is!" exploded Mr. Partridge. "I should just think—"

He was cut short. A hand had fallen on his shoulder.

It was the hand of the conductor, and the next few moments were extremely unpleasant. Mr. Partridge paid up his extra fare, but was unable to clear his character. Lisbeth and Hamilton had also overshot their stage, though only by a penny, and the whole party left the vehicle under a heavy cloud. They had to wait twenty minutes for the last bus back. It was altogether a most peculiar and uncomfortable episode—and what worried Mr. Partridge most of all was a feeling that he hadn't got to the bottom of it.

3

There was another peculiar incident which took place about this time, but of which Mr. Partridge remained ignorant. Ronny took tea, one Sunday afternoon, in Belgrave Square. He sat on a chair of rosewood and petit-point, drinking china tea out of a Spode cup, and eating thin bread-and-butter off a Spode plate. At the other end of the couch Helena presided over a tray set for two. Both her parents were out, but even their joint presence could hardly have added to the decorum of the party. A long serious conversation (on the influence of gangster films) had just come to an end; on the white marble mantelpiece a black marble clock struck half-past five.

The peculiarity of this episode lay in the fact that Ronny was enjoying himself.

He did not know why: asked what sort of things he enjoyed, he would have replied, "Night clubs"; his self-analysis (so impressive to Mr. Partridge) had not gone far enough; he had never consciously realized that beneath his taste for champagne at 2 A.M. lay a much more fundamental desire for the peace and security connoted by afternoon tea at half-past four. He knew only that the calm spaciousness of the Clough drawing-room was highly agreeable to him. It also reminded him of a good many things he thought he had forgotten.

"Did you ever," he asked abruptly, "go blackberrying?"

"Often," said Helena. "When I was about nine. In Dorset." She sat, as usual, very still; but her eyes were intent, as though the conversation had suddenly taken an important turn. "Where did you?"

"In Sussex, When we lived—Lisbeth and I—with the Aunts. We lived in the country for years and years."

"Did you like it?"

Ronny took another piece of bread-and-butter, and considered while he ate.

"It was pretty ghastly, of course. Deadly dull. But there was a sort of—of restfulness about the place. Regular meals, and all that."

Helena silently passed him a plate of home-made macaroons.

"Mind you," continued Ronny, "we had a rattling good time in London. A marvellous time. But somehow we never seemed to settle down."

"Your sister," suggested Helena, "will be settling down pretty soon?"

Ronny nodded. He had long told Miss Clough about Lisbeth and Hugh Brocard—though omitting all mention of Canada.

"I hope she will," he said seriously. "Of course Lisbeth's a year older than I am, but in a way I always feel she's much younger. She doesn't really understand me. She's most wonderfully loyal, and I wouldn't say a word against her, but—well, there is such a thing as bossiness—"

Helena's lids dropped—unnecessarily. Ronny, gazing across the tea-table, saw only the exquisite contour of her face and the exquisite curve of her mouth.

"I gas an awful lot about myself," he said. "You never do. What do *you* want most out of life?"

Helena did not immediately answer. If she had spoken truthfully she would have said, "My own way. An ordered household in which I am the mistress and the master too. A happy household, which I possess." Under her lowered lids she looked back at Ronny and smiled.

"I don't know," she said lightly. "Apart from the regular meals. And my next regular meal's at seven, because we're going to the theatre, and I've a dozen things to do before I dress . . ."

Ronny at once rose. He had passed a very pleasant hour, he liked Helena very much indeed, but he was not aware of having either said or done anything of the least importance. Nor was there anything in Helena's manner to suggest that her mind was now definitely and inevitably made up.

"Lunch to-morrow?" said Ronny.

"Lunch to-morrow," agreed Miss Clough.

She accompanied him into the hall and opened the front door. Rain was falling, and a cruising taxi, seeing a figure emerge from so stately a portal, hopefully slackened speed. For a moment Ronny paused; he turned back towards Helena, and the look in his eye—the intention to borrow half-a-crown—was plain to read. Then he simply grinned at her, and ran down into the wet.

That was quite important too.

Chapter 14

1

ONE week, two weeks, three weeks. Then Sunday, Monday, Tuesday. On the Wednesday evening at five o'clock came a cable addressed to Miss Campion. Mr. Partridge, who had got off early on account of a thunderstorm, and was alone in the flat when it arrived, spent a good deal of time holding the envelope up to the light, but without success; he had to wait till Lisbeth came in to learn that Hugh Brocard was due back on Sunday afternoon.

"Well, well, well!" said Mr. Partridge, highly pleased. "Better late than never!"

"He isn't late," pointed out Lisbeth, staring at the message. "In fact, he's a day early. In his last letter he said he wouldn't be back till Monday."

"It just shows what a hurry he's in," agreed Mr. Partridge. "Hasting, as you might say, to the wedding. I s'pose you'll be married in a church?"

Lisbeth nodded.

"I suppose so . . ."

"He'll be in uniform, I shouldn't wonder? Kilts and all?"

Lisbeth nodded again.

"I'd wear mine too," pursued Mr. Partridge, "'cept that it might seem like putting myself forward. I don't want to take the shine out of *him*. That's the bride's job." He looked at her enquiringly: she had done, so far as he knew, nothing whatever about her wedding-dress, and Mr. Partridge had an idea that wedding-dresses took time. Then he reflected again, and remembered that they also cost money. . . .

"Cheer up," said Mr. Partridge.

Lisbeth's chin lifted.

"What on earth do you mean by that?"

"White satin isn't everything," explained Mr. Partridge. "And you'd look a treat even in your nightgown."

It was not, as he immediately realized, an altogether delicate observation. Looked at one way, it was positively improper. Mr. Partridge blushed. He could not see whether Lisbeth were blushing too, because she had turned away her face—so she probably was. He hastened to put matters right.

"I didn't mean," began Mr. Partridge hastily, "in <u>bed</u>—" and the next instant was quite glad to see Ronny come into the room.

2

Ronny, on the other hand, did not seem particularly pleased to see Mr. Partridge. He fidgeted about, looked once or twice at Lisbeth as though he were going to say something, and then rather obviously changed his mind. Mr. Partridge could take a hint as well as most men, so after about ten minutes of this he withdrew to his own room and pointedly shut the door. He was almost certain that if he had not done this himself, Ronny would have done it for him.

"I'm very worried," began Ronny at once, "about Helena."

"Yes?" said Lisbeth.

Her voice was not quite so sympathetic as usual, but Ronny was too preoccupied to notice.

"She's not," he stated, "herself. She seems upset about something."

With one half of her mind Lisbeth decided that Ronny had been right in considering Miss Clough intelligent.

"Since when, darling?" she asked.

"Oh, just this last week or so. And I had lunch with her today, and they're going down to Windsor for the steeple-chases on Friday, and she rather wanted me to go along too. Of course I can't—we both know that—it was just an idea she had—but her having it at all shows how—how sort of lonely she is." Ronny broke off, and frowned. "She never says a word, of course, because she's so plucky; but I don't believe she's happy at home."

"Very few girls are, my dear."

"Helena isn't like other girls. I mean, she wouldn't fuss about nothing. I'm wondering whether I ought to try and make her talk, or whether I ought to—to respect her reserve. What do you think?"

"Make her talk," said Lisbeth at once. "If possible, make her cry."

Ronny stared.

"You mean it would relieve her nerves?"

"That's right, darling. It also clears the head."

"But how?"

"Oh, tell her a sad story," said Lisbeth impatiently.

Ronny fidgeted round the room and came back to the mantelpiece.

"You don't like her, do you?" he said.

Lisbeth hesitated. Her feelings towards Miss Clough were perfectly defined, and in a sense highly favourable; but the feelings she was at the moment concerned with were not her own, but Ronny's.

"Helena's very beautiful," she said. "I thought that long before you did."

"I don't now. I suppose it's because I'm so completely detached about her, but I've never thought she had more than nice hair and eyes and a good figure. And of course she dresses well. But it's her character that's so—so rare, and that's what you've never appreciated."

"Darling, I hardly know her!"

"And you've never tried to. I never thought you were jealous, or catty—but I suppose most women are jealous of a person like Helena."

Lisbeth succeeded in keeping her temper.

"I suppose we are," she agreed meekly. "After all, she has pretty nearly everything . . ."

"That's just it. And that's why she's so extraordinarily lonely. Women are jealous, and she can't keep a man friend because they all fall in love with her. She simply daren't be nice to them."

"She'd better give up and go into a convent," suggested Lisbeth.

Ronny turned and looked at her. His mouth was set—she never remembered having seen it so before—in a firm line.

"All right," he said. "I shan't ask your advice again. But if only I had some cash—"

The sentence remained unfinished; for at that moment the door of Mr. Partridge's room burst open and Mr. Partridge (who had been out of things quite long enough) rejoined the party.

"Here!" cried Mr. Partridge. "I've remembered something important. Where's your engagement ring? Still with your auntie?"

Lisbeth looked startled.

"Yes," she said. "Yes, it must be. I'd forgotten about it . . ."

Ronny laughed.

"Forgotten!" he repeated deliberately. "It's worth hundreds of pounds, and you forget all about it! My God!"

"Now then!" Mr. Partridge eyed him repressively. "She's got plenty else to think of—you, for one thing. But it did ought to be got back."

"Yes," said Lisbeth again; and sat down on the end of her divan-bed. She looked suddenly very tired.

"If you like," volunteered Mr. Partridge, "I'll do it. I'll wire and explain things, and tell her to bring it up. She'd like to meet the Captain, anyway."

Lisbeth nodded; so Mr. Partridge put on his hat and went out.

3

On the way to the Post Office, it struck him that if he were to do any explaining at all his telegram would probably cost him about five pounds. He decided therefore to confine himself to the simple request, and sign it "Lisbeth."

"Please bring my ring to 7 Horsham Street Paddington by Sunday very urgent. Lisbeth."

The wire dispatched, he did not go straight home, but set off in the direction of the Edgware Road. His mind for some time past had been exercised by the question of a wedding present, and he wanted to look at the shops. The shops in Edgware Road were not of the very highest class, but then neither was Mr. Partridge's stipend. By great economy, and by cutting down his beer, he had managed to save four-and-sixpence. Measured against his wishes the sum was small, but at least he was spared the difficulty of deciding between a pearl necklace and a fur coat. His desire was to give Lisbeth not one of these objects, but both of them, and yet to have done so (supposing his finances permitted) might have looked ostentatious. At any rate he was saved from that: with the best will in the world you couldn't be ostentatious on four-and-six. . . .

Like a moth at a lamp, Mr. Partridge hovered outside the bright windows; but nothing he saw pleased him. He wanted something which would be personal, and as good, of its kind, as money could buy. A large ostrich-egg in a pawn-shop, marked three shillings, momentarily attracted him: it was cleverly painted with a view of Lake Como, and the price was so outrageous that he felt sure it must be a very special egg indeed. Then he reflected that the Captain probably possessed ostrich-eggs already—they went almost necessarily with foxes'-brushes and elephants' feet—and that Lisbeth would therefore be endowed with them, as with his other worldly goods, in the natural course of events. Mr. Partridge passed on. His brow was furrowed; the thought of so many worldly goods was disconcerting. Their abundance left no gap, so to speak, for him to fill. He stood some minutes outside a draper's, contemplating an array of handkerchiefs: some were in boxes, but the superior specimens were displayed individually, puffed out through little metal rings. One of these, in the centre, was priced at no less than four shillings—four shillings for a single handkerchief. It had a deep border of lace, with a scalloped edge; it was such a handkerchief as a bride might carry at her wedding and blow her nose on in the presence of a bishop. Mr. Partridge nearly fell for it. But handkerchiefs are perishable, besides being almost predestined victims of the laundry. Mr. Partridge moved on again.

He moved on past a butcher's, an ironmonger's, a second draper's and a Post Office. The shop which came next was so narrow as to be little more than a booth, but despite this lack of importance it managed to make its effect. The window was plastered with photographs—sheets and sheets of them, twelve heads to a sheet, and over all, in enormous red letters on a white ground, ran the legend "PHOTOMA-TOM." To one side a placard in blue and yellow added its persuasions: "12 positions for 2/6: How to Make Your Friends Happy. The Ideal Gift."

"By gum!" said Mr. Partridge.

He looked more closely. Some of the sheets, besides giving the twelve positions, practically told a story as well. "From Grave to Gay," one was labelled, and another, "Oh What a Surprise!" Mr. Partridge was fascinated. All his doubts were over. Personal, imperishable, and unique—a photograph was the very thing! Twelve photographs would be magnificent! With the spare two bob he could buy a frame! And he had several very good ideas: he wouldn't copy, he would be original. He would be reading a letter— "News from Abroad" Or what about "Seeing a Ghost"—very dramatic? Too dramatic, perhaps: Lisbeth might wake up and see it in the night (he had a feeling it would be kept in her bedroom) and get a nasty shock. . . .

For a moment more Mr. Partridge meditated; then he had another idea still. It was a peach.

"I want to be taken," said Mr. Partridge, entering the shop, "as Dreaming about Angels."

4

When he regained Marsham Street some hour-and-a-half later there was nobody at home; and for once Mr. Partridge was glad of the solitude. It allowed him to take the photographs out and lay them on the table; and it also allowed him to swear.

"Damn," said Mr. Partridge.

For the photographs were not a success. Though he had been concentrating on angels all the time, expressing, as he believed, every gradation of astonishment and rapture, his intention had not properly materialized. You could be quite sure he was dreaming, because his eyes were shut, but he might have been dreaming about anything. Half-way through, when his mouth was fully open to indicate awe, he looked as though he were having a nightmare. And his expression of ecstasy at the end made him look simply stuffed. . . .

Mr. Partridge leaned over the table in an attitude of rueful contemplation. His half-crown was gone, and though he hadn't had the heart to buy a frame, you couldn't do much on two bob. Could anything be done with the photographs? They would be better, he thought, with the eyes open: with a little touching up. All the best photographs were touched up, though one could hardly expect it for two-and-six. Perhaps touching up was all they needed. . . .

On the end of the mantelpiece stood a jar containing Ronny's disused brushes, with a bottle of India ink. Mr. Partridge carried them to the table, and drew up a chair, and set to. A spot of ink in the centre of an eyelid—and behold, the eye was open! A little work on the moustache, to make it blacker and more luxuriant—and twenty years were knocked off Mr. Partridge's age! It was easy as pie!

"I believe I've got a gift!" thought Mr. Partridge joyfully; and gave himself up to the ghastly work.

5

A sound from the kitchen made him start: there was someone at home after all, and in case it should be Lisbeth he hastily drew a sheet of newspaper over his handiwork.

But it was not Lisbeth, it was Ronny—a Ronny who, by the look of his creased and ash-bespattered jacket, had employed the interval since Mr. Partridge last saw him by lying on his bed smoking cigarettes.

"You smoke more than's good for you," remarked Mr. Partridge severely.

"I've been thinking," said Ronny, with dignity. "I find smoking helps."

He advanced towards the table. Mr. Partridge laid a hand upon the newspaper. His artist's soul thirsted for a fellow-artist's appreciation; but he was still too much annoyed with young Ronny to give him such a treat.

"Do you know," asked Ronny unexpectedly, "any sad stories?"

"Dozens," said Mr. Partridge.

"What's the saddest?"

Mr. Partridge considered.

"There was a chap I knew was tipped Jerry M. for the National half an hour before the start. A hundred to one. As he was crossing the road to hand in his slip, he was knocked out by a bus and didn't come to till the race was over. Jerry M. won. How's that?"

Ronny shook his head.

"I call it fair heart-rending," said Mr. Partridge disappointedly.

"Oh, absolutely," agreed Ronny. "But it's the wrong kind. I was thinking of something a bit more sentimental."

Mr. Partridge considered again.

"There was another fellow I knew broke his heart over a girl and gave up a nice little fish-shop to drown himself at Herne Bay. A bit touched in the head, he was. *She'd* been walking out with a milkman, d'you see, at the same time, and it destroyed his faith in human nature. Women seem to have a knack of it."

There was a movement behind him. Lisbeth had come quietly in, and had evidently heard Mr. Partridge's second essay in the pathetic.

"Suppose," she suggested, "the milkman would have drowned himself if she hadn't walked out with *him*?"

"She ought never to have started it," declared Mr. Partridge. "Not with both of 'em—"

Ronny got up and with an abstracted air retired to his own room. Lisbeth took off her hat. She looked more tired than ever.

"Where've you been?" enquired Mr. Partridge.

"On a job. Two hours' child-tending."

"Well, it'll soon be over now," encouraged Mr. Partridge.

She was at the mirror, sleeking her hair. She did it in a funny way, all twisted up on top, as though she were going to wash her ears; and Mr. Partridge, considering her coiffure first from the back, and then, through the glass, from the front, wondered how she managed to look so attractive. . . .

"It's much harder for women than you think," said Lisbeth suddenly. "Suppose you meet a man, and he's nice, and you like him—are you to go right away and never see him again, just because he *might* fall in love with you and get hurt?"

"I thought women had instincts for that kind of thing," said Mr. Partridge.

"But they can't always be sure. And—and they think 'Am I just being conceited? Why should I know I'm going to take just so much interest in a man, and expect him to lose his head about me?' And then before they know where they are they're in a place with no way out. . . ."

"What you're trying to tell me," said Mr. Partridge, "is that women like playing with fire."

"So do men! They may know nothing can ever happen, and *they* don't go away. It's not happy to be loved when you mayn't—when you can't love back. It makes you feel mean."

"Well, you've no call to worry," said Mr. Partridge comfortably. "You're going to marry him."

Lisbeth stood quite still, staring at herself in the glass.

"I must get my hair done," she said. "I must look my best for Hugh."

On which unexceptionable statement the conversation ended.

CHAPTER 15

1

LISBETH'S visit to the coiffeur was paid next day.

Hugh Brocard was not due home for another forty-eight hours, but her hair was so fine that it took that length of time to settle down. She came back with the twist on top arranged in a nest of small curls, looking soignée, charming, and rather unlike herself. The flat was unlike itself too: not a chair, not a cushion had been changed, but the atmosphere was different. There was an end-of-all-things feeling, which both Lisbeth and Mr. Partridge resolutely ignored. Neither looked beyond the next two days—Mr. Partridge at least very foolishly, since he should have been finding himself another lodging; but he could not bear to. Once or twice Lisbeth looked at him speculatively, opened her mouth to speak, and closed it again. (But she went downstairs to the Walkers, and had a long conversation with Sidney, and came back looking more cheerful.) Ronny's card-painting was now a thing of the past, but some of his litter—brushes, wash-pots and ink bottles—was still in evidence. Lisbeth packed it all together in a cardboard box, and when Mr. Partridge caught her at it remarked that the place was really getting too untidy. Mr. Partridge merely nodded, and went into his room: when he came out again the litter had been replaced.

"It's like leaving a boat," said Lisbeth, with a grin. "One always gets ready too early."

It was the first overt reference to the approaching break-up, and again Mr. Partridge nodded. There were sausages for supper, and for something to do he went and took them out of their paper and began carefully pricking them with a fork. There were six sausages instead of the usual three—a mournful plenty, as of funeral baked meats. Lisbeth began to lay the table. They both wanted something to do.

"Where's Ronny?" asked Mr. Partridge.

"Not back yet. He said they were very busy." Lisbeth paused, with an upward look. "We've done that job, you know. We really have."

"He seems to be working pretty steady," admitted Mr. Partridge.

"He is. And he's changed: you must have seen it."

"*That's* his bowler hat," said Mr. Partridge.

"Of course. It's symbolical. When he puts on his bowler hat he's a different man."

Mr. Partridge left the sausages and came back into the sitting-room.

"Are you going to show him?" he asked. "I mean to the Captain?"

"I think," said Lisbeth reflectively, "that I shall let him transpire. But it doesn't matter. Because the great thing Hugh—and everyone else—had against Ronny was that he wouldn't work. And now he is working. So it's all right."

Mr. Partridge looked at her.

"You know as well as I do," he said, "young Ronny can't keep himself. Not by a long chalk. There's something going on in your head that you won't tell me."

"I'm afraid of shocking you," said Lisbeth demurely. "I said once before that Ronny would make an excellent father."

"You talk a whole lot of rubbish," retorted Mr. Partridge, steering away, in spite of himself, from the implications of this remark. It offended, in an obscure way, his male pride. Lisbeth had often pointed out that her view of Ronny was purely objective; but it was carrying objectiveness a bit far (felt Mr. Partridge) to regard any man solely as a procreator. Such a viewpoint detracted from male dignity. It made one wonder what women—the whole lot of them—were really thinking. . . .

"You can't tell," reflected Mr. Partridge aloud.

"But I can about Ronny," said Lisbeth. She drew a long sigh. "I'm perfectly sure about him. He's going to be useful and happy, and—and I'm so thankful I could damn well cry. Whatever comes to the rest of us, Ronny's all right."

There was a tap on the door, and Lester Hamilton came quietly in.

"Where's your brother?" asked Mr. Hamilton.

2

"Not back yet," said Lisbeth.

"Not back from where?"

There was a moment's silence. Hamilton looked from one to the other of them in a peculiar way.

"He left this morning all right," supplied Mr. Partridge. "I suppose you mean he didn't turn up?"

"He did not. But—"

Lisbeth jumped up.

"I know," she said grimly. "He's gone with Helena to Windsor. There was a whole party, and Ronny was talking about it—Really, it's too bad!"

Mr. Hamilton shifted uneasily.

"It's worse," he said. "At least, it looks worse. You see, one of our men arrived in London yesterday, and he came in as soon as he got to town to see the boss. He had a portfolio with his passport and some papers in it, also eighty pounds in cash which he'd just won in the ship's sweepstake. And while he went in to see the manager, he left the portfolio on your brother's desk. There was no one else in the outer office. He collected it again when he came out, and didn't open it again till this morning. The money was gone—"

There was a second silence, and a longer one.

"It's a pity," said Mr. Hamilton, "your brother chose today to play hookey."

The cuckoo cried six.

"Our man," continued Mr. Hamilton doggedly, "says that between leaving the boat and coming to our office he never let it out of his grip. He went from the office to his hotel, the Luxemberg, had a meal in his room with the portfolio lying on a chair beside him, and went to bed with it locked in his suitcase. This morning he came round and just naturally raised Cain. Luckily, he saw me."

Lisbeth moistened her lips.

"What did you do?"

"I stalled. I said Campion was away on the firm's business. I—I pretended to put a call through to him at Denham, and said he was there all right, but couldn't be got hold of. Van Hoyt—our man—is coming back in the morning. He says he thinks your police are wonderful."

"Ronny didn't take it, you know," said Lisbeth calmly.

Both Mr. Partridge and Hamilton looked at her with a flicker of hope. Her tone was so assured, so casual even, that they both for a moment expected her to produce some conclusive and unforeseeable piece of evidence in Ronny's favour. But she did not. She was evidently speaking from a full heart rather than from a clear head.

"What makes you say that?" asked Mr. Hamilton politely.

"Knowing Ronny. It isn't in him to take money. When they told me about the cocaine business I believed it at once, because it was just the sort of idiotic thing he would do. So I'm not foolishly prejudiced about him. But he hasn't taken that money." She swung round upon the hitherto silent Mr. Partridge. "You know him almost as well as I do, and you don't believe it either. Do you?"

Her eyes, bright and intent, searched his face. Mr. Partridge had a feeling that he was being hypnotized. But there was a core of resistance in him as strong as Lisbeth's will: he kept silence. Lisbeth turned her gaze on Hamilton.

"He didn't do it," she repeated.

This time she won.

"Right," said Mr. Hamilton. "He didn't do it. I'm believing you. But I should also like to have it on record that your brother is the biggest gosh-darned nuisance in an Empire on which the sun never sets."

"Hear, hear," said Mr. Partridge.

Lisbeth looked from one to the other of them with an air of mild surprise.

"Of *course* Ronny's a nuisance," she agreed. "He always was. But he isn't a thief. I think I'd better see this Mr. Van Hoyt."

"If you do," said Hamilton, with a return to gloom, "it will probably be in the presence of his lawyer. He's got a whale of a lawyer over here, apparently, and he's just aching to see him in action."

"All the better. A solicitor will tell him about the libel laws. Do you know the man's name?"

"Treweeke," said Mr. Hamilton, "of Lincoln's Inn."

3

As though pulled by the same string, the heads of Lisbeth and Mr. Partridge turned towards the mantel; whence the portrait of Captain Brocard, who would be home in two days, gazed firmly and serenely back.

"I don't think we'll see Mr. Treweeke," said Lisbeth slowly. "We'll have to think of something else."

4

Hamilton looked at the clock.

"I've a date," he said, "With Van Hoyt. I guess—" he smiled wryly—"Mr. Van Hoyt is keeping an eye on me."

"Where are you going?" asked Lisbeth.

"Dinner at the Savoy, and then a show. I'll look in here again afterwards. . . . If you can find your brother—"

"What's the number of his room?" interrupted Lisbeth. "I mean Mr. Van Hoyt's?"

"Fifty-two." Lester Hamilton looked at her uneasily, and Mr. Partridge knew what was passing through his mind: the conviction that any advice, any warning, would be completely useless. "If you can find your brother," he repeated, "and get some sort of an explanation out of him—"

"I will," said Lisbeth. "And—thank you very much."

Lester Hamilton nodded and went out, leaving silence behind. Not a word—as Mr. Partridge suddenly realized—had been said about the impending arrival of Captain Brocard, and in spite of everything else this struck him as being important. He hurried after; but he must have stood gaping longer than he thought, for he reached the street door only in time to see a taxi drive off. He looked up and down the pavement: no young American was in sight. The taxi had evidently been kept waiting for him, ticking up all the time; a circumstance which brought home to Mr. Partridge, as nothing else could have done, the extreme seriousness of the occasion. . . .

"What is it?" asked Lisbeth behind him.

"He's gone," said Mr. Partridge. "In a cab. I wanted to tell him about the Captain. But I suppose it doesn't matter."

"No," agreed Lisbeth. "It doesn't matter."

She stood a moment watching the back of the taxi disappear down Marsham Street, then turned and went slowly up the stairs. Mr. Partridge followed in silence. He could not think of anything to say to her except perhaps, "Cheer up"; and he had a sound feeling that such an exhortation would only irritate. His feet on the uncarpeted treads made a hollow clumping noise, very depressing, which he had never before noticed; when he tried to step more softly it sounded as though there were sickness in the house. . . .

On the second landing the door stood open; through it could be seen a family group of the three Walkers. They made an impressive sight: they sat like three images, old Mr. Walker in the middle, Sidney to his right, young Oswald to his left; before each stood a bottle of cherry brandy and a small glass. They were not drinking, they were not speaking. They appeared to be in some sort of a trance.

Lisbeth paused.

"Let us consult," she said, "the oracles."

5

She went in. Mr. Partridge rather dubiously followed. But their welcome was almost warm.

"Good," said Mr. Walker. "We were just arguing who was going to shut the door."

Lisbeth immediately shut it behind her. Both younger Walkers made a motion to rise, but so elaborately and carefully that Mr. Partridge at once realized that the closing of the door was indeed a matter for deliberation. He looked at the trio with respect: they were evidently dedicating their evening off to really serious drinking. Three more bottles (but empty ones) stood underneath the table. . . .

"No, don't move," said Lisbeth quickly. "We shan't stay a minute. We just wanted to ask your advice."

"Oswald," ordered Mr. Walker heavily, "get the young lady a glass."

Young Oswald again heaved himself up; and again, as Lisbeth prevented him, dropped gratefully back.

"No, please!" she said. "It's just this: you know a lot about hotels, don't you?"

Mr. Walker nodded. His sons nodded also. Mr. Partridge's thoughts, for some obscure reason, flew to his elephant's tusk. Three big heads, gravely nodding. . . .

"Would you say," proceeded Lisbeth diffidently, "that much—thieving goes on in them? I mean, of course, of money?"

"No," said Mr. Walker.

The unoracular precision of this answer was disconcerting. Lisbeth's face fell.

Then the oracle spoke again.

"I wouldn't," said Mr. Walker, "say a thing like that on any account. It might get me into trouble." Lisbeth's eyes narrowed. For the first time since the inruption of Lester Hamilton, she smiled.

"But there have been thefts in hotels?"

"Not in the New Park Lane," said Mr. Walker firmly. "What goes on in the others I can't tell." He paused to ruminate. "But if I was staying at the—" here he named, with every inflection of scorn, a very famous caravanserai indeed—"and they left me with a sovereign to my name, d'you know what I'd do with it?"

"What?"

"I'd have it melted down for a filling and carry it in my teeth. Oswald, get the young lady a glass."

But Oswald was for the third time reprieved. Even as Mr. Walker raised his personal bottle ready to pour, Lisbeth was out on the landing, excusing her lack of ceremony with a backward smile. Mr. Walker stared after her, the bottle suspended in mid-air, then slowly turned his gaze on her less swiftly-moving companion.

He did not speak—his unwonted eloquence appeared to have exhausted him—but his eye was inviting.

"Not for me, thanks," said Mr. Partridge regretfully.

The bottle quivered.

"Not just now," said Mr. Partridge.

"Then shut the door," said Mr. Walker.

6

Lisbeth had already reached the sitting-room upstairs. She had done more: she had got her frock halfway over her head. Mr. Partridge modestly backed out and addressed her from the landing.

"You mind your hair," he said. "What's the idea now?"

"Van Hoyt's hotel," replied Lisbeth, in a muffled voice. "The Luxemberg. It's in Pall Mall."

"And what'll you do when you get there?"

"I don't know. Snoop. Trust to luck."

Mr. Partridge considered this program dubiously.

"Am I coming too?"

There was a slight pause. Miss Campion appeared to be considering also.

"I'm changing," she observed superfluously. "I think I'd better look rather elegant . . ."

"I could wear my kilt," offered Mr. Partridge. (He had long ceased to be ashamed of his garment; he felt rather proud of it. It made him feel—owing to a pardonable confusion between the works of Sir Alexander Raeburn and Sir Edwin Landseer—like a Monarch of the Glen.)

"No, I shouldn't do that," said Lisbeth quickly.

"Well, I'm coming all the same," stated Mr. Partridge. "If you go snooping round hotels alone you'll be in trouble before you know where you are. How long will it take you to titivate?"

"Three minutes," said Lisbeth.

Mr. Partridge listened carefully, and heard the rattle of the drawer in which she kept her powders and creams. She hadn't done her face yet: the three minutes would most likely be five.

"You'll find me in the Walkers'," called Mr. Partridge. "And don't think to slip by, for I've a very quick ear."

He remembered having read somewhere that cherry brandy had an extremely warming, heartening effect.

He hoped it was true.

CHAPTER 16

1

IN THE imposing lobby of the Luxemberg Hotel Mr. Partridge would have paused; but Lisbeth did not. She walked straight across to the desk, looking extremely smart and assured, and in the two seconds before the reception-clerk attended to her ran her eye over the row of keys. 53 was there, 52 was missing.

"My cousin," said Lisbeth sweetly. "Room 53."

The clerk summoned a page-boy, and with one hand on the telephone, hesitated. The Luxemberg prided itself above all on its tact and *savoir-faire*. It never asked for the names of celebrities, or of persons whose pictures appeared in the fashionable weeklies: it was supposed to recognize them. And Lisbeth, in her best clothes, and wearing her most social face, looked like a composite photograph of every debutante since 1936. The clerk was still hesitating while Lisbeth, followed by Mr. Partridge, and walking with a modish slouch quite unlike her usual gait, crossed in the wake of the page-boy to the waiting lift.

"Young lady to see you," said the clerk into the mouth-piece. No. 53 was a gentleman; the clerk had at least enough *savoir-faire* to say nothing about cousins.

"Lady who?" demanded 53.

"Lady Er-Rumph," said the clerk; and neatly cut himself off.

Lady Er-Rumph and Mr. Partridge had meanwhile emerged on the second floor; the page indicated the appropriate door and shot himself down again.

"What do we do now?" asked Mr. Partridge dubiously. "Wriggle through the key-hole?"

Even Lisbeth seemed momentarily at a loss. She looked up and down the corridor, and approached the door numbered 52. . . .

"Sst!" hissed Mr. Partridge.

A room-waiter in a white jacket, moving on noiseless feet, was advancing towards them. He suddenly halted, and turned.

"O.K.," breathed Mr. Partridge. "He's going away again."

But Lisbeth, staring at that tall receding back, did not hear. She stared, took a step forward, and spoke.

"Waiter!" called Lisbeth sharply.

Automatically the man turned. His face was dark and rather ugly, and it was impossible to tell from it whether he was thirty or thirty-five or forty years old.

The waiter was Charles Lambert. Or at any rate, that had been his name when he stayed at the Dormouth Towers Hotel.

2

"Yes, madam?" said Charles Lambert politely.

"Good evening," said Lisbeth.

There was a slight pause. The expressionless and deferential visage showed not a flicker of recognition. "Ashamed to own himself," thought Mr. Partridge, with sympathy: he remembered his own sensations on first wearing kilts. So he advanced heartily, and held out his hand.

"Pleased to see you again," said Mr. Partridge. "It's a small world, and we've come down in it too."

The greeting, he thought, was tactful and neatly turned; but from neither Lisbeth nor Mr. Lambert did he get a smile of approval. They were looking at each other with rather odd expressions. Mr. Lambert also took a swift glance at Lisbeth's left hand. Then he grinned.

"*Touché,*" he said. "What can I do for you?"

"Is this your floor?" asked Lisbeth.

"It is."

"And that—" she nodded towards the door marked 52—"is Mr. Van Hoyt's suite?"

"An American gentleman," corroborated Mr. Lambert. "Very pleasant—"

"Can we get in?" asked Lisbeth. "I just want to talk to you for a few minutes."

Mr. Lambert produced a key from the pocket of his white jacket and opened the door. They all passed through a small lobby into a large sitting-room, the second door of which, standing ajar, revealed a bedchamber. Lisbeth sat down and took out a cigarette.

"Mr. Van Hoyt," she began directly, "has with him a leather portfolio—perhaps you noticed it?"

"Vaguely," admitted Mr. Lambert. With waiter-like promptness he produced a lighter and applied it to her cigarette.

"Well, he had," proceeded Lisbeth. "And in it, amongst other things, was a packet of eighty pounds, which has since disappeared. And for some silly reason he thinks my brother stole it. Ronny didn't, of course, but we don't want a fuss." She paused. "I don't suppose you want a fuss either."

"The management," agreed Mr. Lambert smoothly, "dislikes—fusses—very much indeed. But no loss has been reported."

"That's because he doesn't think it happened here. He's saying that all the time he was in the hotel he never let his portfolio out of his sight. On the other hand, I think it's quite possible that he just stepped into the other room, for instance, while you were serving his dinner in this. But of course that's irrelevant—"

"Quite irrelevant," agreed Mr. Lambert.

Mr. Partridge, however, thought differently. He had an idea.

"Hold on a minute," he said. "If he left the thing in here—"

"*Quite* irrelevant," repeated Lisbeth firmly. "What happened, of course, is that Mr. Van Hoyt absent-mindedly *took* the money out of the case, and mislaid it somewhere in the suite. Or perhaps hid it."

"And then forgot all about it?" interrupted Mr. Partridge sceptically. "It doesn't sound likely to me."

"It's *very* likely," contradicted Lisbeth. "Aunt Mildred was always hiding things and forgetting where she'd put them—" She gave Mr. Partridge a quite unfriendly look, and turned back to Charles Lambert. "Don't *you* think it's likely?"

Charles Lambert nodded. He seemed to be working something out in his mind.

"So what I want you to do is to make a thorough search for the money, and when you've found it tell the manager. That's all."

"Where," enquired Mr. Lambert thoughtfully, "do you think is the best place to look?"

Lisbeth considered.

"I believe," she said, "it all happened when he was half asleep. He reached out, you see, and opened his bag, and put the money under his pillow. And then when they made the bed this morning it slipped out and fell between the mattress and the wall—"

"Then let's look now!" cried Mr. Partridge, jumping up. Lisbeth gave him another glance and he sat down again.

"I think we'll just leave it to Mr. Lambert," she said firmly. "There may be a reward, and after taking so much trouble, I think he ought to get it."

She rose with a pleasant smile, and held out her hand. Lambert took it. In spite of his white jacket he no longer looked in the least like a waiter. Since he was so tall Lisbeth, to smile up at him, had to tilt back her head: and with a quick movement that had yet nothing hurried about it, Charles Lambert stooped and kissed her.

"Now then!" cried Mr. Partridge, outraged, "what's all this?"

"The reward," explained Mr. Lambert. "Miss Campion and I understand each other perfectly. By the way, how is your aunt?"

"Very well," said Lisbeth, who did not seem in the least put out. "Mr. Partridge saw her last. Didn't you, darling?"

"Yes," said Mr. Partridge, He felt thoroughly bewildered: the conversation was twisting and turning too fast for him to follow. It now seemed to have settled down into a pleasant social chat, but he still felt distrustful. He fixed Charles Lambert with a suspicious eye.

"And we had a word about *you*," he added. "You seemed to have made quite an impression on her."

Mr. Lambert smiled reminiscently.

"She reminded me," he said, "of something I'd nearly forgotten." His tone was almost wistful: it made Mr. Partridge suddenly realize that they were all, every one of them, mothers' sons. Perhaps even this peculiar Lambert chap had a corner in his heart for some little old lady who in turn remembered him in her prayers. . . .

"She reminded me," continued Mr. Lambert, "that there are still some women who carry their valuables in their stays . . ."

3

"What did I say?" demanded Lisbeth triumphantly, as they emerged once more into Pall Mall.

"Too much for me to remember," replied Mr. Partridge. He felt he had been left in the dark, that he had not received her full confidence; his tone had a touch of sulkiness.

"'Trust to luck'," quoted Lisbeth. "And I did, and it came off. I had an absolute intuition—"

"Intuition my eye!" retorted Mr. Partridge. "You knew that Lambert chap at the Towers."

"But I didn't know he'd be at the Luxemberg! I just suspected there'd be someone like him. And I didn't know that *he*—I don't *really* know now—"

She broke off. Mr. Partridge snorted impatiently. He was still ruffled.

"You can't deceive me," he told her. "I'm remembering a whole heap of things. I'm remembering that bit in the paper about an actress-woman at the Towers who had her necklace stolen after you'd gone. What you were going to say was that your friend Mr. Lambert is just one of these blooming hotel thieves."

For the second time Lisbeth answered with a quotation.

"'I wouldn't say a thing like that'," she murmured, "'on any account. It might get me into trouble'."

To Lester Hamilton she said even less. There was not indeed time to say much, for that agitated young man turned up in Marsham Street at nine o'clock, having taxied from the theatre during the first interval, with only three minutes to spare for conversation. As a matter of fact he had ten, for Mr. Partridge, still burning with curiosity, conceived the clever idea of bundling Lisbeth into the cab (he himself of course accompanying her) and driving back with Mr. Hamilton to Piccadilly. The American's story was a curious one: shortly after eight o'clock the manager of the Luxemberg, who knew where Mr. Van Hoyt was dining, had telephoned the extraordinary information that a room-waiter named Lambert had discovered eighty pounds in notes lying on the floor, between bed and wall, in Mr. Van Hoyt's apartment. Mr. Van Hoyt was naturally pleased, but he was also puzzled. So was Lester Hamilton.

"It's so simple!" cried Lisbeth. She had, reflected Mr. Partridge, a quite remarkable command of her features. She was looking just as bewildered (though from an opposite point of view) as the young man beside her. "It's perfectly obvious what happened. Mr. Van Hoyt took the money out—"

"He says not," remarked Lester Hamilton, with detachment.

"Because he's forgotten. That's the whole point. As soon as he realizes it—"

"He won't," said Mr. Hamilton. "He thinks there's something queer. He's going to look at the numbers of those notes very, very carefully."

Mr. Partridge kept his eyes on Lisbeth's face. Her expression did not change. She evidently had complete faith in the efficiency of her confederate.

"I think he's being very silly," she said. "Of course the numbers will be the same. And then I hope he'll stop worrying."

"Well, I guess he will," admitted Mr. Hamilton thoughtfully. "After all, there's nothing he can prove. . . ."

"Nothing at all," agreed Lisbeth, with satisfaction.

Mr. Hamilton appeared to digest this remark in silence while the taxi turned into Bond Street.

"He ought," added Lisbeth, "to give the waiter ten per cent. Eighty pounds—just left lying about—is a great temptation."

To Mr. Partridge, knowing what he did and guessing what he guessed, this suggestion savoured of positive immorality. It savoured of hush-money. He nearly protested. But Lisbeth's face, fleetingly illumined by an amber neon-light, was that of a complacent angel. Also, her right toe was pressing firmly into his left calf.

"I'll admit," said Lester Hamilton, "that the idea of a reward hadn't struck me."

Mr. Partridge could keep silence no longer.

"Reward!" he burst out. "He's had that already!"

The toe dug harder; at the same moment the taxi turned into Clifford Street. It did not, in Mr. Partridge's opinion, turn very violently, but Lisbeth's bag was jerked from her lap and its contents scattered over the floor. They all bent and groped—after a powder-box, a key, a handkerchief, and half-a-crown in small change—and by the time all these things were collected Piccadilly had been reached and the cab was slowing down. Lester Hamilton raised his head and looked first at the meter, then at Lisbeth.

"I'd like to know all the same—" he began.

"My comb!" cried Lisbeth.

They groped again. It was Lisbeth who found.

"I *would* like to know," said Mr. Hamilton, almost wist-fully, "just how you fixed it . . ."

But Lisbeth was looking at her watch.

"Exactly in time!" she exclaimed. "You mustn't keep Mr. Van Hoyt waiting."

Mr. Hamilton got out, and paid the taxi. Lisbeth was so anxious that he should not be late that she almost pushed him into the theatre. The interval bell had just ceased ring-ing, the foyer was almost empty; and when Lester Hamilton too had disappeared, Lisbeth and Mr. Partridge found them-selves standing alone, in a sudden silence.

4

It was a moment, undoubtedly, for triumph. A difficult job had been well (if shadily) pulled off; a dreadful crisis had been completely (if narrowly) avoided. The absence of Ronny was by comparison too small a matter to worry about: in a way, looking forward to the Captain's arrival, it was almost an advantage. But Mr. Partridge felt no more than relief. He could not think why; he was not consciously aware that his emotions always took their colour from Lisbeth's. Turning to address her, however, it struck him that in spite of her best clothes and newly-done hair, she had a sort of forlorn look. She was staring at the curtain behind which young Hamilton had just disappeared as though—as though she wanted to be on the other side of it too. . . .

"If you like," said Mr. Partridge kindly, "we'll go up to the gallery and have a bob's worth. We'll soon pick up what it's all about."

Lisbeth shook her head, and slipped a hand through his arm.

"Let's go home, darling, and see if Ronny's back. He's out of this jam, but I daresay he's done something else awful just to make up."

This mood of depression was so unlike her that Mr. Partridge felt quite worried. He cast about in his mind for something to cheer her up, and suggested that they should look about for a nice quiet pub, where he would stand her a ladylike sherry. But Lisbeth did not want a sherry. She wanted to go home, so they walked across to Regent Street to wait for a 112 bus. The Circus lights glittered under a clear sky; the air, in spite of buildings and traffic, had an autumn freshness. It was very different from the windy salt breeze of Dormouth Bay, but Mr. Partridge snuffed it up contentedly. Whatever happened, he thought, he would stay in London. . . .

"It's been fun, hasn't it?" said Lisbeth suddenly.

Mr. Partridge squeezed the hand under his arm.

"Grand fun," he assented. "It's been the time of my life"

"The time of my life," repeated Lisbeth after him. Her voice was thoughtful, almost sad. "I suppose you can never tell—I mean, which really *is* the best time. It may still be coming . . ."

"It is for you, of course," said Mr. Partridge, with cheerful conviction. "And I shan't do so bad. I've got a job. I ought to look about for a room though."

"If I were you," said Lisbeth, as though the idea had just occurred to her, "I should try the Walkers. Mr. Walker was saying only the other day they could do with a nice quiet lodger, to sleep in the sitting-room at half-a-crown a week."

This notion pleased Mr. Partridge very much indeed. He liked the Walkers—more, he respected them. He felt they were Deep. To find out all about the Walkers would take a long time. . . .

"I'll have a word with the old man to-morrow," he promised. "And I shall offer three bob. Half-a-crown's not enough—"

This idea too was pleasing: Mr. Partridge liked to be generous, and for a minute or two he stood happily working out ways and means. He would be far better off, paying three shillings a week to the Walkers, than he was now paying ten shillings to Lisbeth. Two square meals a day were enough for any man, and his meals at the Bonnie Scotland were so square as to be almost cubic. His earnings there came, with tips, to nearly twelve shillings a week: three from twelve left nine, with nothing to pay for except food on Sundays, beer, laundry, clothes and hair-cuts. His wardrobe, since he took most wear out of his kilt, would last for years; his scarlet socks were still inches deep under his mattress. "If I give up smoking," thought Mr. Partridge, "I can live like a blooming Duke . . ."

The bus appeared. He handed Lisbeth on, and in so doing was suddenly reminded of the occasion in Marsham Street when they had left young Hamilton standing on the curb.

"There, now!" exclaimed Mr. Partridge. "We still haven't told him!"

"Told who what?" asked Lisbeth, as she sat down.

"Young Hamilton. About the Captain being back on Monday."

"I'll tell him to-morrow."

"To-morrow's Saturday. I suppose he'll come round?"

"He'll come round," said Lisbeth definitely. "He's coming to say good-bye."

5

They reached home, but Ronny was not there. Satur-day came, and Ronny still did not turn up; but Captain Brocard did.

CHAPTER 17

1

HE ARRIVED just about half-past four. The day had been a depressing one: neither Lisbeth nor Mr. Partridge (expectant of Lester Hamilton, hopeful of Ronny) had stirred out, and neither of the young men had appeared to reward them. Ronny had of course been missing only a day and a night, but so much had happened in the interval that Mr. Partridge felt as though he had been gone a week. So evidently, from her pale looks, did Lisbeth. She put on a new dress and took a lot of trouble with her hair—rehearsing, diagnosed Mr. Partridge, for the Captain—but her spirits were low. Now and then, indeed—and no doubt when the Captain was uppermost in her mind—they became unusually high; but it was plain that most of her mind was given to her brother. Mr. Partridge's dislike of that young man recovered all its pristine strength.

Immediately after tea he went down to the Walkers and concluded a most satisfactory bargain for the use of a camp-bed in their sitting-room. He thought it would please Lisbeth to know that everything was fixed up, and did not linger, as he would normally have done, for further conversation. He went back at once, and it was fortunate that he did so; for there on the upper flight, looking uncertainly about, stood a tall, a magnificent, and a familiar figure. . . .

2

"God bless my soul!" cried Mr. Partridge.

The Captain turned. He was very brown, which made him more than usually handsome. He carried an enormous bunch of red roses. He looked in every respect the beau ideal of the Returning Lover. Mr. Partridge's heart leapt.

"Could you tell me," called Captain Brocard, "if there is a Miss Campion living here?"

From his tone of voice it was at once apparent that he believed himself to be addressing a stranger. Mr. Partridge, already bounding upstairs, suffered a slight shock. The courteous impersonality of those well-bred accents made him suddenly remember a great many things which in the course of the last few months he had almost forgotten. He was made to remember, for instance, the abysmal gap in social standing between himself and Miss Campion. Hastily—between one step and the next—he searched his heart: had he been, all these months, *presuming*? When he checked her for swearing, had it really been his place to do so? But all these questions flashed so rapidly through his mind that he had no time to answer them: he had to answer the Captain.

"On the top floor," he said. "Next landing. She's in."

"Good God!" said Hugh Brocard. Then he looked again at Mr. Partridge, who was now on a level with him, and his expression changed.

"I've seen you before," he stated. "Aren't you—"

"Mr. Partridge," said Mr. Partridge. "We met about six months ago—"

"I remember. You did some business for me about that young fool. And—you say Miss Campion's living *here*?"

Mr. Partridge nodded dumbly. They had reached the top landing.

"Then what in heaven's name has been happening?"

There was no time for an answer, for at that moment the door opened. Lisbeth, within, had heard their double footfall on the stair. She flung open the door expecting to see besides Mr. Partridge either Ronny or Lester Hamilton, and for a moment stood breathless and astonished. But since both breathlessness and astonishment were perfectly appropriate to the circumstances, there was nothing in her face for a lover to object to. The next instant, there was everything that a lover could desire.

"Hugh!" she cried.

She did not, as once before on a similar occasion, disappear into his arms; but she reached out her hands, and took both of his, and so drew him into the room. Mr. Partridge followed. It was perhaps not a very delicate thing to do, but he had a feeling that she might need his support.

"My God!" said Hugh Brocard again.

He stared round the harlequin-coloured room; and Mr. Partridge, following his gaze, and looking as it were through Captain Brocard's eyes, saw that it had somehow got rather shabby.

"My God!" said Hugh Brocard for the third time. "What's happened?"

"I live here," said Lisbeth, in a small voice.

"But—where's your aunt?"

"In the country. She—she lost all her money." (This was quite true: Miss Pickering had lost her money, in 1912.)

"Then where are the Maules?"

"They've gone back to Australia," said Lisbeth.

"But why—my darling—didn't you tell me in your letters?"

"I didn't," said Lisbeth (still truthfully), "want to worry you. . . ."

Captain Brocard was never afraid of a hackneyed phrase. "My brave little woman!" he said; and took her in his arms.

3

At this point Mr. Partridge had no longer any option: he had to retire; but he retired no farther than the kitchen. So far everything had gone well—remarkably, astoundingly well; but he was pretty sure that his assistance would soon be needed, and as he sat on the edge of the bath he revolved half a dozen helpful schemes. For lies, to any extent, he was fully prepared; but a sound instinct warned him that all explanation had better be kept to a minimum. Lisbeth, with the greatest economy, had already put matters on a happy (though precarious) footing; if the Captain could only take her out and marry her straight away, all might yet be well. There were things called Special Licenses: Mr. Partridge did not know how long they took to operate—he thought a week, and a week was too much; he thought of Gretna Green—had the Captain, as a Scot, already the residential qualifications?—And if he had, would he be prepared to pack Lisbeth into a car and set off at ten minutes' notice for the Great North Road? Such a proceeding, feared Mr. Partridge, was inherently foreign to the Captain's nature: only a great peril at his heels would drive him to such a course. . . .

Mr. Partridge sat on the bath and thought about perils. He thought about the Walkers. Could they be presented to the Captain's imagination as three thugs, destroyers of virginity, against whom Lisbeth had to be protected by himself (wielding the elephant's tusk) every time she used the stairs? Or what about kidnappers? Could he have over-heard a plot at The London Apprentice—a plot to waylay Lisbeth that very night, and shut her up in a cellar, and apply to the Captain for ransom-money? "He'd just go to the police," thought Mr. Partridge. "I'm an old fool."

In the end he decided simply to get the Captain alone, point out the extreme unsuitability of Miss Campion's present environment, and add that the bailiffs were expected that evening. He would do this as soon as possible, even if it meant breaking in upon the lovers' reunion, for he was confident that Lisbeth, even uncoached, would at once follow so promising a lead. He got up, and re-entered the sitting-room.

Things were still going well. Captain Brocard was telling Lisbeth about India, and Lisbeth, her hands busy with his roses, was listening with an expression of rapt intelligence. Mr. Partridge caught her eye, and was given a reassuring look. "All right," said Lisbeth's eyes, "all right—so far . . ."

It was just at that moment that Ronny came back.

He simply walked in. He wore his usual air of happy confidence. At the sight of Hugh Brocard he paused indeed, but only for a moment. Then his face lit up.

"You're the very man I wanted to see!" cried Ronny joyfully.

Hugh Brocard at once turned to Lisbeth; and at once he saw that, although surprised, she was not astonished. She was not looking nearly so startled as she had done at the sight of himself. She looked as though she were surprised to see Ronny because she had believed him to be, for example, in another part of London. It was perfectly clear that she had not believed him to be in Canada. . . .

4

Tall as a tower, motionless as the portrait of a gentleman, Hugh Brocard stood there in the centre of the room; and Mr. Partridge at least felt very sorry for him: the bewilderment on his face contrasted so sharply with the strength and poise of his body. He looked like a man who had awakened to a nightmare.

"What," he asked, through stiff lips, "are you doing here?"

"Oh, I've been doing all sorts of things," said Ronny hastily. "I didn't go to Canada, you know—I hope you don't mind—but the point is I want you to come round now and—and meet my father-in-law."

"What!" cried Lisbeth and Mr. Partridge simultaneously; but whereas the cry of Mr. Partridge was followed by an invisible question mark, that of Lisbeth was followed merely by a point of exclamation. She looked at her brother with less surprise than approval.

"Yes," said Ronny. "Helena and I got married yesterday, and I'm going round now to see her people. They don't know yet, because we thought it would save fuss to get married first and tell them afterwards. But the old man may be a bit sticky, and I thought if Hugh came too, and so to speak vouched for me—"

"Darling, you're a fool," said Lisbeth quickly; but she turned towards her fiancé all the same. Hugh Brocard did not meet her glance: he kept his eyes fixed on Ronny.

"Do you mean," he asked, "that you've married into a—a decent family?"

"Oh, rather!" agreed Ronny. "They've got pots of money, and old man Clough wrote a book on the Crimean War. That's why—"

"Clough? Not A.R. Clough, the historian?"

"That's the bird. And that's why—"

"You say you've *married* his daughter?"

"Helena," explained Ronny. "She's marvellous. She's absolutely wonderful to look at, and she's got the brains of a—of a Prime Minister. I know you want to see Lisbeth, of course, but if you could just spare half an hour—"

Hugh Brocard looked at his betrothed. His question did not need to be put into words.

"Helena does," said Lisbeth quickly. "Helena knows everything."

"But not her parents?"

"No. I don't see why they ever should. It would only worry them, and—and what does all that matter *now*?" She took a quick step towards him. "Hugh—you wouldn't tell them?"

There was a long silence. Then Captain Brocard grimly shook his head.

"Not now," he said. "It's too late."

Ronny considered him dubiously.

"Perhaps you'd better not come round after all," he said.
"I thought you'd be rather bucked. Because I mean I really
am settled for life. I know I've been rather a nuisance—"

"Darling," said Lisbeth, "get out."

5

Ronny went. Mr. Partridge nipped out after him. He was
in that state of nervous excitement which can be relieved
only by letting fly at someone, and Ronny presented a highly
suitable target.

"Of all the roaring imbeciles," began Mr. Partridge meth-
odically, "in this world or the next—"

"You and Brocard take the prize," retorted Ronny, with
unusual vigour. "Marrying Helena is the most sensible thing
I've ever done. It's the greatest piece of luck—"

"I'm not talking about you marrying Helena. I'm talking about all the trouble you've given me and your sister in
the last twenty-four hours. For twenty-four hours," cried
Mr. Partridge, "we've been in a fair chaos. First you pinch
eighty quid—"

Ronny's jaw dropped.

"I *what*?"

"Well, you didn't actually," conceded Mr. Partridge.
"Actually it was pinched by someone else—but you ought to
have had more sense than to be missing at the same time.
And more good feeling than to go off and get married without telling your sister. If you're not criminal you're heartless,
and I don't know which is worse."

Ronny clutched the banisters and shook them. He (and
not unnaturally) was in a high state of nervous excitement
also.

"I didn't tell Lisbeth because she doesn't like Helena.
And as for this eighty pounds, I don't know what you're

talking about. As far as I can see only two things happened yesterday: I got married, and you went mad."

He released the banisters and bounded downstairs. Mr. Partridge stood dumb. He had let fly all right, but he had let fly a boomerang. Still feeling slightly stunned, he returned to the sitting-room.

6

The departure of Ronny had changed, but scarcely lightened, the atmosphere. Mr. Partridge, after one glance at the Captain's face, passed directly to his own room—but leaving the door ajar. He could not quite shut it, as the ventilation was so bad.

"It's true, you know," he heard Lisbeth say at last. "He *is* settled for life. And that's what we wanted, isn't it?"

There was no answer.

"If you'd met Helena," continued Lisbeth, "you'd realize how extraordinarily suitable it was. She's a natural boss. She'll make Ronny very happy, and keep him in order, but he'll make her happy too. He's just what she wants—"

"None of that," said Hugh Brocard heavily, "matters."

"Then what does, darling? I know I kept Ronny here when you thought he should go abroad—but look how it's worked out! If you'd been here yourself—"

"I wish I had been, I wish I'd never gone away. Then I shouldn't have found out."

"Found out what, darling? Or . . . do you mean—me?"

There was a long silence, broken only by a sound from Captain Brocard that was like something between a groan and a sigh. When Lisbeth spoke again her voice was very low.

"My dear," she said. "I think perhaps we've made a mistake. Let's just break off our engagement and forget all about it."

"No!" cried Captain Brocard.

On the edge of his bed Mr. Partridge actually shuddered with alarm. The repudiation had been vehement enough, but to offer a man his freedom was, in Mr. Partridge's opinion, like offering a dog a bone. It was too tempting. Whether a man wanted it or not he was almost sure to take it, because the chance might never come again. . . .

"I'm thinking of what's best for both of us," said Lisbeth gently. "And that's true, my dear; you can believe that."

Mr. Partridge writhed. Best for both of them! When she hadn't a penny to her name, and no one to look after her! She was going to sacrifice herself! Self-sacrifice was very well in its way—it won you a heavenly crown—but all that was practical in Mr. Partridge's nature cried out that for a young woman like Lisbeth a good husband on earth was far more to the point. She was throwing away the chance of a lifetime, and the only ray of hope was that she couldn't give back her engagement ring, because Miss Pickering still had it. . . .

"Tell me one thing," said Hugh Brocard. "Do you still love me?"

Mr. Partridge, of course, could not see the Captain's face. Lisbeth could. She looked straight into his eyes: they were puzzled, resentful, above all they were bitterly hurt.

"Yes, Hugh," she said steadily. "That's why—" she tried to make her tone lighter—"I so particularly don't want to make you unhappy. That's why I'm breaking our engagement."

Brocard lifted his head.

"And if I don't let you?" he asked doggedly.

"It's for you to decide, darling. If I have treated you badly, I—I never will again. Only don't decide now. Wait till you've been home a day or two—till you've been up to Scotland—"

Mr. Partridge rose to his feet and precipitated himself into the sitting-room. His feelings of the staircase were totally forgotten: presumptuous or not, out of his place or in it, he was going to take a hand.

"You go down to the Walkers," he said to Lisbeth, "while I have a word with the Captain."

7

She glanced first at her lover. He did not tell her to stay. As she moved towards the door Mr. Partridge was struck by the look on her face: it was a look, which he had never seen there before, of submission. Instinctively he turned to Hugh Brocard, and the reason for it became clear. The Captain was in a bad way. He looked like a man who had taken a knock-out. And Lisbeth, being responsible, was making the only amends she could by putting herself entirely in his hands. She was going to do, in future, whatever the Captain told her. . . .

The door closed, and the two men were alone. Mr. Partridge's heart sank. He was still resolute, still determined to do his best for Lisbeth, but he felt, before such genuine distress, at a disadvantage. He waited for the other to begin.

"What you're doing in all this," said Brocard grimly, "I don't know."

"I sometimes wonder myself," admitted Mr. Partridge. "But I suppose you could say I've been keeping an eye on things."

"I left you with perfectly definite instructions—"

"I know you did. But things turned out different. They do—often. But when they've turned out well it's best to let bygones be bygones and sleeping dogs lie." Mr. Partridge paused, and took the bull by the horns. "You're still engaged to her, aren't you?"

The Captain frowned.

"I don't know. She says she wants to break it off . . ." At the approach of danger Mr. Partridge's spirit returned. He at once launched his attack. "And why?" he demanded vigorously. "Because she's got the best heart, and the properest feelings, in all the world! Because she feels she's let you down—because she feels *you* feel she's let you down—she'll give you back your word! And if you don't mind breaking her heart, I s'pose you'll take it. But if you're half the gentleman I've thought you—"

Slowly, heavily, Brocard shook his head.

"I don't understand," he stated.

Mr. Partridge felt a touch of impatience.

"Why should you?" he asked. "We can't understand everything. Now you, I shouldn't wonder, understand all about rifle-drill—"

"Rifle-drill!" repeated Captain Brocard. It sounded as though he were swearing.

"I was only going to point out," said Mr. Partridge mildly, "that we can't all have the same sort of brain. A man who understood rifle-drill *and* women—he'd be a bit of a marvel. And what we don't understand, we have to take on trust."

"You mean I've got to take my wife on trust?"

"And why not? Isn't it what we all do?"

"But she's deceived me!" cried Captain Brocard.

"Better now than after," said Mr. Partridge sensibly. "If I had your luck I'd be throwing my cap in the air."

This was evidently not the view of Captain Brocard. He turned and began to pace the room. It was too small to give him proper scope: at every fourth stride he had to turn, and the exercise, instead of soothing, merely infuriated. "He ought to be on a horse," thought Mr. Partridge, with sudden insight. "He wants a good gallop." There was a livery-stable at Marble Arch, but it would take too long to get a mount sent round. . . .

"Her letters!" ejaculated Hugh Brocard.

"Ah!" said Mr. Partridge, with more sympathy. "But you liked getting 'em?"

"Like! I've kept them all—tied up! And not a word of truth in one of them!"

"Not a word of *un*truth, you mean," corrected Mr. Partridge severely. "She was most particular. She took endless trouble so as not to write you a lie." He paused: a certain phrase of Lisbeth's came back rather too clearly. Mr. Partridge changed his ground. "Anyway, that's all over and done with. She had a job to do, and she did it—sparing your feelings all the while. You ought to be proud of her."

"If I couldn't be proud of my wife," said Hugh Brocard slowly, "I think I'd shoot myself."

He was now standing motionless, staring straight in front of him: straight, as it happened, at his own portrait propped on the mantelpiece. Mr. Partridge saw another chance.

"Yes, you look at that!" he adjured. "All day it's been there, for six months—and every night under her pillow! I've seen it with my own eyes! Wet with tears too, most like—which is why it's a bit grubby! You look at that, young man, and ask yourself what's your duty!"

By pure luck he had struck exactly the right note. Duty. . . . Never in all his life had Hugh Brocard failed to respond to that call. Either joyfully or doggedly, his duty had always been done. There was not much joy about him now; he actually winced; but the spell still worked. He was duty-conditioned. . . .

"She loves you," said Mr. Partridge, "and you've promised to marry her."

"And I will," said Hugh Brocard.

No bridegroom at the altar could have spoken with greater solemnity. There flashed into Mr. Partridge's mind a phrase from *Piebald, the Broncho King*: "a shotgun wedding." But he did not care. He had secured Lisbeth's happiness. Without another word he rushed from the room, and bounded downstairs, and thrust his head through the Walkers' door.

"It's all right!" cried Mr. Partridge joyfully. "He's going to marry you!"

Chapter 18

1

LISBETH did not speak, but merely nodded. Mr. Partridge hoped that this was because her heart was too full—of gratitude, and joy; but he was conscious nevertheless of a sense of anticlimax. He wanted someone to shake him by the hand, or clap him on the back: if Lisbeth had thrown her arms about his neck he would have been embarrassed, but not displeased. Miss Campion, however, made no move, neither did the two Walkers. They stood one on each side of her, Sidney to the right, old Mr. Walker to the left, expressionless as Gog and Magog. It was disconcerting.

"Well?" demanded Mr. Partridge impatiently.

Lisbeth smiled at him.

"Thank you, darling," she said softly. "Thank you very much indeed. It was just what I wanted . . ."

"Well, nip along," said Mr. Partridge. "He's still upstairs."

Lisbeth moved towards the door. Her step was so slow that Mr. Partridge received a sudden illumination. She was nervous, poor thing! She had a lot on her conscience—or if not exactly on her conscience, at any rate on her mind. So had the Captain. They needed (the thought, all things considered, was an odd one, but Mr. Partridge did not at the moment realize it) something to cheer them up. . . .

"Tell you what," said Mr. Partridge vigorously. "We'll give a party. To celebrate. There's you and me and him and Mr. Walker here and Sid—that's plenty. You three go along up, and I'll nip down to Cubitt's and get a couple of bottles of sherry. We'll have a regular beano."

Obediently, Lisbeth nodded, and turned towards the Walkers. Obediently the Walkers moved forward and joined her. But obedience was not enough. Looking at the three of them, Mr. Partridge decided that he had better go along too and at least perform the introductions; it was important that the right note (of hilarious joy) should be firmly struck from the beginning. None of them seemed to notice his change of plan: they simply followed as he led the way upstairs. He hummed a little song on the way; he looked back over his shoulder, and smiled at Lisbeth, and winked at Sid Walker. For a moment he wondered whether he should tap on the door and in answer to the Captain's question reply "Obadiah," as Ronny did, and enter, so to speak, on the wings of a jest; but he couldn't remember the second half, and there was no time to ask Lisbeth, so they had to go in in a normal way.

The Captain was still standing before his portrait. He looked slightly surprised.

"We're giving a party," announced Mr. Partridge. "Just to celebrate. This is Mr. Walker, and Mr. Sid Walker, from down below."

"Pleased to meet you," said Mr. Walker.

"Pleased to meet you," echoed Sid.

The Captain nodded. They all shook hands.

"If you're wanting a wedding cake," added Mr. Partridge jovially, "I've brought you the very man. Now you all make yourselves at home, while I pop down and fetch the drinks."

He beamed encouragingly upon them and went out. For a moment he paused outside the closed door: the sound of Lisbeth's voice, talking very fast, reassured him. He went down to T. Cubitt's, and on second thoughts procured not two bottles of the grocer's best sherry, but four. T. Cubitt, apprised of the circumstances, not only promised to come up himself as soon as business permitted, but threw in a large bag of potato chips which Mr. Partridge clipped under one arm. He then went out again through the side door, and ran straight into Lester Hamilton.

"Good!" exclaimed Mr. Partridge. "I'm glad to see you. Take a couple of these and come up. We're having a party."

The young man hesitated.

"I just wanted to see Miss Campion—"

"So you will. She's upstairs. And the Captain. We're celebrating his safe return. You take these—" Mr. Partridge broke off; the young man was suddenly looking very queer indeed. His face was white as a sheet, he was leaning, his shoulders bowed forward, against the staircase wall.

"What's the matter?" asked Mr. Partridge. "Wind?"

Lester Hamilton shook his head.

"I just don't feel so good. I guess I won't come up after all. . . ."

Mr. Partridge fixed him with a stern eye.

"Now then!" he ordered firmly. "You've behaved very well up to now, so don't go and spoil it. You come up and meet the Captain, and shake him by the hand, and be glad of the opportunity. You won't often meet such a gentleman as him—not in your trade."

"Thanks," said Mr. Hamilton rather grimly, "for the offer."

Mr. Partridge began to be annoyed. It had already struck him that neither the Walkers nor himself were really fit companions, socially speaking, for the guest of honour; young Hamilton, in spite of being a Colonial, was: his presence would heighten the tone of the gathering to a very marked degree. Mr. Partridge passionately desired that his party should be a success, for the sense of anticlimax was still strong upon him, and he had a feeling that the rest of

the evening, unless socially hilarious, would be very difficult to get through.

"All right," he said. "But I expect it's your last chance
of seeing Miss Campion: she won't have much time before
the wedding. But I'll say I saw you, and that you went off
looking like a sick cat. I daresay it'll worry her, being so
soft-hearted—"

Lester Hamilton seized a bottle of sherry in each hand
and began to run upstairs.

2

The party was not going well. It was hardly going at all.
It was practically at a standstill.

"This," said Mr. Partridge, "is young Hamilton. Friend
of ours."

He looked at the Captain anxiously: he felt (though he did
not stop to analyze the sensation) rather like a dog bring-
ing a bone into the drawing-room: it was a worthy bone,
but would it please? To his relief, however, the Captain's
brow perceptibly lightened; he greeted Mr. Hamilton quite
warmly, and the business of opening the bottles and finding sufficient glasses produced a slight animation. Mr.
Partridge's first toast—"The Happy Pair"—animated the
proceedings still further: young Hamilton began to talk
very rapidly to anyone who would listen, both Walkers, with
great solemnity, offered the Captain their congratulations,
Lisbeth, standing close to her fiancé, smiled and nodded and
began a dozen sentences that all ended in laughter, and Mr.
Partridge bustled round refilling glasses. It was a mistake:
T. Cubitt's best sherry was extremely bad. Mr. Partridge,
unaccustomed to a drink which he had always considered
teetotal, did not know this; but Sid Walker, after the first
sip, quietly went downstairs and came back with a bottle of
cherry brandy. Hugh Brocard emptied his glass with grim

•

politeness, Lisbeth set down hers half-empty, only young Hamilton drank down whatever he was given and held out his glass for more. His gaiety was almost embarrassing: he became, in speech, more American than Mr. Partridge had ever known him, and conversed solely in what Mr. Partridge suspected to be wisecracks. The favourable effect produced on Captain Brocard evaporated like dew under a hot sun; his effect on the Walkers was from the first highly unfortunate. As soon as they learnt of his connection with the film trade they drew together like a couple of cows apprehensive of a barking dog, following him suspiciously with wary eyes. Only once did Mr. Walker address him, and then in tones of deepest disapproval.

"I bin reading," said Mr. Walker sternly, "a piece in the paper. All about film-actresses. It made my gorge rise—"

"I guess it was exaggerated," said Hamilton, placably. "What was it about?"

"It was about," replied Mr. Walker, with bitter emphasis, "their *ephemeral* art. Ephemeral. D'you know what that means?"

"Well—short-lived and soon forgotten?"

"That's right. Ephemeral. Always gassing, they are, about their ephemeral art." Mr. Walker lowered. "Do they ever think about *our* art being ephemeral? Does anyone? Answer me that!"

Lester Hamilton naturally could not.

"I spend an hour, two hours, four hours," continued Mr. Walker, "making an ice-basket of sugar-fruit. My Windsor Castle took three days. And in ten minutes, where is it? If there weren't a lady present, I'd tell you. In ten minutes—"

"I can imagine it," said Lester Hamilton hastily.

"Right. But if that's not ephemeral I don't know what is. That's what I'd like to tell these writing fellows. Compared with my Windsor Castle, Garbo's a pyramid."

There was a brief silence. The *cri du coeur* of an artist, unless uttered amongst his peers, has a stilling effect. Mr. Partridge, who had been about to say, "Have a potato chip," closed his mouth and put the bag down quietly on the window-sill. It was fortunate that he did so, for, glancing out, he saw on the pavement below Miss Pickering apparently asking her way of the grocer's boy.

"My gum!" said Mr. Partridge.

He was not specially surprised to see her; but he had just remembered that she still, to all intents and purposes, knew nothing.

Behind him Lester Hamilton had started to talk again. He had started to tell a story which (if Mr. Partridge were any judge) was going to have an unsuitable ending. But there was no time to stop him now; Mr. Partridge edged past the Walkers, beamed once again all round, and once again made for the stairs.

3

He found Miss Pickering half-way up the bottom flight. She carried a large bundle of country flowers, which at the sight of Mr. Partridge she almost dropped.

"Good gracious!" cried Miss Pickering. "*You* here!"

"Yes," said Mr. Partridge hastily. "It's me all right. And I want you to listen very carefully, because—"

"But isn't this where my niece is staying?"

"Yes," agreed Mr. Partridge. "That's why I want you to listen, because they're all upstairs—"

"Who are?"

"Miss Campion and the Captain and the Walkers and another young chap. We're giving," said Mr. Partridge for the fourth time, "a party. And there's a whole lot you ought to know."

"There is indeed!" cried Miss Pickering vigorously. "Do you mean to tell me my niece and Captain Brocard aren't married?"

"Not yet," said Mr. Partridge. "But they soon will be." He looked at her and wondered how much she could take in. No use going too deep. . . . "All you've got to remember," he said firmly, "is this: you've lost all your money—"

"But I haven't! At least—"

"Don't argue!" ordered Mr. Partridge. It seemed to him that he had spent all day reasoning with people on the stairs. "*You've* lost all your money, that's why you're not living in town with Miss Campion. She *has* been living here, ever since she left Dormouth Bay, with her young brother, who's now got a job and married into the bargain—you'd better not speak of him, for there's still a little unpleasantness. But now the Captain's back home, and all's forgiven, and they're going to get married next week. Have you got that?"

"No," said Miss Pickering.

Mr. Partridge groaned.

"Then you'd better not try. Just come up and have a glass of sherry and give 'em your blessing. Though if you could remember about losing your money—"

"I will not," stated Miss Pickering, "be a party to any deception. If Captain Brocard asks me—"

"He won't. He's got too much else to think of. You just come up and see for yourself."

With an air half-resolute, half-apprehensive, Miss Pickering allowed herself to be shepherded upstairs. Like the Captain, she appeared to be struck very forcibly by the state of the walls and banisters.

"Do you mean to say my niece has been *living* here?"

"That's right," agreed Mr. Partridge. "It's very handy."

"And where do you live?"

"Me?" said Mr. Partridge, quite surprised. "Why, I live here too."

He pushed open the door and revealed the heterogeneous company in the harlequin room.

4

Lester Hamilton was still talking. The cherry brandy in the bottle was perceptibly lower. Lisbeth was showing Captain Brocard Ronny's long silken doll. As the door opened she turned sharply; Mr. Partridge received an odd impression that she wanted to run out through it. Then she saw her aunt, and her face changed.

"Darling! How lovely! And—and look, Hugh's back!"

Miss Pickering, the colour high in her cheeks, marched across the room and held out her hand.

"I'm very glad to see Captain Brocard," she said. "Very glad indeed."

Hugh Brocard stepped forward. His eyes were friendly, and they held also a faint look of reproach. Miss Pickering met them steadily, while her colour rose still higher.

"Yes," she said. "But now that you're home—"

"Aunt Mildred!" Lisbeth slipped between them. "Where's my ring?"

Miss Pickering glanced round. Privacy was impossible: the open door to the kitchen was blocked by Sid Walker, that to Mr. Partridge's cupboard by Lester Hamilton. All men. . . .

"I'm *afraid*, dear," she murmured, "you'll have to wait. It's inside my . . . I mean, it's *inside*."

Without a gleam of amusement, Lisbeth nodded. Miss Pickering turned back to Hugh Brocard.

"There's only one thing I want to say," she stated firmly. "I brought Lisbeth up, and—and she's a good child."

He was nothing if not gallant.

"I know it," he said. "And I'm a proud and happy man."

Lester Hamilton started another story.

In spite of this, however, the social atmosphere now improved. Mr. Partridge seized Miss Pickering and introduced her all round, and Miss Pickering, by behaving exactly as though she were at a vicarage tea-party, went down very well. She asked Mr. Walker if he were fond of gardening, from which question there arose a very interesting discussion on the subject of herbs. Mr. Walker knew a great deal about herbs—he had a friend who mixed the best salad in London—and also about preserving fruit; he gave Miss Pickering some useful hints on bottled strawberries. She had a soothing influence on young Hamilton, who ceased to tell unsuitable stories and listened politely to her account of the Horsham Flower Shows. Lisbeth and her fiancé meanwhile stood side by side at the window, and Mr. Partridge was pleased to see them talking together in a quiet and cheerful manner. He was careful not to interrupt them, even when T. Cubitt at last put in his appearance. "Mustn't disturb the lovebirds!" called Mr. Partridge gaily. The remark, as it happened, fell upon a dead silence: all eyes turned to the window. The two Walkers (now mellowed by cherry brandy) grinned broadly. T. Cubitt ducked and nodded; but over the countenance of Miss Pickering spread a look of startled distress. She had turned like the rest of them, and in so doing had caught sight of Lester Hamilton's face.

"He's feeling a bit queasy," said Mr. Partridge in her ear. "You haven't got a bismuth tablet on you?"

Miss Pickering's hand went to her bag, and came away empty.

"No," she said. "No, I don't think that's it—Have you known him long?"

"Matter of three months," said Mr. Partridge. "He's been very useful, taking Miss Campion about, and so on. Nice young chap—although American."

Miss Pickering nodded. Her flow of small-talk seemed to have dried up; and its cessation showed how valuable it had been, for from that moment the party-spirit noticeably flagged. Mr. Partridge did his utmost—he refilled all the glasses, and jested with T. Cubitt, and even went out and came in again announcing himself as Obadiah. The joke took a good deal of explaining, and seemed, in some curious way, to depress rather than to exhilarate. There was no doubt about it, the party was going rapidly downhill; and it was quite a relief when Mr. Walker unobtrusively took him aside and drew his attention to the hour.

"Six o'clock," murmured Mr. Walker. "They're open."

Like a beautiful vision the Saloon Bar of The London Apprentice rose before Mr. Partridge's eyes. He had no foolish scruples about leaving the ladies behind: he came from a walk of life in which the pleasures of the male did not admit of interference. Seizing an empty sherry bottle he banged loudly on the table and called for silence.

"They're open!" announced Mr. Partridge. "I ask the pleasure of all you gentlemen's company just round the corner."

At once, with remarkable co-ordination, T. Cubitt and the Walkers moved towards the door. Captain Brocard hesitated: he looked at Lisbeth. His principal desire at that moment was for a very strong whisky-and-soda.

"Yes, darling, you go," she said. "I want to clear up this place."

"I'll come back and take you out to dinner," promised Hugh Brocard, picking up his hat.

Lester Hamilton said nothing. He too moved forward, as though to join the pub-party; but in the doorway, and when the others were already on the stairs, he halted and turned round.

"There's a lot to do," he suggested. "You—you don't want to be late for dinner. I guess I'll stay and lend a hand."

Both Lisbeth and Miss Pickering assured him that this was unnecessary, but the young man was stubborn.

In silence he collected the glasses and took them to the sink while Lisbeth put on a kettle and shook soap-flakes into a bowl. Miss Pickering followed them about as closely as she could, but the kitchen was extremely small, and her natural task was the tidying of the sitting-room. There was a great deal of ash about, which she collected into a piece of newspaper, and the whole bag of potato chips had been dropped to the floor, and then trodden on. . . .

"Ready!" said Lisbeth. "Pass me that glass, will you?"

Lester Hamilton passed it. Their hands touched; and the next moment Lisbeth was in his arms.

5

Neither spoke. Hamilton held her close, his mouth pressed against her hair; down Lisbeth's face, buried in his coat, the tears ran silently. Neither moved. They were still standing so when Miss Pickering appeared in the open door.

Miss Pickering did not speak either. She gasped: and at the sound Hamilton's head jerked up. For a moment he stared at her blankly; then very gently his hands moved to Lisbeth's shoulders and he put her from him. She had not yet seen her aunt; she simply stood where he placed her, her eyes fixed on his face, the tears still running down her cheeks.

"Lisbeth!" said Miss Pickering.

Lisbeth turned. Abruptly, as though her knees had given way, Miss Pickering sat down on the edge of Ronny's bed. The whole house was quite still.

"On my honour," said Lester Hamilton, "it's the first time. And the last. I'm going back to New York next week."

"Lisbeth!" said Miss Pickering again.

Lisbeth put up a hand and wiped her eyes.

"It's all right, Aunt Mildred," she said. "It's . . . it's all right."

Miss Pickering glanced from one to the other of them. Her hands, clasped very tightly in her lap, looked as though they were praying by themselves.

"But this is dreadful!" she said faintly.

"No, darling." Lisbeth's voice was faint also, but steady. "It's just an accident. It doesn't affect anything."

"You're in love with each other," stated Miss Pickering.

"We're not. We're very good friends, and—"

Miss Pickering's eyes flashed.

"Elisabeth Campion! I've tried to bring you up truthfully, and I hope I haven't failed. Deceit is bad enough, but lies are worse. You've been deceiving Captain Brocard—"

"I have not! At least—not in that way! I deceived him about Ronny, and I was right to. But this—as Lester says, it's the first time he's ever even kissed me, and it's the last. I shall marry Hugh and make him a good wife and talk about the Army and be everything he wants."

"My dear," said Miss Pickering, more gently. "I know it must be a great temptation. Captain Brocard's position and prospects would tempt anyone. But no girl should marry, however advantageously, while her heart is another's."

The impeccable romantic sentiment, enunciated in Miss Pickering's earnest tones, produced a sudden silence. Lisbeth stared.

"You think I'm *tempted* to marry Hugh?"

Miss Pickering nodded.

"It's quite natural. I'm not—I'm trying not to blame you for it. Although I'm an old woman, I can remember how ambitious youth always is. I once had a notion myself of breeding Pekingese, though of course nothing ever came of it. So I can understand, my dear—"

"You don't understand anything," said Lisbeth wearily.

"And that," retorted Miss Pickering, "is just what *I* said when my dear mother refused to let me buy Champion Ku Lin of Horsham. And she turned out to be quite right, for none of his puppies ever did any good. You must just make up your mind that Providence has decided otherwise for you, and bow to a higher will."

Lisbeth smiled faintly.

"I said," she murmured, "he wasn't a bad harlequin . . ."

Miss Pickering looked at her with concern.

"You want a sedative, my dear. I don't wonder, for this must have been a great strain. And it's—" her face suddenly crumpled—"a great strain on me too."

Instantly Lisbeth was on her knees beside the bed.

"Darling! I'm a worry and a pest to you. I'm a pest to everyone. But I'm going to reform. Isn't it funny—" she smiled again—"I've spent all this time reforming Ronny, and it's I who need it so much more. . . ."

"No," said Hamilton.

It was the only word he had uttered since his first statement. His position had not been an easy one: he had been standing physically constrained by the cooker and the sink, and mentally by the difficult sensations of a male who has got left behind with the ladies. These, moreover, were but superficial embarrassments: his fundamental emotions were more excruciating still.

"No," he said again. "You're perfect. That's all. You're so lovely I guess everyone wants you, but there's only one fellow who can be lucky. If you say it's to be Brocard, then that's just so. You've honoured me with a very lovely friendship, and I'm proud and grateful. I'll have had something in my life—something—"

"Stop!" cried Miss Pickering. She was looking not at him but at her niece. "This is no time for foolish argument. It's a question of right and wrong. You love this young man, and yet you propose to marry Captain Brocard—"

"And I shall be right," said Lisbeth.

"You will be wrong," retorted Miss Pickering firmly. "You will be most wickedly wrong."

"But I've promised!"

"Then you must break your promise."

"Isn't that wrong too, darling?"

Miss Pickering looked slightly flustered, but she stuck to her guns.

"It will be *less* wrong. Of two evils one must always choose the less. To jilt Captain Brocard—"

Lisbeth winced.

"It's not quite so simple, darling. . . ."

"On the contrary, it's very simple indeed. You young people think too much and puzzle your brains too much until you can't see your plain duty. Your duty in this case is to be guided by me. You will break off your engagement to Captain Brocard because—setting everything else aside—I tell you to."

Over her fierce old head the eyes of Lisbeth and Lester Hamilton met. "Was it so simple?" asked the eyes of Lisbeth. "Can it be so simple—just to do as one's told—push off all responsibility? Can I, may I, my dear?" And the eyes of Lester Hamilton answered, "Yes. I'll do whatever you say, but—yes, Lisbeth!"

"*Always,*" said Miss Pickering, clasping and unclasping her hands, "follow your heart. Then you can't go wrong. I learnt that with great difficulty, and I'm not going to have it wasted." She turned to Lester Hamilton. "I haven't asked your intentions, young man, but I presume you can support my niece like a lady?"

"I can," said Lester Hamilton fervently.

"And—and you'll look after her, and be good to her?"

"I will," said Lester Hamilton, more fervently still.

"Have you any relations or connections in London whom I can visit to-morrow?"

"I'll make out a list. I'll do anything you like—"

"Then I think," said Miss Pickering, "if everything is satisfactory—you'd better get married as soon as possible."

She got up; the two young people looked at her with something like awe. She had undoubtedly settled everything, but how had she done it? Was it possible that the tradition in which she had been brought up—the tradition of Victoria the Good—had still some hypnotic power? Did the age-old machinery of matchmaking still work? "But she had it all wrong!" thought Lisbeth. "I *didn't* want to marry Hugh! The only thing she got right was about *us*. . . ."

"That's enough," said Miss Pickering firmly. But she was not (as she might have been) answering her niece's thoughts: she was speaking to her niece's new fiancé, who had just rather unexpectedly kissed her. "That's enough," repeated Miss Pickering, looking pleased nevertheless. "I hope we shall learn to be very fond of each other, but at the moment there are several things to do. About Captain Brocard, for instance—"

"I must tell him," said Lisbeth, on a sigh.

"No, my dear, not you. *I* shall. You can't wish to see him just now—"

"I don't. But I don't see why I should shirk it . . ."

"Then I do," said Miss Pickering. "In such a case a girl's relations should always act for her, so I am the proper person. I must go to him at once, before he comes back and sees you. Where have they gone?"

"To The London Apprentice," said Lisbeth. "The pub at the end of the road."

Miss Pickering blenched. She blenched, but she did not waver.

"Just take Mr. Hamilton into the next room," she directed. "I want to get something out of my . . . inside."

6

The process of getting anything out of Miss Pickering's inside took some time; since she also washed her hands and face, and took off her hat and skewered it on again, it was some minutes before she re-passed through the sitting-room; but even so Lisbeth and Lester Hamilton were still standing just on the other side of the door. They looked at her quite vaguely.

"You'd better go out yourselves," she said, considering them, "and get some food inside you. Something *plain*. And bring Lisbeth back early, Mr. Hamilton, because I'm staying here the night, and I shall sit up for her."

"Isn't she a marvel?" asked Lisbeth, as the door closed.

"Yes," said Hamilton. "Do you remember the round-about?"

"Do you remember the time when Mr. Partridge wouldn't let you get on the bus?"

"Do you remember the time when I had to be away three days?"

Do you remember . . .?

The conventionality of Miss Pickering's catechism—the ritual ceremony with which she had asked intentions—had struck both her hearers as being echoes (though strangely potent ones) from the past; but no less conventional, no less firmly rooted in the traditions of the human heart and the penny novelette, was the ensuing conversation between Lisbeth and Lester Hamilton.

Miss Pickering herself was meanwhile performing one of the most heroic actions of a not uncourageous life. She was pushing open the Saloon Bar door of The London Apprentice.

CHAPTER 19

1

HER first unexpected emotion was one of astonishment. The place was so much more respectable than she had anticipated. It was clean, and bright, yet with an air of great solidity. There were aspidistras in pots, just like the ones she had at home; and as for the company—she never remembered having seen so worthy-looking a collection of males (all talking quietly and earnestly together) save at a vestry-meeting of her own St. Matthew's Church. . . .

Considerably emboldened, Miss Pickering advanced. No one molested her. Several heads turned, and at once, with great decorum, turned away again. A gentleman in a bowler hat, whose outstretched legs barred her path, politely withdrew them; Miss Pickering instinctively bowed. The gentleman (though still seated) bowed back. Only Ruby the barmaid, middle-aged and with the traditionally elaborate coiffure, looked slightly cold, as though afraid that Miss Pickering was about to produce a collecting-box. Fortunately, Miss Pickering had no need to address her, for there at the end of the bar, in the most favoured place, stood Mr. Partridge surrounded by his friends.

They all seemed to be enjoying themselves much more than they had done in Marsham Street. Mr. Partridge's face was particularly bright: he had produced, in Captain Brocard, one of the most distinguished visitors the Apprentice had ever known. Hugh Brocard's fine presence and military bearing, the fact that he had just come back from

India, and also his connoisseurship of whisky, made him the centre of attraction: the habitués of the Apprentice had at once recognized him as a genuine nob and one of the real sort; and since even Hugh Brocard was in many respects human, their ready deference was very agreeable to him. He made himself agreeable in return, talking easily, accepting drinks, always standing a round himself a little before it was due: when Miss Pickering came in he was just about to stand his third.

"Captain Brocard!" said Miss Pickering.

There was a moment's pause: then Mr. Walker (on whom she had made a great impression) stepped ponderously aside to let her into the circle. But Miss Pickering stood where she was.

"Captain Brocard!" she said again. "I should like to speak to you. Just for *one* moment."

Hugh Brocard came out through the gap and looked uncertainly round the bar.

"Here?" he said. "Or outside?"

"Not outside, please," said Miss Pickering. "I've something to give you. Something valuable . . ."

He looked round again, and then, obedient to Ruby's experienced nod, led her swiftly into the Private Bar.

2

The Private was just as respectable as the Saloon, though darker and colder, and it was occupied only by two elderly ladies sipping small ports. Miss Pickering sighed with relief, and sat down as far from them as possible on a narrow horsehair-covered bench that ran round the wall. Then she opened her bag and took out from it a minute package sewn up in pink flannel.

"There!" she said. "Open it."

Captain Brocard shook his head. Even through the flannel his fingers had told him what it contained; and he looked at it speechlessly.

"Open it," insisted Miss Pickering. "Please! I know it's very valuable, and though I don't think anyone could have chloroformed me on the way up, we'd better to make sure—"

He took out a penknife and ripped apart the stitches. One big emerald, held close in the curve of his hand, glittered like a green flake of fire. . . .

"Lisbeth," proceeded Miss Pickering steadily, "has asked me to give it back to you. And to say that she is very sorry, but she asks to be released from her engagement."

Hugh Brocard stood up. He almost stood to attention. His fine jaw quivered.

"Why?"

"Because no girl should ever marry one man," explained Miss Pickering gently, "when her heart is another's."

The features of Captain Brocard set into a mask. This was because they were not used to expressing more than one emotion at a time: having now to cope with no less than three, they threw up the sponge and became simply wooden. But behind that mask the emotions were there: relief, astonishment and—jealousy. Lisbeth had given him, by proxy, the only word of release which he could in honour accept; but—

"Who is it?" he demanded.

Miss Pickering told him. She drew a little—not on her imagination, but on her knowledge of Lisbeth's character; she expatiated on the struggle that had taken place between love and loyalty, and also upon Lisbeth's growing sense of her own unworthiness. The implication that though unworthy of the Captain she was quite worthy of Mr. Hamilton, struck neither Miss Pickering nor Brocard as at all odd. The difficulty was not there.

"But she told me," he stated, "that she loved *me*."

"Then I am afraid," said Miss Pickering apologetically, "that she told a fib. Though I'm sure she does love you too, as—as a brother. She respects and admires you. But the heart, dear Captain Brocard—"

"The heart be damned!" he cried.

It was the first ungentlemanly act of his life: he had sworn in front of a woman—of three women, in fact, for the two port-sippers, who had hitherto had to strain their ears, simultaneously jumped. Captain Brocard looked round; he had forgotten the presence of those silent witnesses. The awfulness of the situation struck him afresh: the fact that he had been driven to discuss his most private affairs in a Paddington pub filled him with more dismay than the fact that his whole future had been thrust out of course. And who had so driven him—who had so dislocated his life? Who had made him so forget himself as to use strong language before ladies? Lisbeth. Tenderness was swallowed up in resentment. It was entirely her fault that he swore again.

"I *think*," said Miss Pickering gently, "you'd better go straight away. . . ."

Instinct reasserted itself.

"I can't," said the Captain wretchedly, "leave you here."

"Yes, you can. I just want a moment to compose myself, and then I'm going quietly to an Anti-Vivisection meeting." Miss Pickering smiled brightly. "Such a piece of luck, don't you think? I mean that there should *be* one to-night, when I so rarely come up to Town. But I saw the poster at the station, and said to myself, 'Don't forget, it's at eight-thirty. . . .'"

For a moment Hugh Brocard forgot his own misery and looked at her. She was very white: the events of the evening had told on her, and her social gallantry, her brave attempt to ease the situation, shamed him. Then his misery returned. It would be best to do as she said—to go, to get away, to get out. . . .

With an odd, constrained gesture—as though he were trying to salute her—the Captain went.

3

Miss Pickering clasped her hands and closed her eyes. The need for repose was very real, but even the moment she had claimed was not allowed her. Hardly had the street door stopped swinging when the inner door opened, and Mr. Partridge, afraid that he might be missing something, impetuously entered.

"Where's the Captain?" he asked at once.

"Gone," said Miss Pickering—reluctantly opening her eyes.

"Gone where? To fetch Lisbeth?"

"Just gone," said Miss Pickering.

The next instant Mr. Partridge had leapt towards the door. With surprising agility Miss Pickering jumped up and caught him by the jacket. Mr. Partridge made an instinctive movement to thrust her off; but she held fast, and he could not struggle with a lady. The two port-sippers exchanged congratulatory looks. They felt they were seeing life. . . .

"Now you *have* done it," gasped Mr. Partridge. "He'll jump in the first taxi he sees. Whatever made you let him go?"

Miss Pickering also was rather short of breath; but she retained her dignity.

"I came here," she explained, "specially to tell him to go. To tell him that my niece wishes to be released from her engagement."

Mr. Partridge gaped.

"You've never been and given the ring back?"

"Certainly I have. I know it must be a surprise to you—"

"Surprise!" exploded Mr. Partridge. "Surprise be blowed! I knew about that all along! It's the one thing I've been striving to prevent! And I had, too, until you turned up! The surprise is that you haven't more sense!"

"I may not have sense," retorted Miss Pickering, "but I have principles."

"Principles!" ejaculated Mr. Partridge. "She can't marry a principle!"

Miss Pickering smiled.

"Certainly not. But she *is* going to marry that nice Mr. Hamilton . . ."

There was a muffled thud as Mr. Partridge's knees gave way, and he dropped abruptly onto the horsehair-covered seat.

4

The rest of Miss Pickering's evening may be briefly described. She dined lightly off a cheese sandwich and a glass of milk, and passed an interesting (though harrowing) hour with the Anti-Vivisection League. At the same time Lester Hamilton was spending three-pounds-fifteen on a meal which neither he nor Lisbeth tasted. Hugh Brocard went straight to his Club and merely sat there—soaking himself, as it were, in his native element. There was a bison's skull on each wall; nobody spoke to him because nobody spoke to anyone; and at the end of thirty minutes, he was able to face another whisky-and-soda.

The worst off of them all was Mr. Partridge. For some time he was too stunned even to move back into the Saloon Bar. He just sat where he was, amid (so to speak) the ruins. Miss Pickering's explanations had been convincing enough; he was no longer bewildered—and that, indeed, was the trouble. She had made everything so plain that he felt himself to have been as blind as a bat and as silly as an owl not to have seen it all himself. But the Captain, even in retrospect, had dazzled him. As soon as his first suspicions were allayed he had never thought seriously of young Hamilton again. He had backed, in fact, the wrong horse. . . .

To err is human. A fallible creature will fail somewhere. But Mr. Partridge had for so long been in the habit of considering himself an exceptional person, that no such saws could now comfort him. At the moment he agreed, though unconsciously, with a more modern writer: he saw hope only in malt.

He pulled himself together and stood up. The two port-drinking ladies looked round, their glances expressive of mingled curiosity and concern: they were evidently quite ready to call him "dearie" and listen to his woes. But Mr. Partridge had had enough of women. He glared at them sternly, and stamped back into the Saloon Bar. If he could unburden himself to anyone, it was to old Walker.

Mr. Walker, however, was gone. So were Sid Walker and T. Cubitt. The abrupt departure and long absence of the host had not unnaturally broken up the party, but Mr. Partridge was in a mood to take their disappearance as a personal insult. He ordered a half of half and half and bore it away to a remote table. Though there were several of his other acquaintances present, he did not wish to speak to them. He wished to brood.

Even in this he was unsuccessful. He had been brooding barely ten minutes when his privacy was intruded upon by a voice bidding him good evening.

"Good evening," said the voice. "You look as though you'd had a brush with the harlequin . . ."

Mr. Partridge glanced up. It was a long gaunt chap speaking—a long gaunt chap whom he remembered with discomfort. A silly fellow, very depressing in his talk. . . .

"What are you drinking after that?" the long chap asked.

"Naught," replied Mr. Partridge.

He hunched himself round unsociably. But the chap had no manners: he sat down too, and set his can on the table, and took out a packet of cigarettes.

"Got a light?" he asked.

There are some things no civilized man can refuse, and a light, if such happens to be in his possession, is one of them. Mr. Partridge produced a box of matches. But he would not accept a cigarette.

"You seem," observed the stranger, "to have come round to my point of view. I thought you looked like a sensible man."

"Then you thought wrong," snapped Mr. Partridge. "I'm an old fool." This was, at the moment, his genuine opinion; at the same time he felt a strong desire to contradict everything the stranger said. The pleasure of being contradictory seemed to him the only pleasure left. "I remember you quite well," he continued disagreeably. "You talked more rubbish than any chap I've ever met, and you seem to be at it still."

"What did I say?" asked the stranger, with interest.

"You made out that life wasn't worth living. I daresay it isn't—to a booby."

The stranger grinned at him.

"You don't seem," he suggested, "to be enjoying it much yourself . . ."

"Ah," said Mr. Partridge, "but then I don't blame life for it. I blame myself—which is just the difference between us. Life's all right."

"If you believe that—"

"I do," affirmed Mr. Partridge stoutly. And suddenly it was true; quite suddenly his black mood lightened. He felt better. His rudeness to the stranger had relieved his feelings; his contradictoriness had forced him into optimism, and optimism was his natural mood. Thinking of Lisbeth, he realized that however wrong he might have been in detail, his general philosophy was still gloriously right. By marrying an American, when she might have married the Captain, Lisbeth had simply illustrated his lifelong conviction that one never could tell. He at least had always perceived—had never lost sight of—the fact that the fundamental trait in her character was its unpredictableness; and he had been right about that too. That she should be happy with young Hamilton was all Mr. Partridge now asked; and casting his mind back over the last few months, he thought she stood a good chance. Young Hamilton had merits. He wasn't the Captain—Mr. Partridge heaved a last, loyal sigh—but he was honest and industrious and fairly good-looking, and he loved Lisbeth. He had been very helpful about those stockings. For a moment Mr. Partridge tried to picture Captain Brocard being equally helpful—inking in, for example, a brassière: but for once his imagination failed. The Captain would never have done it. He had every good quality, but he lacked . . . elasticity. And for the purpose of making Lisbeth happy, Mr. Partridge had begun to feel that elasticity might count for a great deal. . . .

"I believe," said Mr. Partridge slowly, "it's all for the best."

The stranger looked quite disappointed.

"You're a backslider," he stated.

"Put it like that if you want," allowed Mr. Partridge. "Anyway, I'm going to slide back home and see what's going on. I may be missing something."

He stood up. He looked at the stranger with positive benevolence.

"D'you know what's amiss with you?" he asked. "You've got a poor circulation. You ought to get yourself some red socks. They're warming to the blood."

His own circulation now in perfect order, his own feet properly furnished, Mr. Partridge nodded affably and passed out through the swing-doors.

THE END

FURROWED MIDDLEBROW